CLUTTER FREE

CLUTTER FREE

An
Organized Crime
Cozy Mystery

Jackie Layton

LeVel
BEST BOOKS

This book is lovingly dedicated to Sherrinda Ketchersid, Rhonda Starnes, and Cate Nolan for meeting me for writing sprints and always encouraging me. You all are amazing.

I'd also like to dedicate it to Shawn Simmons, my wonderful editor at Level Best Books, and I must include my incredible agent, Dawn Dowdle.

Last, this is dedicated to my husband who supports me every day of this writing journey. Tim and I met while living in Georgia, we fell in love and got married in Georgia. I'm excited to be writing a series set in Georgia.

Praise for Clutter Free

"Completely charming and exactly what a cozy mystery should be."—Hank Phillippi Ryan, bestselling author of *The Guest House*

"Kept me guessing till the end. Andi Grace is an excellent amateur sleuth... and *Caught and Collared* is an engrossing and enjoyable cozy mystery."—The Book Decoder, Best Books of 2022

"Andi Grace is adorable, resilient, and has a doggedly curious need to solve a murder. A pleasure to read."—C. Hope Clark, award-winning author of *Edisto Tidings*

Chapter One

Zones, lovely zones. Areas for designated purposes. Pantries work best when organized in specific sections. There are many ways to accomplish such a task. Baskets, clear containers, and under-shelf baskets were a few of my tools as a professional organizer.

Before moving back to Fox Island, families had been my typical clients. I was familiar with the zones they preferred. Healthy snacks, junk food, baking supplies, drinks, pasta, canned food, dry goods, and desserts.

Today's job was for a man. A single man.

Men fit into the zone of family, friends, and clients. At fifty-three, there was no room in my life for dating and romance. I'd been hired to organize Reid Barrett's pantry by his mother. He was an old friend. Nothing more.

I checked expiration dates on every food item in Reid's pantry. Granola boxes, near-empty chip bags, soups, more chips, whole grain bread, and bottles of sports drinks filled one wall in the walk-in pantry. The man definitely needed a "first in, first out," system to avoid wasting food. After tossing expired items, I cleaned and attached liners to the wire shelving. Often in the past, I hired a crew to reconfigure the work space and add track shelving. Not today. The budget was tighter for this project, but a thrifty plan had never deterred me from doing my best work.

In my opinion, Reid had tried to be somewhat organized. Gold star for effort, but he didn't have the tools to make it work. It was also possible he gave up due to time constraints or possibly exhaustion from a stressful job. Organization was my thing, and whipping his pantry into shape made me happy. Still, it was always important to keep the homeowner in mind.

The more I stuck to Reid's semi-system, the more likely he'd follow my organizational structure.

A lazy Susan was the perfect place to store his oils, barbecue sauces, and ketchup. Stackable organizers held cans of hearty soups and vegetables. Spices filled a rack. All these items went on a high shelf, probably eye-level for Reid, but I stood on my tiptoes to verify it looked nice. I filled clean glass storage jars with rice, chia seeds, whole wheat pasta, and dates. By transferring these items to glass containers, there was less opportunity for island bugs to get into his food. These were placed on the next shelf.

Now to start on the other items. Mismatched food storage products belonged in the trash and were replaced with a graduated system of stackable square containers.

Mail spilled out of a tattered old shoe box. Insulated water bottles galore needed to be thinned out. Who needed that many bottles? Although, to be fair, Reid was a contractor. Hot Georgia days required lots of cold water for a man who spent hours working outside.

I paused and studied the drink bottles. Some had logos from 5K races, and others advertised businesses. It'd be in poor taste to toss one if he was sentimentally attached to it. When Reid got home, I'd convince him to sort through the drink bottles and ditch some. For now, I arranged them on his kitchen counter near the sink and verified each bottle had its appropriate top.

Fanning myself with a sales circular, I leaned against the counter. The kitchen was more closed off than I would've liked. Although there was an interior window in the wall between this and the living room, a vaulted ceiling made the area seem bigger.

I sipped icy water from a Tervis tumbler advertising my business, Let's Get Organized. My best friend from childhood, Bess King, and I had recently started the company together when I returned to Fox Island.

An exterior door slammed, and I jumped.

Reid appeared wearing dusty faded jeans and a grungy T-shirt. He stopped dead in his tracks. His eyes widened, and his mouth dropped open.

"Hello, Reid. It's me. Kate Sloan. Paul's sister." For some silly reason seeing Reid for the first time in years created a weird sensation in my belly. My younger brother and Reid had been best friends all their lives. There was absolutely no reason to feel nervous. Except for the fact his mother had hired me with the intention of surprising her son with an organized pantry.

Reid smirked. "Um, I know who you are, Katie. Just don't know why you're here."

My heart skipped a beat. Nobody had referred to me as Katie in decades. After I left home for college, I rarely returned to the island. How was it possible Reid still affected me? He was in the friend zone. Nothing more. "I live here now."

"Welcome back to town. I guess I should've been more specific. What are you doing in my kitchen?" He elbowed me out of the way to wash up at the kitchen sink. He scrubbed his hands, splashed water on his face, dried off with a threadbare hand towel, then stared at me.

Ugh. "Do you dry your hands on the same towel you use for dishes?"

"Not that it's any of your business, but no." He raised the solid gray tea towel. "Faded towels are for after work only. Nice towels are intended for drying dishes. I need a shower in the worst way. For the last time, why are you in my kitchen? Also, why are my water bottles out? Were you snooping in my pantry?"

My face grew hot from embarrassment and a little bit of anger. "Surprise. Your mother hired me to organize the pantry." Joy Barrett doted on her son, and she'd always been kind to me. In fact, she was our first customer at Let's Get Organized.

Reid muttered his reply.

I turned to hear him with my good ear. "I'm sorry. What?"

This time his face reddened. "Man, I'm the one who should be sorry. Paul told me you lost the hearing in your right ear years ago. Some kind of tumor, right?"

"Acoustic neuroma." He knew about my disability, and he even knew which ear had been affected. "It's fine, though. I don't hear everything, but I've learned to cope."

"I'm really sorry you had to go through that." He ran a hand over his face.

"Don't get soft on me, Reid. You need to treat me the same way you did when we were growing up." I shook my finger at him.

He laughed. "That brings back memories. Annoying older sister it is, then."

"Not that much older." Barely two years. "I can still probably out-swim you."

"Challenge accepted. How do you feel about the Memorial Day Triathlon?"

"Not great." Running, biking, and swimming. Not on my wish list.

"I need to clean up; then I guess you should explain this plan of yours."

"Take your time." I entered the pantry. What had possessed me to challenge him? Memories rushed over me from my youth. Because of his friendship with my brother, Reid had been a big part of my life. I'd never thought of him as a brother, but I hadn't dated him either. It wouldn't have been appropriate because of his friendship with Paul. Years had changed both of us. The thing I hadn't counted on was Reid's charisma or his good looks. He was more muscular than when I'd seen him twenty years earlier at Paul's wedding. If possible, he'd grown more handsome.

It didn't seem fair. I worked out, colored my hair, used sunscreen, and I still looked my age. Silver streaks and lines around Reid's eyes added to his appeal. Nope. Life wasn't fair.

I adjusted cereal keepers in a line on a shelf. They were what I predicted was eye level for Reid, making it easy for him to see when a selection needed to be added to his grocery list.

I'd returned to Fox Island to get to know myself again. I could be Kate Sloan here. Not David's wife, a widow, or Ethan's mom. Just me.

"Hello, Kate?" Joy's voice rang out with a musical lilt. "I ran and got us some smoothies. Land sakes, but it's warm today. Eighty degrees, according to the clock at the bank. Is Reid here?"

I joined her in the kitchen. "Yes, and he wasn't happy to discover me in his kitchen. You told me this was going to be a surprise gift, but I figured you might have given him a little warning." I propped my hands on my hips and struggled to give her a stern look. Who could get mad at a seventy-something woman wearing a kiwi-green top over bright, flowery multi-

4

color leggings? Her silver hoop earrings dangled so low that they almost touched her shoulders. Wavy silver hair and wide blue eyes added to her timeless beauty. Reid had his momma's eyes. The woman was precious to me and always would be.

She laughed it off. "Sorry about that. Good thing I brought three smoothies. Try the blue raspberry." She slid a drink to me, kept one, and placed the last smoothie in the refrigerator.

I took a sip of the icy drink. Tangy, sweet, and cold. It hit the spot. "Yum. Thanks."

"You're welcome. How's it going?" Her eyes twinkled with mischief. "It was a mess, wasn't it?"

"Joy, you wouldn't have hired me if Reid didn't need a little help tidying up." I never criticized a client.

"He keeps a neat worksite, but his home is a different story. He's working himself to death, and he's drained by the time he gets home." Her black cat eye sunglasses dangled on a gold chain around her neck.

"I heard that." Reid entered the kitchen with damp hair, wearing khaki shorts and a clean blue polo. "Having a cluttered pantry is not a character defect."

I laughed. "Depends who you ask."

Reid pointed to the counter on my right. "Your phone's ringing."

Paul's name lit up the screen, and the theme song from *Hawaii Five-O* played. I swiped at the display. "Hey, what's up?"

"I'm in big trouble. Can you meet me at your place?" He sounded breathless. Not much rattled my brother, the police chief of Fox Island. This must be bad.

"Are you okay?"

"Hurry." His ragged breathing alarmed me.

"Sure. Be right there." I slid the phone into my pocket and faced Joy and Reid. "I'm so sorry, but I've got to run. Reid, can you get rid of about half of those travel cups?"

He stepped close enough for me to get a whiff of Irish Spring. "What's wrong?"

"It sounds like we've got a family emergency. I'll come back as soon as possible."

He met my gaze. "Don't worry about me. Family comes first. Call if I can be of any help."

"Thanks."

Joy handed me my smoothie and purse. "We'll see you later. Be careful, hon."

I made it home in record time. It wasn't like my brother to overreact. Paul's panicked tone pushed me to drive faster than normal, and I reached my long-term rental in four minutes. Paul's truck filled my little driveway. I parked my blue VW Beetle in the first available space on the street and hustled along the sidewalk. I ran up the wooden stairs to my downtown apartment located steps from the Atlantic Ocean. Waves crashed on the beach. The harsh pounding warned of a storm brewing.

The apartment's door tended to stick in damp weather, and I shouldered my way in. I dropped my purse on the entry table. Paul stood looking out the window but turned toward me. His face looked almost as gray as his short hair. "Hey, sis."

"What's wrong?" Closing the gap between us, I placed my smoothie on a coffee table coaster, then hugged Paul. It didn't matter that he was fifty years old, he was my little brother.

The tremor in his shoulders alarmed me.

"Is it Susie?" Could his wife be sick? Hurt? It'd explain why he'd come to me instead of her.

"I can't believe this is happening." He stepped back and rubbed his temples.

I moved to the tiny kitchen and pulled out a Coke, and passed it to him. Normally, I'd pour it over ice and hand him the glass and a pretty cocktail napkin, but it didn't seem like the right time for social graces. "Have a seat and tell me what's going on."

He plunked down into a chair at the small eating table and chugged his soft drink.

I retrieved my smoothie and took a sip. When a topic was hard, Paul usually paused before speaking. I didn't rush him. The good Lord knew

Paul had been more than patient with me years ago when my husband died suddenly.

The room darkened. Thunder rumbled in the distance.

Paul finished his drink and hunched forward over the table. "There's a woman in town. Young enough to be my daughter."

My throat constricted. Paul had been with me when I'd discovered my husband hadn't been faithful. After his death fifteen years earlier, the *other woman* had shown up at my house and asked if David left anything to their daughter in his will. Paul had been furious. He believed in staying faithful to one's spouse. "A woman?"

Paul said, "She's posted on social media that we're engaged. There are pictures of us together to back up the claim. Of course, they're doctored, but it'll take time to prove the lies."

"Oh, no. Why would she do that?" Not even for a nanosecond would I believe Paul had stepped out on Susie.

He shook his head and stared at the table. "Don't know."

My stomach dropped like the time I'd ridden the Tower of Terror with my son, Ethan. "Who is this woman?"

"Carissa Ruffalo." He crushed the aluminum can in one hand, and a dribble of remaining liquid ran down the side.

The name meant nothing to me. "Have you met her? Given her a speeding ticket? Arrested her for breaking the law?"

"No. That's the weird thing. She seems vaguely familiar, but no altercations come to mind. I even looked it up. I haven't arrested her for anything. So what is her motive?"

"Does Susie know about this?"

Paul squeezed his eyes shut. "Yeah, she's the first one who confronted me. It caught me totally off guard."

"What's her stance?" My heart thundered as I waited for his response.

"Well, she didn't cuss me out and throw my clothes on the lawn. But she's confused. And embarrassed." He opened his eyes and met my gaze.

"I imagine she's hurt, too. People treat you differently when they find out your partner is a cheater." I took a deep breath. My unfaithful husband had died years ago. This situation wasn't about me. "You two need to talk, but first, I have another question. You say there hasn't been trouble with you and this woman, but have you investigated Carissa Ruffalo? Where does she live? Where does she work? How can we find her?"

"At this point, I need to stay as far away from that woman as possible."

I opened my phone and searched for the big fat liar who was accusing my sweet brother of having an affair. No, worse than that. She'd claimed they were engaged. There she was. Young and slender with a hardness in her gaze. "Here's a picture of you two at the art gallery's coffee shop."

"The art gallery?" He ripped the phone from my hands and held the screen close to his eyes. "I've been in there, but I usually carry my own coffee from home to save money. That photo has been digitally altered."

I took back my phone and continued to scroll.

Paul said, "She works at Fox Mart."

I stood. "Then that's where I'm heading. You stay here."

His fingers circled my wrist just tight enough to get my attention. "You're not going alone."

"I'll be fine." I pulled away from him.

He moved with speed and finesse and blocked me from exiting the front door while typing on his phone.

I glanced at the only other means of escape from this living space. I didn't relish the thought of jumping from my balcony. "Paul, it's daylight, and there are tourists out and about. I'll be fine."

"No can do." He met my gaze. "I texted Reid. He'll meet you at Fox Mart."

Arguing with Paul was hard enough, but when those two teamed up against me, they presented a formidable force, and I needed to save my fight for Carissa. Momma had taught us to respond with grace. "Okay, but Reid can be intimidating. I might learn more if I approach her by myself."

"The buddy system is always the best way to go." He pressed his lips together.

"Safety in numbers. I get it. Tell Reid to meet me in the parking lot."

Paul moved to the side, allowing me to walk out the door. "Thanks, sis."

"Anytime." I kissed his cheek and headed outside before he saw me cry.

My apartment was in the business district of the island, and it was an easy walk to the store. I played out different scenarios in my head of how to confront the young woman. I had one son and knew how to lecture boys. Dealing with girls was a different matter.

I sat on a bench and blew my nose. Checking my reflection in my compact mirror, I blotted away smeared mascara and applied my favorite shade of orchid lipstick. Better, so I continued my trek to meet Reid.

He pulled into the public parking lot and joined me. "Paul wants me to have your back. Kate, have you been—"

"Please don't ask. I'm barely holding it together." If I was this torn up, it must be so much worse for Paul and Susie.

"Understood. What's your plan?" He crossed his arms.

"Thanks for asking my thoughts." My appreciation for Reid rose.

"It's a courtesy you didn't extend to me at my house." His eyes sparkled in the same teasing way, like when he was a child.

"Maybe I should've checked with you before taking the job. Would you like me to back out?"

"No, it's all good. If I fire you, Mom will find another way to—what's a nice way to say interfere?"

I laughed. "There's no nice way to say that."

"You're probably right. Now, what's the plan?" His posture relaxed, probably relieved I hadn't burst into tears. He'd done a great job of changing the mood.

"How would you feel about waiting on the sidewalk just outside the front door? If I run into trouble, I'll say a code word real loud."

"What's the word? Liar? Scumbag? Home wrecker? No, that's two words." He rubbed his chin.

"Your loyalty to Paul is admirable. Thanks." Dark clouds moved over us. "Let's use tourist, because they carry T-shirts, sunscreen, beach chairs, and all that jazz. I think I can squeeze it into a conversation without alarming the woman."

"Fine by me. I'll stand near the door with my phone out and pretend to have a text conversation. Let's get a move on." Reid motioned for me to take the lead, and he hung back a few steps when I entered the tourist trap.

The woman who'd made false accusations against my brother was easy to find in the near-empty shop. Tall, dark hair, slim, busty, and not afraid to flaunt it by the sight of her low-cut top. Definitely the same woman who'd posted pictures on social media.

I wandered around the store, pretending to look at T-shirts. In reality, I watched my brother's accuser.

Carissa folded beach towels, not crisp, but decent. She smiled at a mother with young daughters. The tender expression threw me. She was supposed to be a monster, right? After all, she was spreading lies about Paul.

I bumped into a display of beach toys. Wooden paddles crashed onto the concrete floor.

Carissa gave me a toothy smile and approached. "How can I help you?"

I picked up the items. "Sorry about that."

"It happens. Is there anything I can help you find?"

"Actually, you're the reason I came into the store. I'm Kate Sloan, Paul Wright's sister." I straightened my shoulders and lifted my chin.

"So?" Carissa's smile disappeared, and she turned and walked toward a display of stuffed sea turtles.

"I'd like to discuss your recent posts on social media."

"There's nothing to say." She turned away from me so fast she walked right out of a flip-flop on the way to the cash register, where she tapped some keys.

"The things you've posted online aren't true, and the photos were edited."

"I'm not a liar." She slipped her foot into the abandoned sandal and headed to the employees' room. "Arden, I'm taking the rest of the day off."

The woman folding T-shirts behind the counter did a double take, then frowned. "You're on the schedule to close the store tonight."

"Sorry." Carissa opened the door.

I followed her into the private area before the door swung shut. "Paul would never cheat on his wife."

"It makes sense you'd believe him, but we're engaged. As soon as he can ditch his wife, we'll get married." She snatched her purse and left the room, walking toward the exit.

I'd never wanted to stop a person by yanking their hair before, but there's a first time for everything. Instead, I blocked Carissa's escape with my body, just like Paul had stopped me at my apartment. Standing in the doorway, I pointed at the young woman. "No. You. Weren't. I don't know why you're lying, but I'll prove Paul is innocent."

"Good luck with that. The pictures show I'm telling the truth." She pushed me aside and headed down the sidewalk.

I glanced at Reid. "Tourist."

He nodded.

At the risk of twisting my ankle, I jogged after the young woman in my two-inch wedge sandals. "Stop. This conversation isn't over."

Reid followed without crowding me.

Carissa ignored me as she dug into her purse, continuing to walk down the sidewalk.

I caught up and strode beside her. "You're destroying a good man's reputation. Think about his family. Please, take down your posts about the affair. Tell everybody it isn't true."

We reached the same public parking lot where Reid's truck sat. Carissa pointed her key fob at a little white sedan with a dent in the rear bumper. The car beeped, and she jumped in it, slamming the door.

I watched her drive away. She'd won this round, but my brother was innocent. Carissa hadn't heard the last from me.

Reid touched my elbow. "What just happened?"

I crossed my arms. "I blew it. She didn't confess."

His eyes widened. "Fine, but did you learn anything?"

"She's still lying, and I hate to go back to Paul with nothing." Wind blew my hair, and I pulled it into a ponytail, fastening it with a holder from my pocket.

Reid said, "It could be a bumpy ride for your brother until the truth comes out."

"Let's go back to the store and question the other employee. She wasn't thrilled when Carissa left." I fanned myself with my hand but found little

11

relief from the heat.

"I bet it didn't get this humid in Kentucky in March."

"You can say that again. We never knew what to expect weatherwise in March." At a more sedate pace, I walked to the store, at least until I reflected on what was at stake. My brother's reputation, his career, and his family. It wouldn't kill me to perspire, so I kicked it into high gear and soon reentered the gift shop.

The blonde with too much eye makeup glared my way, probably blaming me for her employee's departure. Carissa had called her Arden.

"Hi, Arden, I'm Kate Sloan."

Her frown deepened. "I take it you're a friend of Carissa's."

"Today is the first time we met." I glanced at Reid. He moseyed around the store, pretending to shop. "What can you tell me about her?"

She pointed at Reid and turned away from me. "I've got a customer to help."

"Sorry, he's with me."

Arden stopped mid-stride, and her shoulders slumped. "It's not like we're friends. In fact, she isn't a very good employee. What do you want to know?"

Reid and I approached the clerk, who stood by a display of sunglasses. I said, "Carissa posted about a romantic relationship on social media. Do you know who she's dating?"

"I don't see how she has time to date. She works two jobs and is trying to get back into professional dancing." She blew a purple bubble and sucked it back into her mouth before it stuck to her light peach lips. "Carissa used to date a guy with a weird name. Disc jockey? Radio man? No, it was, uh, Anchorman. That's it."

It sounded like a good clue. "Do you know Anchorman very well?"

"Not really, but he's easy enough to spot. He's a super tall Black man who used to play basketball. He's even taller than you." She reached a finger toward Reid as if she was going to touch his chest, but he sidestepped her ploy. "He's in a band now, though."

Reid said, "I'm sure that's his stage name. Do you know his real name?"

She smiled at him in the way flirty women do. "I'm afraid not, but if you'd like, I can try to find out for ya' sugar."

Reid's face grew red. "Thanks."

A group of giggling teenage girls entered the shop and beelined it to the bikini rack.

Time to go. "We'll let you get back to work. Thanks for your time, Arden."

She stared at Reid. "Come back soon. Maybe I'll have that name for you."

"Sure." He beat a hasty retreat.

"Thanks for your help. We'll be in touch." I left the store clerk with a dreamy look on her face.

I found Reid standing on the street corner. A single cold raindrop plunked onto my nose, and I wiped it away. "What do you think?"

"It's a start. We need to talk to Paul."

"I'm renting an apartment over there." I pointed in the direction of the beach. "Shall we walk? Or run if it starts seriously raining."

"Walking is fine. Why are you renting?" He fell into step beside me.

"I wanted to be sure about buying the right place, and Sand Piper Apartments seemed like a good option." We hurried down the street leading to my long-term rental. "I've been gone for decades and wanted to readjust to beach life before picking my forever home."

"I hope you consider buying an older house." A family with a double stroller approached, and we darted into the entryway of a café, allowing them to go past.

My wedge slipped into a sidewalk divot, and I wobbled.

Reid cupped my elbow. "Steady, there. You okay?"

"Fine. You know how the kids always called me an easy out in kickball? I'm still on the clumsy side."

"Oh, Katie. They were mean, and you're not clumsy. You need to let it go."

"Easier said than done." I moved onto the sidewalk, now clear of tourists, and continued toward my temporary home. "Are we going to tell Paul everything we learned?"

"Absolutely. He has resources at his disposal that we can't touch. Most of the officers will believe your brother is innocent. His track record is impeccable."

"I'm not so sure. One of his men was fired for having an affair a couple of months back. Paul might be in deep trouble."

"Hey now, where's the optimistic girl I grew up with? Besides, that guy was guilty of the affair, and he didn't try very hard to hide the relationship."

I'd suffered some hard knocks, and returning to the island was supposed to be my fresh start. New beginning and all. "You're right. We're going to prove Paul is innocent."

Thunder rolled, and a streak of lightning over the ocean brightened the sky. "We need to hurry before it turns into a gully washer."

I slipped off my sandals and ran. I wanted like everything to believe Reid's words. We'd prove Paul was innocent. What could be worse than having a woman accuse him of an illicit affair and becoming engaged?

Chapter Two

Before moving to Fox Island, I had a coffee station at my home. The house's large kitchen had allowed for the indulgence. My current place didn't permit for luxuries. Instead of a coffee nook, I had a flat handwoven natural seagrass basket. It held a variety of coffees, my coffee bean grinder, filters, and heathy sweeteners. Most days preparing my morning cup of joe was a sweet way to ease into the day. This particular Friday wasn't most days.

A night with very little sleep caused me to miss the alarm, and I stopped at the Island Perk for my first java of the day. Coffee in hand, I entered Let's Get Organized and removed my sunglasses. My best friend stood at the shiny white counter where we planned to greet customers. "Morning, Bess." I passed a skinny vanilla latte to her and took the first sip of my cinnamon dolce latte.

"Morning." She cocked her head. "Sister, what's happened? You look terrible."

Oh, how I'd missed her southern accent the years I'd been away. No, I'd missed Bess. Pure and simple. "You're not going to believe it."

"Sure, I will. Tell me." She lifted her perfectly-shaped eyebrows.

I shared the basics of the horrible situation then took another sip to fortify myself before continuing the story. "Last night, Paul, Reid and I studied social media posts and tried to figure out a motive for why Carissa did this. Before she posted about the fake engagement, she often discussed her opportunity to dance in Atlanta. She even shared pictures of herself in the city."

"Hmm, it doesn't make much sense. What did you learn?"

"We know she has been a drug abuser. She may be clean now, but we don't know for certain. Reid left around eleven, and Paul crashed in the guest room. I started making a list of what we know about Carissa. Do we have any appointments this morning?"

Bess shook her head and pointed to a piece of paper full of names and contact information. "No, but we need to call these people who emailed questions to us."

"Great. So, it can wait for a little bit." I glanced at her list. "Will you please go with me to question Carissa Ruffalo?"

One eyebrow lifted, and she picked up her drink. Bess was beautiful with unflawed black skin and no visible wrinkles. "Thanks for the coffee."

"You're welcome, but you didn't answer my question."

"Paul's a grown man. Why do you feel the need to butt into his business?"

"He reached out to me, and I can't turn my back on him. I promise to throw myself into work as soon as we clear Paul's good name."

"Even when we prove he's innocent, this will put a strain on his marriage. Have you talked to Susie?"

"When I suspected my husband was involved with another woman all those years ago, I didn't want to talk to anyone about. I'm trying to respect Susie's boundaries. So, will you go with me?"

"I poured my life savings into our business. I need you to be focused."

I reached for her hand. "I am focused on Let's Get Organized, but this is Paul."

Bess sighed. "I get it. Family should come before work. Give me a minute."

I drank my coffee and reviewed my plan. One way or another, I needed to extract a confession from Carissa.

Bess returned carrying her big denim purse over one shoulder and a can of pepper spray in her hand. "Ready."

"We're not going to attack the girl, just question her."

Bess reached for her coffee. "She may decide to attack us if you pose the wrong question. I'm even carrying my daddy's pocketknife. You know the one he gave me when we graduated from high school?"

"Good to know. It's a short walk to Fox Mart."

"Let's go before it gets too humid." Bess set the store alarm, locked the door, and we strolled to the gift shop.

"Thanks for going with me. If it makes you more comfortable, I can do the talking, but help me listen to her answers. And feel free to jump in with questions of your own. I need her to confess the truth and take her posts off social media."

"People are still liable to think Paul is guilty."

"Yeah, but I can only tackle one issue at a time." We arrived at the store, and I ran a hand over my navy polka dot shirt and khaki shorts. After another fortifying sip of coffee, I entered the store.

Arden stood at a table removing plastic-wrapped swimsuits from a cardboard box. "May I help you?" Her smile disappeared. "Oh, it's you again. Where's the hunk from yesterday?"

"Uh, he couldn't come with me. Are you the only one working again?"

"Carissa's a no-show. She didn't even have the courtesy to call in and warn me."

I folded a wadded-up T-shirt and placed it on a stack of similar shirts. "I hate when that happens. Do you want me to check on her, you know, just in case she's sick or something? When we find her, I'll make sure she calls you."

Arden's angry expression cleared. "That would be great. We're starting to get more tourists, and I can't run this place by myself."

Now to get her address. "Okay, we'll let you know when we find her. Oh, yeah, I don't know where she lives." I returned two pair of abandoned sunglasses to their display rack.

"You don't need to help me in here." Arden smiled. "She lives in the new apartment complex. Pelican Shore Apartments. It's number five-twenty-six."

"We'll be in touch." We walked outside and toward my place, but I didn't say a word until there was no possibility Arden might hear me. When it was safe, I glanced at Bess. "What do you think? Why didn't Carissa show up for work?"

Bess said, "Maybe she skipped town. She stirred up a hornet's nest, then disappeared."

"You could be right. I'll drive us over."

"That's fine, but we need to alert somebody just in case we disappear."

"We'll be safe. It's broad daylight."

"The day after Carissa posted an affair on social media, she didn't show up at work. Don't you think it's strange?" Bess tossed her empty cup into a trash can.

"Not showing up at work isn't the same as disappearing." We arrived at my driveway. "Do you need to run inside for anything before we leave?"

"I'm good."

We hopped into my VW Bug and took off. "We'll pass the Fox Island Art Gallery and Coffee Shop on the way to the apartment complex. Can you stand another drink?"

Bess laughed. "You're not going to help my coffee addiction at this rate, but why not? Also, why?"

I pulled onto Ocean Boulevard and mashed the gas. "One of the photos Carissa posted of her and Paul makes it appear they're in that coffee shop. It's been altered, but Paul said he's been in there before. Just not with Carissa."

"Are we going in to question the employees or just to get drinks?"

I signaled then turned into the gallery's sandy lot and parked beside a black Volvo sports car. "Today we're going in to get a feel for the people. No questions. Have you been here before?"

"A couple of times." Bess shrugged. "The art is too modern for my taste. I like pictures with a Caribbean flair."

"Oh yeah, I'm aware. You have a beautiful art collection." I hopped out and followed Bess into the building.

Bess said, "Izzy Reynolds is the main artist, and she owns the gallery. Every time I've seen her, she's worn black clothes and chunky gold jewelry."

"Black outfit. Got it." I paused at the door. "Let's split up. Do you want to order coffee or look at art?"

"Art. I'll take another skinny vanilla latte."

We entered the old refurbished building.

A petite woman with beautiful white hair and big glasses greeted us then turned back to leafing through a magazine. We returned her greeting then followed through on our plan.

The wood floor tilted at a slight angle. Soft rock played over a good sound system. I moseyed toward the coffee shop on the right. Six wood tables were scattered around the dining area. A glass door led to a patio with umbrella covered tables. Inside, two men sat together, each looking at their laptops. They were in a big, animated discussion, but I couldn't hear the topic. A lady sat in the corner reading a cozy mystery and sipping from a large mug. A young couple sat in the corner. The woman appeared to nurse a baby, and the man was on his cellphone. At the other occupied table sat a man with a thick moustache and graying hair. Reading glasses were perched on his nose, and he read a Bible while taking notes on a yellow pad. This place had a serious vibe compared to Island Perk.

"What can I get you?" A woman wearing a red apron asked. Her nametag indicated she was Marie B.

"Hi, I'd like whatever your iced tea of the day is, and a skinny vanilla latte."

"Raspberry iced tea sweetened with local honey is today's special."

"Perfect." I tugged my credit card out of my wallet.

"For here or to go?"

"How about to go cups?"

"Yes, ma'am." I paid her then sat at an empty table.

Marie's wholesome appearance contrasted with some artists I knew personally. Cornsilk blond hair pulled back into a ponytail, no piercings, and no tattoos. Artists usually had a flair that us mere mortals couldn't achieve. Of course, I grew up with brothers and raised a son. What did I know about fashion or flair? And maybe Marie was a barista and not an artist working in a coffee shop.

Marie placed the drinks on my table. "Can I get you anything else?"

"I've got a quick question. Do you by any chance know Carissa Ruffalo?"

"Yes, ma'am. She used to be a dancer. Now she's working part-time jobs all over town while rehabbing." She twisted her mouth to the side. "Actually, she wants to get back to dancing."

"Rehab? As in drugs? I thought she was clean now."

Marie shrugged. "Carissa hurt her shoulder in New York. I think her family lives in Savannah, but I could be wrong. Although, why else would she come here while rehabilitating? I think the injury led to drug addiction, and now maybe she's recovering from both."

"It makes sense to me. So, you say she works here?"

"Yes. France, our manager, allows her to have a flexible schedule. I guess she feels sorry for Carissa."

"Why do you say that?"

"When France hired me, it was clear this place was my first priority." Marie looked around the coffee shop. "I'm okay with that. They allow me to be creative in what I serve, and I meet artists from different places. It's all good."

"Do you bake the pastries yourself?"

Her chin lifted. "You bet. It's all homemade. Nothing frozen at a factory then thawed and sold here."

"That's impressive. I'll be sure to come back when I have more time."

Bess appeared but stopped by the man reading his Bible and spoke to him.

Marie said, "Sounds good. I'm going to check on the others." She crossed paths with Bess, and Marie also spoke to the man who'd by now closed his Bible.

"You should see the new artwork. They're featuring a couple of artists from Jamaica." Bess sat next to me and whispered, "Did you learn anything?"

"Carissa works here part-time." I leaned closer to my friend. "Who's the man over there?"

"He's the pastor at my church. No need to think he's involved in any nefarious dealings."

"Good to know. Do you mind sharing what you learned while we drive to Pelican Shore Apartments?"

"I didn't learn one iota. Let's go."

Reaching for my untouched tea, I stood. "I'm ready." I exited with a wave to Marie, and it didn't take long to drive to the apartment complex. My phone buzzed. Bobby's name appeared. He was my other brother and tended to be overly dramatic.

"Aren't you going to answer?"

"If I know Bobby, he's upset about how Paul's affair is affecting him." I sighed. "And I do know Bobby."

"I can just imagine his reaction. It's amazing how he turned out so different than you and Paul."

"Yeah. I'll call him back later." I whipped into an empty parking place and pointed at a white dented Camry. "That looks like Carissa's car."

"Are you positive you want to do this?"

My heart beat hard enough I could feel it. "If our visit helps Paul, it'll be worth it."

We entered the building and rode the elevator to the fifth floor. Not a soul questioned our appearance, probably a perk to living in a vacation destination. Exiting the elevator on the fifth floor, we found our way to Carissa's apartment.

Bess grabbed my arm. "I've got a bad feeling."

I glanced at her. "About what?"

"Not sure. This girl could report us for stalking her."

"We're here to check on her health. You know, like a wellness check."

"Except we're not the police, and you want her to confess she lied about your brother." Bess squeezed my arm tighter.

I sighed. "True. Let's get this over with." I stopped in front of five-twenty-six and raised my hand to knock.

The door moved a bit inward before my knuckles touched it.

"Hello, Carissa?" I pushed the door, but it didn't move an inch before stopping. A security door chain prevented us from entering. I tried to turn the knob, but it didn't budge. "Carissa, it's Kate Sloan. Can we talk? Arden's worried about you."

The only reply I heard was the muted sound of a dog barking. With my hearing impairment, the dog could've been anywhere. My focus needed to remain on Carissa.

Bess pulled out her knife. "She might want to avoid you."

"I see your point." I knocked again and leaned my face near the small opening. "Carissa, I don't want to argue. I'm only here to see if you're okay."

The door to the next apartment whipped open, and a bare-chested man appeared wearing nothing but athletic shorts and running shoes. "Ladies, can you hold it down? I'm trying to get some work done."

My voice had probably been loud, and I hadn't considered the other residents on this floor. "I'm so sorry. Do you know Carissa Ruffalo? The girl who lives here?"

"Yeah." He came closer, and Bess backed away.

"She didn't show up for work, and we agreed to check on her. The door is chained."

"Can you believe this building still has chains? I don't remember Carissa using it before though. Whenever I knock, she opens the door. I've never heard a deadbolt or chain being moved." His gaze bounced from me to Bess who was having some kind of moment.

Bess averted her eyes. She was most likely embarrassed. She'd been single all her adult life and hadn't spent as much time around men as I had. It'd been nothing for Ethan and his friends to workout in my basement and run around the house shirtless.

"I'm Kate Sloan, and this is Bess King."

"Ian Wilson. Why is the door open? Did you try to go inside?" His stance showed off his sixpack, a move he may have perfected to impress women closer to his age.

"No, it was like that when we got here."

"Let me call her from my phone. Be right back."

Bess slipped the knife back into her purse. "Put on a shirt too, if you don't mind."

He glanced down at his muscular chest and patted himself. "The AC's on the fritz, and I wasn't expecting company. It's hot as—a campfire in there." He disappeared into his place.

Bess shook her head. "There's a bad vibe here. I'm texting your brother."

"No. If you have to alert anybody, get Reid." I handed her my phone. "He's in my contacts." I turned back to the door and pounded with my fist. "Carissa, we're getting worried. Please, come to the door." I tried to insert my hand through the small opening, but my wrists were too big.

Again, the only reply I heard was possibly the sound of a dog barking. Maybe we were disturbing other residents too. "Bess, can you wiggle your skinny little hand in and unchain the door?"

"You must be off your rocker. If this goes sideways, I don't want my fingerprints all over the place." She crossed her arms.

Ian returned, wearing a faded red University of Georgia T-shirt. "It went straight to voicemail. Say, were you here last night?"

I shook my head. "No, why?"

"Carissa was arguing with a woman. Something's whacked." He reached for the doorknob and pushed. The chain prevented his entrance into the apartment. "Stand back ladies."

Before I could ask why, Ian kicked the door. The chain busted, and the doorframe cracked. The door swung open. I ignored my inner voice warning me of laws like breaking and entering.

The young man entered the apartment first. "It's a one-bedroom place. Just like mine. Open living space, a bathroom, and a bedroom pretty much wraps it up."

I followed him inside, but Bess remained in the hallway talking on her phone to Reid.

Ian breezed past the kitchen with a quick glance, then he ducked into the bathroom. Shower curtain rings scraping a rod sent chills up my spine.

My heartbeat sped up, but my steps slowed.

"No!" Ian screamed.

There were sounds of water splashing.

I darted to the bathroom.

Ian pulled a limp body out of the tub. Water flowed off Carissa's body. "Get out of my way."

I stood frozen.

He sped past me. "We need to do CPR. Someone call for help."

His words spurred me to action. I pulled a bath towel off the counter. An open vial of pills spilled, but I ignored the mess and hurried to the other room. I yelled for my friend. "Bess, I'll help Ian. You make the call."

She appeared and tapped on her phone.

I knelt beside Ian and Carissa on the bedroom floor and draped her body with the towel. I felt her wrist for a pulse. Nothing.

Ian tilted Carissa's head back and pinched her nose. He gave her two breaths then looked at her chest. "Did you see it move?"

"No. I'll begin chest compressions." With both hands, I pushed hard and fast. After thirty times, I nodded at Ian.

He gave her two more breaths. We continued the cycle despite no signs of life until the paramedics arrived and took over.

Ian and I joined Bess in the family room, and I sank onto the couch beside my best friend. Ian plopped onto a chair.

Despite our best rescue efforts, I didn't see how Carissa could survive drowning in her bathtub. What were the odds she accidently drowned the day after she'd announced to the world she was engaged to my brother?

Besides the gloom settling over us, something felt off. "Ian, you said Carissa never used the door chain?"

"Not as long as I've known her." He shuddered. "Maybe if she hadn't chained the door, we could've gotten to her sooner. She might still be alive if not for that blasted chain."

"We can't blame ourselves. There's no telling when she took her bath." I leaned closer to Bess. "Look for evidence."

"For what? The last thing you need is for the police to walk in here and catch us looking for clues." She stepped out of the bathroom.

I saw truth in the Bess's words, but people didn't just drown in their bathtubs. "Ian, did Carissa ever have a seizure?"

"Not around me. Why? Do you think that's what happened?"

"It's possible. Did she drink excessively? Take drugs?"

"No way." He leapt to his feet and walked toward the balcony. "You know she cleaned up her act."

If it wasn't an accidental drowning, she was murdered. If so, Carissa's death might make Paul look guilty of more than just having an extramarital affair. Who else would have intentionally harmed the girl? If the police viewed it as a homicide, they were bound to suspect Paul.

I remembered the spilled tablets. If Ian was correct, Carissa hadn't taken the pills on her own. I tiptoed to the bathroom to look for signs of a struggle.

The towel was cattywampus on the bar. There were other green prescription vials scattered around the single vanity and a few white tablets on the counter. They might have been the ones I spilled earlier. I snapped a picture of the area, including a black tank leotard.

I met Bess by the kitchen. She said, "The cops are down in the parking lot."

"Good." I studied the kitchen. There was an open bottle of wine and a plate of brownies. It didn't appear any had been eaten. I took another picture. Ian had said he heard Carissa and another woman argue. It seemed very possible the evening had started out friendly before turning deadly.

Chapter Three

O
fficer Emerson Diaz arrived at Carissa's apartment complex, wearing a frown. He'd worked on the police force for years with my brother. Officer Diaz ordered Ian, Bess, and me to sit at the kitchen table and wait until he could question us. He also confirmed what we already guessed. Carissa was dead.

I texted Reid. *No need to come. The cops are here. Take care of Paul.*

After sending the message, I remained in my seat and took pictures of the main living area. The kitchen, eating, and living area comprised the bulk of the apartment. Sliding glass doors led to a balcony with an ocean view. There were no signs of a struggle in this area.

If Carissa had asked my advice, I could've given her tips for storing her books, comforters, and magazines in an attractive and functional manner. Instead, they were scattered around the apartment with no particular organizational scheme.

Ian ran his hands through his wavy blond hair. "Do you think she killed herself?"

"I don't know." I swallowed hard. "It seems like the options are suicide, accidental drowning, or murder."

His eyes widened. "But the door was chained. That's got to mean something."

"Does anything else seem unusual?"

"You mean besides my dead neighbor?" His tone was harsh. "Where's the dog?"

I shrugged. "If she has a pet, you should tell one of the officers."

Ian left us sitting at the table.

"I don't believe it was an accident, Bess."

My friend leaned close and whispered, "If the cops say it was murder, you and Paul will be the first two people they accuse. If they rule it a suicide, it's one less problem for Paul to deal with."

My mouth grew dry as a biscuit. Leave it to Bess to cut through the fog. Even so, if there was evidence to point us to the killer, I needed to help. "We can't let them accuse Paul—"

"Or you."

I gulped. "Or me. Or even Susie. It'd be easy to lay the blame on one of us instead of searching for the true murderer. Look around for clues. What do you see?"

The door had a lock on the round knob, a deadbolt, and the chain. Why would a person go to the trouble to lock and chain the door but ignore the deadbolt?

I walked to the door and studied the doorknob. The lock button was up and down, so the place should've been impenetrable. How had the locked door come open?

"Going somewhere, Mrs. Sloan?" Officer Diaz looked down at me.

"No, sir. Did you notice the doorknob was locked even though the door was open?"

He leaned down and eyed the knob. "I see that."

How could that have happened? "In my house in Kentucky, there was a double click when it shut. If I didn't have the door completely shut going out to the garage, and then I opened the garage door, the air pressure sometimes pushed the house door open. Does that make sense?"

"Let's have a little conversation."

"Wait. What if Carissa thought she'd shut the door? Then she chains it? What would cause the door to pop open?" I followed him to the table and sat between him and Bess. His skin was almost as dark as my friend's even though he was of Hispanic descent, and she was African American.

"I don't have an answer for you." He opened a notepad and clicked his pen. "Let's start with why you two are here."

I folded my hands together. "Do you know I'm Paul Wright's sister?"

"Of course, I know who you are. It's a small island." His mouth twitched. "Is there any particular reason you announced the relationship?"

"Just thought you should be aware of the facts, but don't worry. I'm not asking for any favors, except one." I pointed to the empty chair. "Can I move? I'm deaf in my right ear, and it'll be easier to hear from there."

He motioned for me to change seats.

After getting situated, I smiled at him. "Thank you."

"Sure. Now, why are you here?"

I lifted my chin. "We went to Fox Mart to ask Carissa to take her lies off social media. Another employee, Arden Something, said Carissa hadn't shown up to work. We came to check on her."

"Then what? You decided to break into the apartment?"

"No. The door was ajar but chained." I reported what we'd one, and Bess inserted a comment or two. At last I asked, "Officer Diaz, do you believe it's suicide?"

"It looks like an apparent suicide." He leaned back in the chair.

"Don't you think it's odd that she'd work out right before killing herself?" I placed a hand over my queasy stomach.

"What makes you think she was working out?"

"There's a towel on the couch, and a large water bottle on the table. There's also a speaker. Oh, and there was a black Leotard on the bathroom floor but no other dirty clothes. It makes me think she had just exercised or danced before taking her bath."

"There were plenty of spilled pills. It could be an intentional drug overdose." The officer glanced over his shoulder, then wrote in his notepad. "Did you know Carissa well?"

"I met her yesterday. It's warm in here, and Ian said his air conditioner wasn't working. Can we open the sliding glass doors and get a breeze going?"

Bess nodded. "Fresh air might do us all some good."

I moved toward the balcony and glanced at the track for a security bar. There wasn't one, but maybe living on the fifth floor, Carissa had felt safe.

"Stop right there. I don't want your fingerprints on the handle." Officer

Diaz opened the door with a gloved hand.

I gasped. "It's not locked."

A dog barked not too far away. Was it Carissa's dog or a neighbor's pet?

"Nope." Officer Diaz crossed his arms. "Your point?"

"I'm not sure, except there wasn't a backup to keep the door secure. She had three methods to keep the main door locked."

"I don't ever recall a reported break-in from a balcony. Ever. This isn't some spy thriller movie. Ms. King, do you have anything to add?"

Bess shook her head. "I'm good."

"You ladies are free to leave. Call me if you remember any important details." He handed us each a business card and escorted us out of the apartment.

I started to knock on Ian's door to check on him and see if he'd found the missing dog. Voices from inside the apartment stopped me. "I guess the cops are still talking to him."

Bess tugged on my arm. "Let's get going while the gettin's good."

My stomach still hadn't settled, and my legs shook. "I'm with you."

Once we were alone in the elevator, Bess leaned against the wall and met my gaze. "Kate, now I'm just gonna tell you the truth. You're no detective, and you're certainly not a cop. It's one thing to think about convincing a woman to retract a lie. It's another thing to catch her killer."

"Who said anything about catching Carissa's killer?"

"Your eyes said it all. Plus, I heard the questions you asked the detective. You may read mysteries and watch them on TV, but you are not a detective."

The elevator doors slid open, and we exited. There was no use arguing with Bess when she'd made up her mind. I wouldn't debate the issue, but I would look for clues to solve Carissa's murder. Her death right after she'd posted having an affair with Paul was a little too convenient. I had a hunch somebody was pulling her strings. The real mystery was who and why? When I found the answers to these questions, I'd be closer to clearing Paul's name of being engaged to the victim. Chills covered my arms. Bess had been right. If the cops determined Carissa's death was murder, it'd raise the stakes. I'd need to also prove neither Paul nor I had murdered his alleged mistress.

My investigation would be methodical and efficient. Lack of training didn't deter me from launching a search for the true killer.

"Ladies!" Officer Diaz's voice boomed across the parking lot.

My heart jumped like it did after I drank a double shot of espresso. "Bess, if he arrests me, call Reid. He can break the news to Paul. Then call Bobby. He's bound to know a good attorney." I was too old to go to prison for a crime I didn't commit. *Lord, help me.*

Chapter Four

Officer Diaz jogged to where we stood by my blue VW. Beside him was a dirty Westie. Poor thing was more gray than white. "How would you like to foster this little furball until we can reach the victim's family?"

Bess's nostrils flared. "The victim had a name. Carissa Ruffalo."

Oh man, I hated when she used that tone. "We'll foster him. Or is it a her?" What I didn't know about dogs would fill a college textbook. Still the little dog was adorable.

"Snowball is a girl. I'll give Doctor Arkin a call. He likes to examine pets we place in foster care." He passed the leash to me then pulled a crinkled business card from his wallet. "Here's his information. One of the officers will bring Snowball's paraphernalia down in a bit."

The Westie tugged on the leash, and I followed her to an old pink azalea at least four feet tall and unruly.

Bess walked over. "Daylight's burning. This ain't no way to run a business, Kate."

"I know, but would you have allowed them take Snowball to the pound?"

"Fox Island has a perfectly acceptable animal shelter. Can you keep a pet at your apartment?"

I shrugged. "It never occurred to me to ask. If the owner won't let me keep her, I'll figure something else out." I glanced at the card. "Noah Arkin? What a fun name for a vet."

"He attends my church, and he's a great guy. It doesn't surprise me that he takes time to examine animals in compromised situations."

A young cop arrived carrying a pink dog crate. Inside was a bag of food, treats, pink dog dishes, and pink pillows.

I laughed and handed the leash to Bess. "I sense Carissa's favorite color was pink."

"You got that right." She reached down and rubbed the dog's head.

I pressed the VW symbol and opened the trunk. The young man collapsed the crate and placed the items in back. I smiled at him, figuring he was near the same age as my son. "Thanks."

"Yes, ma'am. Thank you for taking the dog." He jogged to the building.

My phone vibrated. "It's a message from Paul."

Diaz said go straight to Arkin's office. What's happening?

"Well?" Bess held the dog.

"We're supposed to go the vet now. Do you want to drive or hold Snowball?"

Bess said, "I'll hold her and give you directions."

On the way my mind dredged up the memory of Carissa's dead body. I fought the image all the way to the vet's office.

* * *

It was early afternoon before I returned to Fox Mart. Snowball had been checked out and sent home with me. She was hanging out at the apartment with my brother. In the tourist store, Arden was folding beach towels into quarters and struggling to fit them all on a display table.

"Hi, Arden. If you fold them in thirds, I believe they'll fit." I took a stack of towels and began folding them one by one.

"Where's Carissa?" Her gaze was fixed on my actions.

"See?" I rearranged the stacks. "It looks neater and plumper. Shoppers will be drawn to them, and the towels will all fit."

"Interesting." She reached for a neon orange towel with Fox Island spelled in blue letters and copied my actions. "So, what about Carissa?"

I sighed. "There's no easy way to say this. Carissa is dead."

Arden dropped the towel and gasped. "I don't believe it. Did you kill her?"

"No." My heart leapt.

"How? Are you sure Carissa is dead?"

"I'm sorry, but it's true." I gave her minimum details.

Kyra Hodge, another employee, overheard our conversation and fell apart. "No! You're wrong. We had plans to hang out." She wailed.

"Pull yourself together," Arden hissed.

A couple with three kids entered the beach store, watched Kyra's hysterics, and rushed out to the street.

Arden glared at me. "Can you get her out of here? I'll try to handle the store by myself. Again."

I nodded. "Kyra, I'm Kate. Why don't we go for a walk?"

Mascara trailed down her cheeks. "Okay."

"Would you like to splash cold water on your face?"

She sniffed and left me standing at the counter while she disappeared into the employees' office. She returned fresh-faced but pale. We left Arden taking care of a group of girls who appeared to be vacationing on their college spring break.

We remained silent as we strolled down the street. After we crossed over a public access, I decided it was time to begin a conversation. "Better?"

"I can't believe she's gone."

"Were you and Carissa close?" The beach was where I gravitated to when life got overwhelming. The rhythm of the waves, flowing back and forth soothed me, and I felt closer to God at the beach.

Kyra secured her long red hair on top of her head. "I'm a musician, and she was a dancer. We were both into the arts and didn't care about sports. We had a lot in common."

I moved to her right side to hear better. "Do you believe she was suicidal?"

"Heck no. She was close to getting back to dancing. Not Broadway, but there was a huge opportunity in Atlanta. She auditioned and was called back for a second audition. We dreamed about both of us making it big there."

"Maybe she accidentally overdosed which could have led to her drowning." I dodged an abandoned beach chair.

Kyra wrapped her arms around her waist. "No way. She got hooked on prescription pain killers after her shoulder surgery. Once she cleaned up, she never took anything stronger than ibuprofen."

Her words added strength to my theory. "Tell me what you know about Carissa's love life. Please."

"She broke up with Anchorman a few weeks ago, and she hasn't mentioned a new guy in her life." Kyra stopped and looked toward the pier. "She was low on cash after the two trips to Atlanta."

The change in subject surprised me. "What did she do?"

"She helped cater events at Fox Island Art Gallery, or she'd do whatever France Granger, the manager of the gallery, asked her. Sometimes France pays attractive people to mill about showings and talk up the artwork. Carissa was tall and beautiful. When she entered a room, people would turn to watch. Did you ever meet her?"

"As a matter of fact, I met her yesterday at Fox Mart. Except for the tall part, she was different than you described."

"That place sucked the life right out of her." Kyra slapped a hand over her mouth, and a tear ran down her face. "That's not what I meant, but Carissa was destined to be a star. Not sell cheap clothes to tourists."

Two police officers leaned on the pier railing and looked in our direction. I repositioned myself to face Kyra and avoid being seen by the cops. "Did you notice her posts on social media this week?"

"About being engaged to a married man?"

"Yes. I need to be upfront. The man is my brother, and he doesn't know Carissa. There was no affair."

"How dare you accuse my friend of lying. If she said they were dating, then they were."

"Think about it. Carissa wanted to start her career in Atlanta. Why would she get engaged to any man with roots here? Much less, why date a married man?"

"I need to go back to work." Kyra turned and left me standing there. I'd give her time to cool off, but surely, she knew the situation didn't make sense.

I returned to my apartment and found a note from Paul saying he'd gone to meet his wife. I stepped onto my balcony. The ocean breeze was nice, so I sat in an Adirondack with Snowball at my side. "You sure have a funny name for a dog living in the south."

Her tail wagged, and she watched a large group of people walking to the beach.

I opened my journal and wrote about my day. In my opinion, Carissa had been murdered. Once the police reached the same conclusion, would Paul really be a suspect? What about me? There was also Paul's wife, to consider. She'd never resort to murder, but did Officer Diaz know this? We were all innocent, so who was the culprit?

I needed to dig into Carissa's life and look for clues, but first I had to go to the store and smooth things over with Bess. I was an organizer, not a detective. My gut instinct told me to create my own list of potential killers. It'd be the best way to prove my brother and I were innocent.

Chapter Five

"Say what?" Bess sat at the consulting table in the front room of Let's Get Organized.

"I want to go to Fox Island Art Gallery and meet Izzy Reynolds." I sat beside my friend. "My plan is to tell them they won a small-room organization package."

"And just how did they win this prize? They're bound to remember they didn't enter a contest."

"One step ahead of you. We made a list of local merchants and randomly picked them. It's a way to introduce our new business to local merchants. We can take pictures of before and after to promote what we do."

Bess reached for a piece of paper and began writing. "We'll do this like Old Maid."

"We don't have time to play cards."

"Hush up. It'll become clear in a minute."

"I'm going to look for France Granger on social media." I opened a search engine on our work computer.

"Go ahead. This won't take long."

Online, there were artistic photos by France, but the post that caught my eye was France and a guitar player. I screenshot the image. "What are the odds that our victim and France Granger dated the same man?"

"It's a small community." Bess cut the sheet into rectangles. "Fox Island, Georgia isn't like Lexington, Kentucky where students come and go. Yeah, we have tourists for about four to six months each year. Otherwise, most of the locals know each other."

"Meaning it's possible they both dated Ryan Ford, also known as Anchorman."

"Exactly." She arranged the pieces of paper in her hand like a deck of cards. "Now you're going to pick one of these names. Whoever you pick will get a free makeover of a small area. This way you'll be telling the truth when you announce to France that she won this opportunity."

"How do I know which one to choose?"

With her thumb, Bess slid one card higher than the others.

"Aha, just like old times." As children, we spent many hours playing cards. I reached over and picked the highest card. "Oh, look. It's Fox Island Art Gallery. I should go discuss it with them. Don't you think?"

"Sure do, but I've got an appointment with a potential client this afternoon. As in a real client who will pay us to work. Why don't you call Paul or Reid to go with you?"

"What can possibly go wrong in the middle of the day in a public place?" We chatted a few more minutes and went our separate ways. Once my brother's name was cleared, I'd make it up to Bess. For now, I was off to see what secrets I could discover at the Fox Island Art Gallery.

The first kink in my plan was finding Reid in front of the art gallery. "Hiya, Katie. How's it going?"

"Let me guess, Bess called you. Don't you have a job?"

"Besides babysitting you?" One side of his mouth quirked up.

"Haha, very funny."

"I do have a job, but it's on the island and I was able to scoot over here to protect you. If Izzy Reynolds shows up, you will need to protect me."

I leaned closer. "I'm sorry. Can you repeat that? I'm sure you didn't say you might need my protection?"

Reid looked right then left. "She has a thing for me."

I laughed. "Oh, honey, I'm sure most of the single women on the island have a crush on you. Except of course for Bess."

"Where does that leave you?"

My face grew warm. "You can still play the role of annoying little brother quite well. Let's go inside before I have a heat stroke."

Reid held the door open, and I entered the cool building. He chuckled, "If you're this hot in March, how are you going to survive July and August?"

"I'll manage by staying in air-conditioned buildings."

"How may I help you today?" A thin young woman with long curly blond hair greeted us.

I stuck a hand out to shake. "I'm Kate Sloan, co-owner of Let's Get Organized. May I speak to the owner or manager?"

"France Granger, manager of Fox Island Art Gallery." She shook my hand with more strength than I would've imagined given her small stature. "What can I do for you?"

"You won a free simple small-space makeover. It can be a storage closet, pantry, or art supply closet."

"Why would you do that?"

"We're trying to get word out about our business, and we drew your name. Are you interested?"

Her stoic expression transformed into a wide smile. "I would love to have you work on my office. It's a disaster, and there's never enough time to get it under control."

"How about I take a look, then we can schedule your appointment." An office was bigger than I'd bargained for, yet it might pave the way to obtaining more information.

"You're sure it's free? No hitches?"

"This will be a simple makeover to get you organized. I won't replace the carpet or paint the walls, but I will bring supplies to make your workflow function."

"Cool." She motioned for me to follow.

Reid stuffed his hands in the pockets of his faded jeans. "I'll get something to drink. Don't leave without me."

"Text me if you need assistance." I winked at him before following France. "Are you an artist, too?"

"Not like Izzy, but I'm a pretty good photographer." She opened the door and turned on the light.

Disorganized didn't begin to describe her space. I surveyed the dark room.

Absolute chaos. "You need more lighting, clear storage bins, and organizers. Your desk doesn't work well because of the piles of paper and all the framed pictures. How would you feel about a credenza?"

"I'd love one."

I opened my work notebook and jotted down ideas. "Do you have a favorite color?"

"Red."

"Let me guess, you love cheering for Georgia."

"You guessed it. My grandpop used to take me to the football games when I was little."

I looked at the photos closer. One was of her and a Black man with bouncy curls. "Is this your boyfriend?"

"Yes, that's Ryan. Can I keep his picture there?"

"Absolutely. He looks familiar. Does he play in a band?"

"Yes." Her voice rose enough that I wanted to cover my good ear to protect it. "His stage name is Anchorman. He'll be stoked when I tell him you recognized him."

"Next time he performs, I'll try to catch the show. Oh, I see a Rolodex. Do you use it?"

France ducked her head. "It belonged to my granddad. He gave it to me when I graduated from college. I keep important contacts on my phone, but it's also nice to have this at my fingertips when I'm working in here."

"I'll definitely keep it on your desk then along with the photo of you and Ryan."

"That'll be great."

"Right now, it looks like I've got enough to prepare for the makeover." It was more extensive than I'd originally planned, and Bess wasn't going to be happy with me. "When would be a good time for you?"

"Anytime but the weekend."

The sooner I got in her office alone, the sooner I could determine if she was involved in Carissa's shenanigans. "I'll be here tomorrow morning. I'd like to take before and after pictures for our portfolio and maybe to put on social media."

"No problem. It'll be good publicity for both of us. Thanks again."

"Spoken like a woman with good marketing skills. See you tomorrow." I headed to the coffee shop.

Reid had his back to the wall. Literally. A woman with smooth brown hair was putting the moves on him. Oh, boy. I pressed my lips tight together to avoid laughing.

I hurried over and inserted myself between the two, wrapping my fingers around his arm. "Honey, sorry that took so long. Who's your friend?" I batted my eyes at him and grinned.

"Katie, this is Izzy Reynolds."

"Oh my stars. How exciting to meet you in person." I lapsed into my Georgia accent that had slowly disappeared over the previous thirty years. "I'm a huge fan of your work."

"We recently had a booth at the art festival, but I don't remember meeting you."

"I'm new to town. Sorry I missed it."

"How new? Are you two dating?" She dared me with her gaze.

"You might refer to us as star-crossed lovers." Not that we'd ever been lovers. Great day. I better dial it back a notch. "We've known each other forever, but life took us in different directions."

Reid took my hand in his and inched away from the artist. "We need to hit the road, sweetie. Good to see you, Izzy."

"Call me." Her voice practically purred.

"Nice to meet you." I struggled to keep up with Reid's six-two frame. His long legs didn't have to work as hard to escape as mine did. "Slow down."

He paused long enough to hold the door for me. "Where's your car?"

"I walked." I adjusted my new sunglasses and studied him.

"Then I'm driving you because I won't risk Izzy running after me with some pretend excuse." He didn't release my hand until I was settled in the passenger seat. "Those are the most ridiculous sunglasses I ever saw."

Oversized square sunglasses in a shade of teal emitted a sense of whimsy. "At the rate I lose sunglasses, you won't have to see me wear them for long."

"Good to know." He rounded the front of the truck and slid into the driver's seat. "So, what'd you learn?"

"Ryan Ford is her boyfriend, but I didn't learn much more. Tomorrow, I'll have unlimited access to France's office. That's my golden opportunity to snoop."

"Mission accomplished. I hope you have a plan for what you are going to search for." He relaxed into his seat and drove with one hand on the steering wheel.

"You'll soon discover, I always have a plan. When I don't, I create one. It's part of my charm." I gave him a sassy smile.

"Oh, brother." Fox Island was small, and we covered the distance in no time. Reid parked in front of my store. "Well, there's no doubt you're charming. However, if you need to brainstorm ideas for what you should search for, let me know. I want to prove Paul is innocent, too."

I squeezed his arm. "I may take you up on your offer."

"See you around Katie."

"Bye, Reid." I hopped out and watched him drive away in his pickup truck. My motivation for moving home to Fox Island had been to end loneliness and rediscover myself. Yeah, I had worked hard as a real estate agent, but true friendships had been non-existent. On the island there was my family and Bess. The idea of renewing a friendship with Reid Barrett had never occurred to me. It probably wouldn't have happened if not for Paul's dire situation, but I found myself thankful for Reid's friendship.

Chapter Six

Back in Reid's pantry late that Friday, I lined up his insulated bottles in a handwoven natural seagrass basket that matched the one holding his coffee supplies. "I'm proud of you for weeding out your supply."

Reid's reply was garbled, and I went into the kitchen. "I'm sorry, what?"

He sat at the table with his laptop open and papers scattered around him. "You didn't leave me much choice, but I agree. There were plenty I never use." He removed his glasses and rubbed his eyes.

"It's been a long day, and I appreciate you going with me to the art gallery." Our little adventure was probably the reason he was working at home tonight.

"Paul's my best friend, and I'll do anything to help prove he's innocent."

"Thanks. Who do you think might be trying to frame him?"

He turned in the chair and stretched out his long legs. "Have you asked Paul who he's arrested lately?"

"Kinda. He can't think of anyone angry enough to set him up for the affair." I sat beside Reid. "Do you think Carissa's death is related to the fake engagement, or is it something else?"

"I don't believe it's a fluke that Carissa died right after posing as Paul's secret fiancée."

I pulled out my phone and searched her posts. "Maybe we'll learn something in the comments from her followers."

Reid rubbed his eyes again.

I checked the time. "I can't believe it's after ten. Go to bed, and I'll head home."

"Not yet. If you focus on Carissa's posts, what can I do?"

"Review Paul's posts. Maybe someone tagged him in a rant." I took time to retrieve my journal and sat back down. Seconds turned into minutes, and soon it was pushing eleven.

"I found something interesting, but it could be random." Reid cleared his rumbly voice.

"What is it?" I clicked my pen, ready to add his thoughts to my notes.

Reid glanced toward me. "Is that your personal journal?"

"Yes."

His footsteps thudded like a person too tired to pick up their feet, and he disappeared for a moment.

I'd never solved a murder or done any kind of investigation. It made sense to buy a new notebook to keep track of what I was learning, but there hadn't been time.

He reappeared and handed me a spiralbound sketchbook. "One for you, and one for me. As I was saying, Brandon Cross has left multiple comments about your brother. He says Paul isn't fair and targeted him."

"First, targeted him for what? And second, I saw his name on one of Carissa's posts." It took a moment to find. "Brandon commented that Carissa couldn't get engaged to a man who was already married. Carissa shot back that Paul had mentioned marriage hundreds of times."

"We can ask Paul about a possible confrontation with Brandon."

I met Reid's gaze. "Returning to Fox Island is a homecoming for me. It's where I'm comfortable, but it's changed. There are so many people I don't know. When this is over, I need to start making new friends."

"There's nothing wrong with making more friends, but you've got Bess, me, and your brothers. Some people never have solid relationships like you do. If you come to me with a problem, I'll do whatever I can to help."

I touched his arm. "You're right. I had a ton of friends in Lexington, but nobody like you and Bess."

Reid ran his hands through his graying hair. "Let's see what we can learn about Brandon. What's your day look like tomorrow? When are you going to the art gallery?"

"I'll go there first thing in the morning. The supplies are already in my car. I want to see what I can learn about Carissa. Can we keep this to ourselves though? Paul wasn't thrilled when he learned we'd already been to the art gallery."

"You were there twice. Paul must have a good reason for you to stay away."

I yawned and closed the sketchpad. "He only wants to hide out at my place. The less people he's around, the less likely he'll say something that can be misinterpreted. It'll give the police more time to catch the killer."

"What does he believe you're doing tonight?"

"Working on your pantry."

"If you plan to stay safe, you've got to be honest with us."

I stood. "There's no need to worry Paul any more than necessary. Please, don't ruin my chance to help him."

"Fine, as long as you keep me in the loop. Safety in numbers."

"Yeah, I know."

"I mean it, Katie. You've got to promise to keep me informed of what you're doing."

"Okay." I grabbed my purse and keys and headed to the door.

"For starters, text me when you get home."

"I was a single mother for years, and I'm perfectly capable of taking care of myself."

"True, but you weren't trying to catch a killer then."

Chills broke out on my arms. Being a strong and independent woman didn't mean I'd take stupid risks. "Point taken. I'll text you."

Heavy traffic slowed my journey home. The majority of cars were heading north, and I decided to follow. Soon little signs appeared directing people to Fox Island Lighthouse Festival. I pulled over and called Reid.

"You home?"

"No, have you heard about tonight's festival?"

"Yeah. A group is trying to raise money to restore the lighthouse grounds by holding a big concert featuring different local bands. The lighthouse keeper's cottage is in bad shape. Seems like the historical society decided tonight's concert would be a good fundraiser since the art fair is tomorrow."

My mind raced faster than two motorcycles whizzing past stalled traffic. "Carissa's ex-boyfriend plays in a band. He dates France now. I'm heading over there."

"Whoa, whoa, whoa. I thought you were tired. It's closing in on midnight."

"Yeah, but this could be important." I pressed the phone against my good ear.

"Wait for me. Please."

"There are tons of people. I'll be safe."

"Don't forget the buddy system. We'll go together. Where are you exactly?"

"Parking lot of Burt's Gym. I'll wait for you." After my husband died of a heart attack years earlier, I learned to stand on my own two feet. We had grown apart when I was diagnosed with a brain tumor, but I hadn't known for sure how bad things were until his mistress showed up after the funeral.

I took a deep breath, willing myself not to remember the heartache he'd caused me over the years. One thing I'd learned was not to depend much on others. Reid, Bess, and Paul were teaching me the exact opposite. Lean on each other.

Who had Carissa leaned on for support? Kyra, Arden, Marie, and France all knew her. Kyra had provided the most answers to my questions. Both were artsy, and both struggled financially. But how tight was their friendship?

Reid drove into the parking lot and tooted his horn.

I locked my car and jumped into his truck. "I could've driven."

"No way I'm getting into your little death trap. Besides, my truck will be less conspicuous."

I buckled up, and he eased into the line of traffic. "What's the plan?"

"Walk around the crowds, and maybe we'll overhear something. Hey, thanks for joining me. You'll probably pick up on more than me."

"You have good instincts, and I'm sure we'll make a good team."

His words warmed my heart, but I shifted mental gears until he parked under a tree a few blocks from the event. I rubbed my hands together and hoped for a clue. A confession would be even better.

Chapter Seven

Unaccustomed to late-night events, crowds, and the noise, I found myself grateful for Reid's presence. "Thanks again for coming with me."

He slid his arm around my shoulders. "You're welcome, but you should know that I'm an early-to-rise kind of guy. It's easier to get started working before the heat of the day. What about you?"

"Ethan, my son, often kept me up late. I could never fall asleep until he was home. I learned to become a night owl."

Reid chuckled. "Aw, so you were one of those mothers."

"Guilty as charged." The crowd thickened, throwing off my equilibrium. "The problem with only hearing in one ear is you never know what direction sounds are coming from. Let's go toward the music."

The all-girl band thanked the crowd and introduced Anchorman and the Freak Band.

Anchorman took the stage, and the crowd cheered.

Teenagers and young adults stood shoulder-to-shoulder on the lawn to the west of the lighthouse. At the rear of the throng of people, not blending in or cheering, stood France Granger. Her head turned back and forth as if searching for a friend. If she was Anchorman's girlfriend, why wasn't she backstage or in the front row?

"Thanks, everybody." Anchorman motioned for the audience to quiet down. "I know we're here to support our Foxy Lady." He pointed to Fox Island Lighthouse, standing tall and regal with spotlights on her. "But I'd also like to dedicate my set to a good friend who just died. Carissa Ruffalo.

We love ya, girl, and we're going to miss you."

A band member said, "Ah, one, two, three."

I glanced toward France, expecting a frown or some negative reaction. Instead, she stood farther back with a tall bald Black man and a woman.

She pulled a white paper bag from her sleek black tote and handed it to them.

The band broke into a song I'd never heard and one I'd probably not listen to again. I tugged on Reid's sleeve.

He leaned down near my face. "What?"

"France is over there. What do you think she's doing?" I pointed in the direction where I'd seen her.

After a quick glance, he shook his head. "No idea."

"Let's do a selfie and see if we can get their picture." I pulled my phone out, and we stood close to each other, but I really tried to capture France and the others.

"Let me try. I don't think you have a good angle. I'll pretend to take pictures of the band." Reid raised the phone high and snapped pictures of the crowd behind us.

"Dude." From behind us, a kid wearing nothing but a pair of tropical swim trunks and untied Converse shoes tapped Reid's shoulder. "Your phone is turned around."

Reid dropped his arm and chuckled as he turned to the young man. "Thanks. There's a lot to learn on these new phones."

"Hey man, I'm impressed you're at a concert this late. Rock on!" He fist-bumped Reid.

Reid laughed again and leaned toward my good ear. "I don't know if he made me feel older or younger, but I can't take any more pictures."

I looked at the young man. "Did you know the girl Anchorman mentioned?"

"I heard of her, but nah." He pointed to his group of friends. "One of them may know her."

A bikini-clad girl standing closest to Converse shoe guy smiled. Her hair was in a messy bun, and she pointed to her swimming attire. "She helped me pick this out. I bet it was the cop who killed her."

My head jerked back as if the girl had punched me in the face. "Why?"

"The affair."

It wasn't easy to hear over the music and crowd, but I understood the word affair. "What if it's not him?"

Converse guy said, "I think she broke up with Anchorman to date the cop. Maybe Anchorman did her in."

My experience with Kyra had taught me not to defend Paul to strangers, but my legs trembled.

Reid pulled me closer to his side. "Anchorman doesn't seem like the kind of guy to let a broken relationship rattle him."

"Don't know what to tell you, dude, but I'm here for the concert. Not conversation."

"Sorry, my man. Take our spots. We need to find something to drink." Reid led me to the back of the crowd before removing his arm from my shoulders. "I'm proud of you for not going ballistic on him."

"It wasn't easy, and it's probably good I didn't hear everything the kid said." I scanned the crowd but didn't spot France. "Do you see her?"

"No, let's move toward the food."

"We can cover more ground if we head in different directions."

"Two words for you."

"Buddy system. I know." I took off toward the concession area, knowing Reid would keep up. "I'm still learning to depend on you."

"You're making progress, Katie." After twenty minutes of perusing the people, Reid reached for my hand. "There are too many people to see her. Plus, she may have left."

"Yeah, it was lucky I spotted her earlier. Maybe we should call it a night."

The music faded as we walked to his truck. After we were inside, I glanced at Reid. "Thanks for coming with me. I wouldn't have gathered as much information by myself. It hurts to know people believe Carissa's story about the affair."

He met my gaze in the light of the dashboard. "You did good with them. You've got to continue being smart. The way you handle people's reactions will affect your ability to prove Paul is innocent."

I fisted my hands. "You're right, but playing it cool isn't easy for me. I work to make things nice and neat—"

"And it's why you're so good at your job, but police work is messy. Crime is messy. Murder is messy."

His words turned a switch on inside me. "Oh, Reid. That's it. I like to create order out of untidy situations. Paul is in the middle of two chaotic circumstances, so I'm the perfect one to help bring order to his life."

"My plan was to convince you to let the cops solve the murder. It was one thing for Paul to ask you to help prove he wasn't having an affair." Reid sighed. "Carissa's death has elevated the crisis to a much higher level."

"I can't hear you." I pointed to my right ear and smiled. "Seriously, I promise to be careful."

"It doesn't sound like you're walking away from the challenge."

I shook my head. "Paul's been too good to me, and I'll do whatever possible to prove he's innocent."

"Fine. I have one request, though."

"What?"

His gaze speared mine. "Don't do anything alone. Call me before going into a dangerous situation, and I'll drop everything to help."

I swallowed hard. For years I'd had trust issues, but it was easy to give in to Reid. "Okay. I'll always have someone with me."

"Thanks." He drove me to my VW in silence. "Good night, Katie."

"Night, Reid." It didn't take long to drive to my rental, but I reflected on the concert. I hadn't looked at the pictures yet, and Reid had taken some too. I yawned. Who were the people France had met? Passing off a large envelope late at night during a concert seemed suspicious. I needed to study the photos. Maybe Paul would recognize the two who'd met with France.

When I got home, Paul lectured me on safety as if I was a child instead of his older sister. When he finished, I fell into my bed, fully clothed, without placing the throw pillows neatly on their designated stool. Tomorrow would be a new day.

Chapter Eight

I woke up Saturday morning with Brandon Cross on my mind. I stumbled to the kitchen in desperate need of coffee.

There was no sign of Paul who I'd left sitting on my couch five hours earlier. Snowball was missing, too.

Most of the belongings I'd brought to Georgia were in storage, but my espresso machine wasn't leaving my sight. I ground Jamaican beans, then added enough coffee for double shot espressos for Paul and me.

The door burst open, and my brother entered wearing a black ballcap pulled low, dark sunglasses, a T-shirt, and shorts. "Beautiful morning. I need to bathe this little rascal, though. He loved playing in the waves." He placed a brown paper bag on the kitchen counter. "Blueberry muffins from a food truck."

"Yum. I'll have coffee ready when you return."

I started the machine then sat in a light blue Adirondack chair on my little porch. By now, the police probably had concluded Carissa's death was murder. While a small part of me hoped they would announce it was an accidental drowning, I didn't believe it. Most likely, Paul, Susie, and I would be on the suspect list, but we were innocent. Once the authorities cleared us, who would they investigate?

Arf, arf. Snowball tore through my little apartment, chased her tail in front of the couch, then joined me on the balcony.

"Look at you all nice and clean again." I rubbed her head.

Paul appeared carrying two white mugs. "Espressos are ready." He placed them on the matching blue table. "Be right back with our muffins."

After he returned and took his first sip of coffee, I began my questions. "How's Susie holding up?"

"Not a happy camper, but she's hanging in there. We found a secluded place on the beach and had a long talk. She's doing her best to believe me."

"Um, I've watched more than a few true crime TV shows. There's no way Susie is involved with Carissa's death, right?"

"Have you lost your mind? Of course, she's innocent." His face reddened.

"In different circumstances, you'd have to ask the question. Moving along, do you know Brandon Cross?"

His head jerked back. "Yes, why?"

"He claims you targeted him. What's that about?"

Paul gave a dismissive wave with his hand. "He's a preacher's kid. Brandon's also an alcoholic. Despite multiple visits to rehab, he can't seem to kick the habit. I pulled him over a while back, and he failed the sobriety test which led to losing his driver's license. He's angry, and it sounds like he's blaming me for his problems instead of taking ownership. I didn't target him, but I couldn't let him drive around the island impaired."

"Makes sense. Where does Brandon's dad preach?"

"Fox Island Community Church."

"I saw Pastor Cross at the art gallery's coffee shop with Bess, but I didn't meet him." I sipped my espresso, and my skull tightened. Definitely a double shot.

"Stay away from there." Paul frowned. "I'm serious."

"I hear you."

He narrowed his eyes. "Not the same as agreeing."

"Listen, there's no need to worry, but I'll be there this morning. I'm working on the manager's office. Have you met France Granger?"

"You're too old to forbid, but I'm not comfortable with you being there, especially alone. Can Bess help you?"

"She's handling the store and taking care of a job where we'll make some money." Not only were we not making money on the project for France, we were losing money. I was good at keeping receipts and track of expenses. I predicted our accountant might say it counted as a tax write-off.

51

Paul clamped his lips together and frowned.

"I'll ask Bess to drop by on some pretext or other."

"Good." His frown diminished. "I also want you to stay in constant contact with me."

"I feel like you're going to lose your mind pacing around this tiny apartment."

Paul pointed at a snoozing Snowball. "We can take another walk, and I'll try to learn more about social media."

"Facebook, Twitter, and Instagram are popular sites to start with. You can use my laptop."

In less than an hour, I'd taught Paul the social media basics. I left him with the dog and drove the short distance to Fox Island Art Gallery. After a quick prayer for wisdom and protection, I gathered plastic totes and entered the building. Time to snoop for clues. My stomach twirled, and I didn't know if it was from excitement or fear.

France held the door open for me. "Good morning, Kate. I'm so thrilled about my office makeover. The credenza arrived almost as soon as I got to work this morning. The men took it to my office. Hope that's okay."

"It's perfect. The older I get, the less I like to lift furniture." Storage containers in hand, I followed France to her office. "Besides the picture of your boyfriend and the Rolodex, is there anything you don't want moved?"

"Nothing I can think of. Call if you need me." She turned on the toe of her wedge sandal and closed the door behind her retreating back.

I whipped out my phone and snapped photos of everything in sight. Before any steps could be taken to organize the space, I needed to declutter. Large clear document cases would help me get started. At least those and a big garbage bag. There were empty and half-empty containers from fast food restaurants.

I got lost in the work of decluttering the messy room. During my time as a real estate agent and stager, I had discovered joy in helping others create order out of their messes. There was also less stress involved in organizing than in selling homes.

I placed all of France's sticky notes on a blank piece of paper. At least right after I read each one. The amount of personal information people had on sticky notes was dangerous. Encouraging clients to put the material on electronic calendars was a must.

A stack of folders slid off the ledge over the desk, so I went ahead and removed boxes and binders precariously sitting on the wobbly shelf. A colorful metal donkey rested on large white envelopes. There was also brown paper along with tape and address labels.

Carissa Ruffalo's name was written in thick black letters on one of the folders. I opened it and snapped pictures of each page to study later, but I couldn't help glancing over the information.

Carissa had been twenty-four years old, six feet tall, and one-hundred-forty pounds. No wonder she seemed frail. Had she suffered from an eating disorder, or was she too busy to eat?

Her work experience consisted mostly of jobs in New York City. Ryan Ford was listed as her emergency contact. Under relationship status was the word boyfriend.

"Ah-hem."

I dropped the files and looked up. Bess stood there with eyebrows raised, shaking her head. "Sister, it's a good thing I came. What would you say right now if I'd been France?"

"Honestly? I would've lied." My heart drummed hard in my chest. "You nearly gave me a heart attack."

Bess tsked. Honest to goodness, tsked. "Let's get this over with. Land sakes, that's a lot of garbage."

I lifted my chin. "It was a pigsty when I got here."

"Shall I carry it out to the dumpster?"

"No, I may take it to Officer Diaz in case he needs the DNA."

"You sure that's legal?" She propped a hand on her skinny hip.

"No, but I have permission to be here. She hired me to clean up and establish a workable office. It seems legit, but Diaz knows the law."

Bess turned on a radio app and played some gospel music, and we worked together in a comfortable rhythm. Underneath the desk was a black tote, similar to the one France had in her possession last night. It was flat, but I peeked inside anyway. Nothing. Oh, well. "Hey, Bess, do you know Brandon Cross?"

"Sure do. He did some odd jobs around the church after his first attempt at rehab. He's a good worker. Strong. At least physically strong. If he could stay away from the booze, he'd be a real catch."

"He got mad at Paul when he lost his driver's license."

"That's the whiskey talking. When he's sober, he's a charmer."

"Help me scoot the desk over here." Moving the desk revealed dust bunnies, spilled coffee, and a white smear. "This will take more than dusting. I've got a bucket and floor cleaner in my car, but I was hoping they wouldn't be needed."

"Won't a mop work better?"

"Probably, but I only brought rags, thinking the place would at least be clean. Most businesses have cleaning crews." The dark-engineered flooring was worse than I'd predicted before we moved France's desk.

"I'm sure they do in the public areas, especially the coffee shop."

I retrieved the extra cleaning supplies from my car and went to work on the floor. Two hours of cleaning and organizing left me breathless. "Don't let me offer a free service again without conditions."

"You got that right." She straightened items on the desk.

"A stranger would never guess what a mess this space was before. Now if we can just convince France to implement a clean desk policy, so it'll last."

Bess repositioned the red stapler. "You added enough red office supplies to be cheerful without overpowering the room. I'll find France for the big reveal."

I chugged the remaining water in my drink bottle and leaned against the wall. It's possible I dozed off, standing upright because France's squeal startled me. I hadn't even heard her enter the room.

"You guys, this place is amazing." France hugged us. "Can I take some pictures of the three of us?"

Bess checked her reflection in the mirror for the impromptu photo shoot. Me? I was ready to hit the road and question Pastor Tom Cross. My best friend wouldn't be thrilled to learn I needed to speak to her pastor, but I'd do whatever it took to clear Paul's name.

Chapter Nine

I found Tom Cross in the church's vegetable garden. He was a tall man with dark hair and a thick mustache, both containing streaks of gray. "Pastor Cross?"

He stood, towering over me. "Yes, pardon me for not shaking hands. I've been working on our outreach vegetable garden for those in need. How may I help you?"

"I'm Kate Sloan."

"You're Bess's friend. Right? I saw you two at the coffee shop, and she often mentioned you when she worked at the church." He motioned for me to follow him. "Please, have a seat."

We sat at a concrete picnic table, and I wiped dead brown leaves off the bench. "I guess you know Paul Wright is my brother."

"Yes, I'm praying for your brother and Susie."

"He's innocent." I explained how angry Paul had been when the truth about my husband came to light. "He's also in love with Susie. I believe somebody framed my brother to get him fired. Citizens like to believe their chief of police is of good moral character."

"I feel like there's more to our visit than you defending your brother." His deep voice had a soothing quality.

"Yes." I didn't add sir because Tom appeared to be about my age, and I didn't want to lay it on too thick. "I don't know if you follow social media, but Brandon has made some unkind remarks about Paul."

"And?" The pastor lifted his hands in a helpless gesture. "I can't control my son."

"Nor can I tell my adult son how to behave. Brandon appears to blame Paul for losing his license." I swept a couple more leaves off the table, and they fluttered to the grass. "Do you think Brandon might have been angry enough to talk Carissa into framing my brother?"

The pastor pounded a fist on the table. Thick eyebrows lowered. "Brandon would never stoop so low. If you'll excuse me, the garden won't weed itself."

Not wanting to end on a sour note, I followed Tom. "I'm sorry, but I needed to ask. I'm desperate to clear Paul's name."

"I know how it feels to be desperate over a loved one, but Brandon's innocent of your accusation. Maybe you should speak to the girl."

"That's impossible. Carissa Ruffalo was murdered."

His mouth dropped open, then he shook his head. "I'm sorry to hear she passed."

"Yeah. Me, too. Were you and Brandon together Thursday night?"

"That is none of your business."

"Well, thanks for your time." I didn't agree, but I left the pastor alone and drove to the store.

On the way over, my phone buzzed, and I pulled over to answer it. The Hands-Free Georgia Act made it unlawful to hold my phone while driving. The last thing I needed was to get a ticket for breaking that particular law. "Hi, Paul. What's up?"

"The coroner's report is in. Carissa Ruffalo died from drowning."

"Do I hear a but?"

"She drowned, but there was a significant amount of drugs in her system."

Oh, dear. "I don't understand."

"Yeah. I don't have a theory yet."

"Kyra Hodge said Carissa was hopeful about her new opportunity in Atlanta, and she wanted to return to show business. I can't believe she'd risk her chance to get back to dancing. How'd you get the report?"

"A buddy texted me a copy. Now shush."

I remained quiet.

"Okay, a muscle relaxer, cyclobenzaprine, showed up in her blood work. Benzodiazepines too. Both could make her drowsy."

"I've been led to believe Carissa got hooked on pain killers after her shoulder surgery, but she was clean. It's a relief that she didn't turn back to narcotics." What was I doing? "Oh, Paul, I'm so sorry. She accused you of horrible things. Shame on me for feeling sorry for her."

Paul sighed. "Hey, she did a bad thing—"

"Very bad."

"True, but her death was tragic. It's okay to mourn her loss." He paused. "What are you doing?"

I caught him up to speed over my morning with France and my conversation with Tom. "I kept France's garbage, just in case we want to sort through it."

"You've done enough. Emerson is a good cop, and he'll find the killer. We only need to be patient."

"Okay. I'm heading to work. Do you need anything?"

"Snowball and I are fine. Keep your eyes open, and stay safe."

"Ten-four." I disconnected and thought about Paul and Susie. Would she be receptive to a call from me? My heart beat faster. I hadn't done anything wrong. If she didn't want to talk, she didn't have to answer. I dialed her number.

"Kate?" Susie's voice was soft.

"Yeah. Are you okay?"

"No." She sniffed. "But we'll get through this."

"How can I help?"

"Paul said you're trying to prove he's innocent. Keep it up. That's the best thing you can do." She sighed. "I've gotta go."

"You can count on me." Multiple people wouldn't be happy that I was firming up my commitment to solve the murder, but too bad. The call ended, and I drove to Let's Get Organized. Signs advertising the art fair could be seen on every street corner.

Paul had warned me to avoid the art gallery. I didn't have a valid reason to return now that France's office had been transformed. The art fair was a different story. It could provide a good way to see a lot of different people in a short time. After checking in with Bess, the fair would be next on my list.

Chapter Ten

At work, Bess and I inventoried our supplies and decided what we needed for a young couple expecting their first baby. We'd promised to help organize their pantry and the baby's nursery.

Bess said, "We need to find affordable ways to market."

I sat beside her at a consultation table. "The pictures we took of France's office will make for interesting posts on our social media and our website."

"I assume Reid will let us post pictures of his pantry. What else?"

"Maybe we could see how much cardboard coffee sleeves cost. If they are affordable, we could ask the local coffee shops if they'd use them if we supplied them."

She shook her finger at me. "I'm on to you, sister. It sounds like another reason for you to go to Fox Island Art Gallery."

"Hey, you can't blame me for trying." I smiled. "Although, I believe it might be an affordable way to market."

"See if it's affordable, and we'll discuss it more."

I made myself a note. "Okay, so how would you like to go to the island lighthouse festival with me tonight?"

"I've got a date."

"Oh la la. Tell me more. Do I know him?"

She stood and reached for her purse. "He's a banker from Savannah. I want to go home and get ready. Will you lock up here?"

"Yes. You should wear your emerald green dress. It looks fabulous on you."

"I'll consider your suggestion."

"Have fun." A banker from Savannah? I hoped he was worthy of Bess. "How'd you meet?"

"A dating website. Ruth kinda pushed me into trying, and I figured it was the only way to shut her up."

Pushy was a perfect description of Bess's sister, Ruth. "Either way, you win, right?"

"I guess that's one way to look at it." She glanced at her watch. "I'm going to be late. Tomorrow, I'll tell you more." She swooshed out the door, and I locked it.

Bess and Paul couldn't go to the art fair with me, so I tried Reid. He'd hammered in the need for me to use the buddy system, and it was worth a shot. After shooting him a text message, I performed the closing routine and set the store alarm even though it was a tad early. Reid's reply appeared while I walked to my Bug.

I'll go. Give me time to clean up. Let's meet at your apartment.

I would've been okay on my own, but it was a bit of a relief to know someone was going with me. *Thanks.*

At home, I found a note from Paul. He and Snowball were out for another walk. If anybody needed to adopt the Westie, it was my brother.

I tidied up, then took a quick shower and slipped into a mocha polka dot skirt and a white short-sleeve V-neck. Fun earrings with matching bracelets, my spoon ring, and Cole Haan tennis sneakers completed my outfit.

A pounding on the door alarmed me. I looked through the peephole before opening the door for Reid. "What's wrong?"

"I was going to ask you the same thing. What took you so long to answer the door?"

I turned off the music on my speaker. "Sorry, I didn't hear you. I tend to play my music too loud."

His hand went to his chest, and he heaved a sigh. "The main thing is you're okay."

"Aw, you care. How nice." My face warmed.

"Of course, I care about you." Reid's neck turned red, and the color crept up to his cheeks.

Uh, oh. We needed to change the subject, and fast. "I'm ready if you are. Shall I drive?"

"Not going to ride in that little bitty bug. Come on." Reid drove us in his truck, and we parked in the same place as the night before. "Are we here for fun?"

"Ha-ha, you should know by now that I'm not relaxing until we prove Paul is innocent." I pulled the sketch pad from my crossover body bag. "Here are my goals. Look for France and the two people we saw her with last night. Speak to Anchorman. I hope we'll bump into him because he's performing tonight. It'd also be fabulous if we crossed paths with Brandon Cross."

"Hold on. Those are some high expectations of this little old art fair."

"Go big or go home." I insisted on paying our entrance fees, and Reid bought us each a strawberry lemonade. We sat on a bench and watched people walk back and forth.

"Kate, your brother doesn't want you to solve this case. It'll kill him if you get hurt. I think the best move is to just be there for him. Listen, pray, listen more, and feed him."

"He does like to eat." I nodded. "Snowball is doing a good job of keeping Paul distracted."

Minutes ticked by.

The people I wanted to see weren't going past us, and my stomach churned. "Time's a wasting. Let's walk around."

Reid stood and held out a hand, helping me to my feet. "Eventually, all the people will walk past us if we stay here."

"I'm too antsy to just sit, but you can stay."

"No, we stick together." He walked on my left side and occasionally commented on a booth or artist. "Abort. Trouble ahead."

Izzy Reynolds stood in front of a booth speaking to potential customers.

We turned and walked in the opposite direction. The lighthouse festival was arranged in a horseshoe shape, with both ends stopping at the stage. People who paid to attend the art show were also allowed to climb to the top of the lighthouse. "It's been years since I climbed to the top of Foxy Lady. What do you say?"

"One-hundred-fifty-four steps? Why not? We might see something important from the observation deck."

By the time we reached the top, I was huffing and puffing. I leaned on the rail of the observation deck and looked at the fair. "It's nice and peaceful up here."

"Sure is. I've got a season pass and try to climb up here once a week. It helps me put my life in perspective."

I nodded while still trying to calm my breathing.

"Kate, see the house over there with the faded red roof?"

With a little, all right, a lot, of squinting, I picked out the house to which he referred. "Yes."

"The place has good bones. I'd like to show it to you."

"For me to live in or for you to flip?"

"You. It's a raised house, but most of the living space is on the main floor, including the primary bedroom suite. The other bedroom on the main floor could be a guest room or your office. The house has a lot of potential, and I think it could be amazing."

I rested my forearms on the black railing. "It couldn't hurt to look. Will it take any repairs or updates? I can declutter and organize, but I can't tear down a wall."

"Yes, it needs to be updated, and that's what I do. I'll listen to your dreams of what you want in a home, then I'll sketch a plan with an estimate of the expense. Saving old homes is good for the environment and good for the island. I'm glad you have an open mind."

"I won't agree to anything until I see it."

"Understood." He smiled.

The ocean breeze tussled my hair, and it smacked my face. I pulled it back into a ponytail. "I usually avoid crowds, but…."

"Why?" He tilted his head.

"I get confused trying to decide where noises come from."

"Is there a special hearing aid that can help?" Reid met my gaze.

"The hearing in my right ear is completely gone. I tried a special device that transfers all sounds on my right to my left ear, then I kept looking to the left at every little sound. I lost all sense of direction."

"Sounds frustrating."

"Kinda, so I don't use it." I looked at the crowded grounds one-hundred-fifty-four steps below us. "I'm ready to return."

Reid held the door open. "After you."

The journey down was easier on my lungs but harder on my knees. At the bottom, I found the screenshot of Anchorman. "This is who we're looking for. He's taller than you, more muscular than you, and he has fluffy cornrows."

"You're about to give me a complex. Why don't you come right out and say I'm old and out of shape?"

I gave Reid the once over, and my face warmed. He fit the cliché of tall, dark, and handsome. "Fishing for a compliment from me? Don't hold your breath, Reid Barrett. I know there are plenty of women singing your praises, starting with Izzy Reynolds and the young Arden Sapp at Fox Mart."

"Ouch." Reid's hand covered his heart. "You really know how to hurt a guy."

"Don't forget I just saved you from an encounter with Izzy."

"Point taken. Let's go find your rapper." Reid stayed at my side while walking around the booths.

"I'll need artwork in my new house. I sold most of my belongings in Lexington."

"Do you want a beach theme in your home here?"

"Possibly. Look at the big red canvas with sunflowers in that booth. It's cheerful and makes me happy. Can we go see what the price is?"

"Go ahead. I'll stand here and text my buddy about showing you the house around the corner while you speak to the artist."

It didn't take long for the woman with short red hair and glasses to approach me. "How are you today?"

"Couldn't be better. I'm interested in your sunflower painting. How much is it?"

The artist went into a lengthy spiel about her education and background. Every time she made a point, I heard ka-ching in my mind. Savannah College of Arts and Design. Ka-ching. Studied abroad. Ka-ching. The price of fancy paints. Ka-ching. On and on, she went until she named an exorbitant price.

Before I could answer, Reid appeared. "I spotted Anchorman."

I turned to the artist. "I'll think about it. Gotta go."

We caught up with Anchorman at a tent where pottery was sold. "Excuse me, Ryan?"

The young Black man turned to me. "What's happening?"

"I'm Kate Sloan, and this is my friend Reid Barrett."

"Cool." He nodded non-stop.

My hands grew damp, but I forged ahead. "I'd like to talk to you about Carissa. Can we buy you a drink or snack?"

"That girl broke my heart." He stood tall. "What do you need to know?"

"I don't believe she'd gone back to using drugs. You were her boyfriend. What do you think?"

"No way. She was hooked on hydrocodone for a year or so. She stopped cold turkey. It was horrible. The withdrawal was wicked. Sweats. Shakes. Vomiting. If a person saw what she went through, they'd be more careful about taking pain meds. If you want my opinion, she was clean. No way she'd put herself through all that again."

"Your heart must've mended quickly."

His eyes widened. "What do you mean?"

"You're dating France, aren't you?"

Anchorman shook his head. "France and I are friends. Nothing more."

"France told me that you're her boyfriend."

"Nah, man. We're only friends. Nothing else. I gotta bounce. My set is coming up. Nice to meet you." He loped away.

"He was friendly." I stared at Reid. "Although, he was quick to deny a romantic relationship with France."

"Yeah, he was clear on that subject. I've got a favor to ask." He stuffed his hands in the front pockets of his jeans.

"What is it?"

"Can you put off talking to France? I'd like to show you the house while the light is good." He had dark circles under his eyes. Probably from staying out with me so late the night before.

"Are you sure it's not because you're afraid we'll run into Izzy?"

"No comment."

I walked toward the gate and glanced back at him. "Hurry up, Reid. I want to see my potential future home."

He shook his head and laughed but caught up with me. "I'm starting to remember you used to be a lot of fun."

"Used to be? You ain't seen nothing yet, buster."

Chapter Eleven

Reid tapped a code into the lockbox on the front door, then led me into the house. "This place is only steps away from the ocean. There's a trail over there. You can walk or bike to the beach. You can also drive a golf cart around the area."

"For real? It's legal to drive a golf cart? I've seen people do it, but who knew it was legal?"

"A lot of beach towns allow carts to drive on public streets. You have to apply for a license, and there are rules, but yeah. It's legit. Another bonus to purchasing an electric cart is it protects the environment."

Reid seemed to have a theme in his life. Protect the environment. I gazed around the room. "It looks so big. I don't need this much space."

"Raised houses give the impression of being larger than they are. Everything below us is a garage and storage space." His eyes sparkled. "There's so much potential here. Three bedrooms and four baths. Front porch, side porch, and back deck. Outside shower so you don't have to track sand into your house after a day at the beach."

From the entry, we walked into the living room. "I'm not a fan of small, choppy rooms."

"No problem." He patted one wall. "This one isn't load-bearing. It'll be easy to knock it down as well as the wall between the dining room and kitchen. If you prefer an open floor plan then it won't be a problem because that's the load-bearing wall over there." He pointed to another wall.

"What's back there?"

"Your bedroom and one guest room." Reid walked taller as he toured me through the beach house.

I remained dubious until we stepped onto the side porch. Charming. There was no other way to describe it. "You just might sell me on this house with the porch alone. I can picture myself having breakfast out here, listening to the surf."

"Wait until you see the roof deck." He took the stairs two at a time. "Here's your loft and extra bedroom. And for the piece de resistance. Ta-da." He opened the door to the deck, and I followed him.

The sight of the ocean from here completely hooked me. "Reid, it's fabulous."

"I agree. We can install a bar area for food prep and add a sink. Imagine a grill, outdoor eating area, maybe a hammock. Add a pergola for shade on blazing hot days."

"Oh, Reid. I want to buy into your excitement." My husband had always picked out our homes. Job transfers in his career as a reporter forced him to move before Ethan and I could join him. We stayed back until the current home sold, and David usually bought our houses. It'd never bothered me, and now I wondered why.

"What's holding you back?"

"A few things. What's the price? What will it cost to remodel? I've only looked at a couple of other homes on the island. There might be a better option."

"All valid points." He quoted the price and looked toward the ocean. "You won't find anything else in this price range this close to the beach. It just went on the market, and it won't last long."

My heart fluttered. Would I pass this opportunity up just for the ability to look at other homes? "If it doesn't turn out the way I hope, we can consider it an investment and sell it for a profit."

Reid's shoulders slumped. "True. Do you want me to put in an offer for you?"

"Let me walk through at my own pace. I'd like to get a feel for it by myself. No offense."

"None taken. I'll take off. Call me when you're ready." His gaze met mine.

"And Katie, there's really no pressure from me."

"Thanks for understanding. I'd like my next place to be my forever home." I rubbed my empty ring finger. Wearing the wedding ring from David had seemed appropriate for my previous life, but I'd removed my wedding and engagement rings when I left Kentucky. They'd been sold at a private auction with instructions not to reveal my identity. A friend tried to convince me to save the rings for Ethan. Not that I was superstitious, but why would I burden my son with rings symbolizing an unfaithful spouse?

"Kate? Did you hear me?"

"Sorry, what?"

The crinkles on his forehead disappeared. "Don't feel any pressure from me. I want you to feel comfortable wherever you choose to live, and I'm sorry for expecting you to feel the same level of excitement as I do for this place. In fact, we can both leave now."

I reached for his hand. "You're a good friend, Reid. There's a lot to like about this place, and I need a little time to absorb it all."

He gave me a one-armed hug. "Take your time. I've got nowhere to be this evening."

Once he left, I explored at a slow pace and took pictures of every room. I tried to imagine how the house would work for me. The loft would be a great place for me to get back to watercolors. It'd been decades since I'd painted anything. Or maybe I could host artists and authors who needed a place to get away and be inspired. Low key and private.

On the main floor, I imagined Reid's vision for one big open room. It'd make a great space for parties. Throwing good parties was one of my talents, probably because organization is key to hosting a gathering.

Was I up to living through a renovation? Move-in ready held tremendous appeal. Although remodeling this place would allow me to put my personal touch and preferences all over the house. Then again, who needed so much stress at my age?

I moved to the side porch with its wide plank floor. I could paint the floor a soft gray to disguise sand and dirt, or a bold turquoise blue and furniture with vibrant cushions. I paced the long, narrow area and imagined myself drinking my morning coffee and eating a warm juicy blueberry muffin.

A breeze fluttered my hair. The sound of the surf gave me goosebumps. The place wasn't in the thick of things like the apartment. In fact, it was fairly secluded.

Would I be safe here alone? Carissa had been murdered in an apartment building with neighbors close by. Although, it probably hadn't been a random killing. I shivered. It was time to get back to finding her killer.

I called Reid.

"Hey, Katie." His deep melodic voice assured me he'd still be my friend no matter what I decided about the house.

"Are you ready to make an offer for me?"

He laughed. "All right. I'll be there soon."

"I'm going to walk around the—neighborhood. Is that what you call the haphazard placement of homes here?"

"Why not? Katie, I'm proud of you for buying a fixer-upper. Not only is it good for the environment, but it preserves the history of Fox Island. I truly believe it'll be a great home for you. See you soon."

I locked the house and took pictures of it from the street. Then I sent all the pictures to Ethan with a short message. *I found my forever home.*

"Lady, look out."

I jumped into the grass and landed on my backside. A bike rider skidded to a stop. When his gaze met mine, my pulse skyrocketed.

Chapter Twelve

"Are you okay?" The muscular twenty-something man asked.

"Yes. What about you?"

He pointed to blood running down his calf. "The anti-skid nails on the pedals scrapped me, but this isn't the first time it's happened. No biggie."

"I'm so sorry." I pulled a clean packet of tissues from my purse and handed it to him. "Are you Brandon Cross?"

"Yeah. Have we met?" He dabbed at the blood with a tissue.

"No, but I've seen some of your posts on social media. You must really hate the police chief."

"Hate may be a little strong, but I wouldn't mind if he left town. The guy's got it out for me. Do you have any idea how hard it is to get a job when you're not allowed to drive?"

I held back the motherly lecture on the tip of my tongue. "What about Carissa? Were you two good friends?"

"More like acquaintances."

Knowing Reid would return soon, I took a chance and pushed Brandon. "Where were you Thursday night?"

"None of your business. Who are you?" He frowned, and his eyes narrowed.

Brandon wore a workout tank, and his bulging muscles convinced me it wouldn't take much effort for him to snap me in two. The kid probably wouldn't even break a sweat.

Where was Reid?

Brandon propped his bike against the white picket fence. "Well?"

"I'm Kate. I heard the ladies are fond of you."

He tilted his head. "I do all right in that department. Have I dated your daughter?"

"I don't have a daughter. When was the last time you saw Carissa?"

He snapped his fingers and pointed at me. "That's it. You're Carissa's mom. We weren't dating, if that's what you're getting at. Anchorman was her last boyfriend. Correction. Chief Paul Wright was her latest boyfriend."

I tamped down my temper. "Did you ever see the two of them together?"

He chomped on gum. "No, but I saw pictures on her posts. Lady, you're kinda freaking me out. Why'd you ask me about Thursday night?"

"It's the night Carissa was murdered, and I thought you might be involved in her death."

He jumped back and grabbed his bike. "You must be out of your mind."

"No, but I am looking for answers." I kept my voice calm and steady despite the fact I wanted to take him by the shoulders and shake a confession out of him.

"Look somewhere else. I got nothing for you." He took off on his bike. I sat on the house's front porch steps and wrote down my thoughts on Brandon in the sketch pad. I wasn't convinced one way or the other, but his name went on the suspect list.

Reid pulled into the driveway, and I hopped in. "You'll never believe who I just met."

"Buckle up. Paul needs us."

I fastened my seatbelt. "Wonder why he didn't call me."

"He said he tried." Reid hurried without being reckless.

I checked my phone. "It's dead. Ethan always gets on me for not keeping it charged. Did Paul say what's wrong?"

"No, but he sounded worried. There's a portable phone charger in my glove compartment." He slowed at a stop sign.

"I've got one at the apartment, but thanks."

"Who'd you meet?"

"Brandon Cross." I caught him up on my short confrontation with the preacher's son.

Reid parallel parked near my temporary home, and we raced to find Paul. Snowball barked when we entered the apartment.

"Paul, what's going on?" I retrieved the portable charger from my desk drawer and attached it to my phone.

"Susie is swamped with reporters at her place, and Emerson Diaz came by to question me. As a courtesy, he didn't make me go to the station."

Reid stood near the balcony and watched outside.

I patted Paul's back. "How did the conversation go with Officer Diaz?"

"He asked tough questions, and he wants to talk to you. In his mind, the top three suspects in Carissa's death are you, Susie, and me."

The supposed fiancé, his wife, and sister. "It makes sense, but you could've told us this over the phone. Why the urgency?"

"Diaz is a buddy and suggested I lay low. I'm going to use my paid time off until the department is convinced I'm innocent. So, I've got nothing but time. I can't go home, but I shouldn't stay here any longer. I need to find a place off the beaten path."

Reid said, "I've got the perfect solution. I'm flipping a place from 1929. It's on the marsh and was in rough shape, but the old house is far enough along for you to stay there."

"What about contractors coming and going?" Paul picked up a whiney Snowball.

"I'll come up with reasons to reschedule them. How soon can you be ready to roll?"

"Less than five minutes. Can I take the dog?" Paul's gaze met mine.

"Sure. No problem." I was surprised to discover I'd miss the Westie even though she'd just come into my life.

In less than five minutes, we were on the road. Reid drove Paul's truck while my brother and Snowball lay down in the backseat. I followed them to the marsh side of the island, down dirt roads, and through the woods. Our only stop was at a service station where fishermen often stocked their coolers with food, water, and beer. Reid bought bags of ice and food staples for Paul, and we continued to the safe haven.

Once there, Reid opened the door for us. "The electricity and water work. Sorry for the mess, but if you want to stay off the grid, this is the place."

I studied the house. There was a trash can and a recycle bin. Sawdust had been swept into a corner. "Your mom was right."

Reid cocked his head in a way I was becoming familiar with. "What do you mean?"

"She said you keep a neat workspace, but where will Paul sleep?"

Snowball sniffed the hardwood floors.

"Sis, I can curl up in a corner. No problem."

"I wouldn't do that to you. Follow me." Reid led us to the primary bedroom. "I'm using this as my office for now. There's a TV and a recliner. Sometimes I get stuck here waiting for contractors to arrive. It's only local stations, but it's better than nothing. There's a hammock on the back porch."

"Thanks, man. You don't know how much I appreciate you." Paul squeezed Reid's shoulder. "Do you have a project I can work on while I'm here?"

"If you're handy with a paintbrush, the upstairs bedrooms need painting. It's fine, though, if you only want to hike, fish, or veg out in front of the TV." Reid took Paul around the house, and I studied the pantry, linen closet, and bathrooms.

When they returned, I waved my hands around the kitchen. "Have you sold this place yet?"

Reid stopped moving. "Why? Would you rather live here?"

"Oh, no. I'm just curious."

"I'm building it for a few homeless veterans."

"How can they afford it?"

"Some non-profit groups are helping with the expenses."

If homeless veterans were going to live here, they'd need a good system to give each person the space they needed. Even if only two men shared a bedroom, they needed their own space. Many couples fought over closet space. How much worse might it be for strangers? I paced and studied the area.

Reid said, "What are you doing?"

"If you're giving veterans a home after living on the streets for who knows how long, they will probably be anxious about the few personal belongings they own. I was thinking lockers or wardrobes that can be locked."

"Good idea."

Paul picked up Snowball and rubbed her head. "It's getting late. You two should go."

I hugged my youngest brother tight. "I hate to leave you all alone."

Snowball jumped to the floor and barked.

Paul hugged me back. "I'm the one worried about you. Trust Emerson to do his job and find the killer. You should only be concerned with your new business."

Reid tapped my shoulder. "Let the man breathe. I'll keep tabs on him."

I released my brother and swiped at a tear. "Paul, call if you need us."

"Will do. Now get out of here."

I headed to my car and dropped a pin on my phone in case I needed to find Paul by myself one day. Had Carissa had family and good friends she could depend on? Marie had believed Carissa left New York to be near family during her surgery and recovery. So, who was her family? Had they stood by her side or turned their backs? Could it be the reason she worked so many jobs? She needed money until her big break came in Atlanta. How desperate had she been to make money?

"Reid, do you think somebody else paid Carissa to spread lies about Paul?"

"It's possible. Why?"

"I'm trying to figure it out." An owl hooted, and I shivered. "What did they hope to accomplish by smearing his name?"

"I don't know." Reid stopped and shook his head. "I'm not riding in that little death trap."

"My Bug? It's perfectly safe."

"I don't know why it didn't occur to me we'd leave here in that." His voice shook.

"Are you serious? It's got a good safety record." My stomach growled. "Come on, and I'll treat you to dinner on the way to my place."

"Pizza?" He circled my car and looked it over.

"Sure. Hop in. We need to discuss what you found out about my potential future home." I'd learned, raising a son, that sometimes distraction worked better than an argument. So, why waste time arguing?

Reid checked his phone. "The agent texted and wants me to call him back."

"That sounds promising. Call while I drive."

Success. He placed the call and quit grumbling about my car.

My thoughts drifted to a list of suspects and what I was going to feed Reid. It'd been a long day, and I craved carbs. Just carbs. No salad. There'd be no redeeming qualities to my dinner.

Chapter Thirteen

After dinner, we met the listing agent for the cute beach house. He came to Reid's home to meet us. With butterflies swirling in my belly, I signed a contract on my forever home. Hopefully.

The agent left, and Reid and I sat in rockers on his front porch. I took a deep breath. "It's peaceful here."

"One of the reasons I bought the place, but I never allow myself to fall in love with a property or house."

"Why?"

"It's the curse of a contractor. If somebody offered me above-market value to buy my place, I'd sell it and makeover another home."

"Have you ever built a new home?"

"No. Restoring older homes leaves a smaller carbon footprint. My goal is to be a good steward of the earth, but we can talk about me another time." He rotated his shoulders. "I know you're concerned about Paul. Who is on your suspect list?"

"I'm not saying they all make sense, but I need a starting point." I opened my sketchbook. "Brandon Cross because he's mad at Paul. Tom Cross because he's protective of his son. Anchorman is Ryan Ford and rejected love is always a motive for murder. The last person on my list is France Granger, because she could've been jealous that Ryan wasn't over loving Carissa."

"Let's rule one of your suspects out. Tom Cross is a pastor, and murder is a firm no for preachers."

"Firm but not impossible." I wouldn't cave in to his philosophy until I knew more about Pastor Tom Cross. Neither would I get into an argument over the preacher.

Reid rocked in the swivel rocking chair and rubbed his chin. Memories returned. Reid often rubbed his chin when deep in thought, even as a child.

I smiled. "Bess is a member of Tom's church. I should attend with her tomorrow."

"Not the best reason to go, but it couldn't hurt."

A dark SUV pulled into Reid's driveway, and a man stepped out. "Bear, you home?"

"Yeah, come on up." He glanced at me and lowered his voice. "This is Emerson Diaz."

"I know who he is. Let me freshen up in case he decides to arrest me." I hurried inside to check my appearance. If Officer Diaz was going to take me in for questioning, I'd go looking my best in case a mugshot was involved.

When I joined the men, they both stood until I was seated at an outside table. Great. No handcuffs. Yet. "Hi, Officer Diaz. How are you tonight?"

"You can call me Emerson when I'm not in uniform. Paul and I are more than work colleagues. We're friends. In fact, Bear takes the three of us fishing out on his boat."

"Bear?"

Reid chuckled. "On a camping trip one winter weekend with the guys, I took an early morning leak, and when I returned, one of the men thought I was a bear."

Emerson laughed. "They yelled bear and scrambled. It's a lucky thing we were fishing and camping. If we'd been on a hunting trip, he might've gotten shot."

Goosebumps popped up on my arms. "That would've been tragic."

"With a last name of Barrett and the camping story, I get called Bear a lot."

It made sense in a manly way, and Reid was tall and broad-shouldered. "My son and his friends have fun nicknames for each other too."

Reid leaned forward and propped his forearms on the small wrought iron table. "Emerson has an update for us."

"This is an unofficial visit, and I'm not revealing anything that's top secret.

Carissa Ruffalo drowned. Kate, I agree it could've been murder. We're hoping the killer will feel more relaxed if he or she doesn't don't know we're looking for them."

"Do you have any suspects?" I'd learned the cause of death earlier from Paul, but I wouldn't get anyone in trouble.

"Do you?" The smoothness of his skin made him appear younger, almost boyish.

"As a matter of fact, I do. Brandon Cross, Tom Cross, Ryan Ford, and France Granger. What about you?"

"Officially, we're looking at alibis for you, Paul, and Susie. I'm not at liberty to share more."

I sighed. It made sense he wouldn't share official information, especially if I was a suspect. "How long do you think it'll be before you look for more suspects? And what can I do to help?"

Emerson scooted his chair back. "Fox Island Police Department is handling the case. Where were you Thursday night?"

"Home. Reid was with us until around eleven, then Paul spent the night. Paul is my alibi, and I'm his."

"Not good. We'll check security cameras of some of the businesses if it comes to that."

"They'll confirm my story. What was Paul's most current case?"

"Looks like you have the same stubborn streak as your brother. Let me handle the investigation." Emerson stood. "Y'all have a good evening."

We didn't say another word until he drove away.

I met Reid's gaze. "Paul keeps telling me to stay away from the art gallery. Do you think there's something fishy going on at Fox Island Art Gallery? France seems nice enough, even if she's high-strung. Izzy has a crush on you. If she killed anyone, it'd probably be me because she thinks we're a couple."

Reid busted out laughing. "I've never given Izzy a reason to hope for a relationship."

"It doesn't always matter to some people. You're a nice man, and she may have read more into an innocent gesture."

"Even if she misunderstood the situation, Izzy is a talented artist. She also supports herself with a career in art. I don't understand why Paul wants you to avoid the place." He popped his knuckles. "There's something we need to discuss."

"About the case?"

"Yeah. For instance, our conversation about the art gallery. Paul doesn't want you involved in solving Carissa's murder. On the other hand, he wants me to keep an eye on you. So here you are, wanting to prove your brother is innocent. You two have put me in a bad position. If I help you catch the killer, Paul won't be happy. If you and I don't work on the case together, you'll do it by yourself."

I stood. "I can make it easy for you."

Reid jumped up and grabbed my hand. "No, that's not what I mean. Paul is innocent of both the affair and the murder. He's my best friend, and I'll do whatever it takes to prove he's not guilty. None of this is coming out right. I'm better using my hands than my words."

My pulse raced and thumped my neck. "It sounds like you want to help without making Paul mad."

"True, but mostly I don't want to endanger you in the process of proving Paul is innocent."

"Where does that put us?" My voice sounded more like a whisper.

"I want to follow you home and make sure you get in safely, especially since you'll be entering an empty apartment. I'd also like for us to attend church together. Let's do as much as possible tomorrow on your investigation, because Monday I need to work."

"You're a good friend, Reid. I'll agree to your suggestion." It wasn't fair to place Reid in the middle, and I'd be as agreeable as possible. "Is church still casual?"

"You know it is."

"Then let's go casual and swing by the festival afterwards. I'm even agreeable to be your girlfriend if it'll protect you from Izzy. We need to check out her booth for anything suspicious."

"Okay, honey. We'll be a couple in love spending an afternoon at the festival."

I laughed. "Looks like you're going to have fun playing the role."

He walked me to my car and opened the door for me. "I'll follow you home tonight and pick you up in the morning. May as well play it up right."

The biggest obstacle to acting like Reid's girlfriend would be not to fall for the act myself. It'd been a very long time since a man had paid so much attention to me. It would be too easy to get used to the attention, especially with Reid. He wasn't the one who got away. Instead, he was the one it'd been impossible to date.

Not dating Reid had been the right decision. He and Paul were lifelong friends, more like brothers. Starting tonight, I'd be his pretend girlfriend. Nothing more.

Chapter Fourteen

After the early service, Reid and I lingered so we could be the last in line to shake hands with Tom Cross.

The pastor smiled and chatted with the people ahead of us. It didn't seem to matter if it was a child or an older adult; he connected with each person.

It was obvious the minute he spotted me. His posture stiffened, and a frown appeared. "Kate, I heard you spoke to Brandon."

"Good morning, Pastor Cross. I enjoyed your sermon on having a servant's heart."

His face reddened. "What do you want?"

"If you'd give me your alibi for Thursday night, I'd feel much better about joining your church." I squeezed Reid's hand. Confronting a preacher wasn't comfortable.

"I was home alone, preparing my sermon. You know, we have a right nice Methodist church up the street. The Catholic priest has been here for years, and that could be another option for you."

"Father Joe?"

"That's him. You should pay him a visit."

I got his meaning. "You've got an interesting way of saying don't let the door hit you on the way out."

Reid stuck his hand out. "Morning, Pastor."

"Good morning, Reid. Nice to have you join us today."

I didn't hear Reid's reply. When the much more polite conversation ended between the men, Reid and I strolled to his truck, hand-in-hand.

"He's pretty insulting for a man of the cross." I slid into the passenger seat.

"At least you know where he stands." Reid circled the front of his truck and whistled on the way to the festival. Once we parked, he looked at me. "You need to shake it off if we're going to manage this charade."

"You're right. Happy couple. Fun day. Got it." I flashed him a fake smile. "Oh, that's terrible."

"I'll do better. Thanks for coming with me." We exited the truck and headed for the entrance. "First stop, Fox Island Art Gallery tent."

Reid reached for my hand. "May as well get it over with."

There was already a crowd, and we worked our way past popular booths like the man who carved decorative wooden boats and the apron makers with salty expressions stitched on their products. I paused at the tent featuring special olive oils. Nope. I couldn't get distracted. I turned my sights to the art booth.

Izzy waved to us before we were close enough to speak.

I waved back while we walked toward her. "Hi, Izzy."

Her eyes darted between Reid and me. The sun emphasized tiny wrinkles around her eyes. "Hi, Reid, and I'm sorry, tell me your name again."

"Kate Sloan."

"Right. How are you today?" Her gaze returned to Reid, who wore sunglasses, and his expression remained neutral.

I said, "Izzy, you're such a talented artist. Do you have a website so you can reach more people?"

Her chin lifted a fraction. "Yes, we ship all over the world. I'm quite popular in Jamaica, Haiti, and Trinidad. I've even shipped a few paintings to France and England."

"Very nice. Reid helped me find a house, and soon I'll be in the market for pictures. Do you mind if I look around?"

"Absolutely. Shop away, and I can be commissioned to paint something special for you." She handed me a business card. "Feel free to give me a call."

"Thanks, Izzy."

Reid said, "How'd you like the work Kate did on France's office?"

"I'm impressed, and it takes a lot to impress me." She curled her fingers around Reid's other arm even though he and I were holding hands.

If I was a jealous person, and especially if I was Reid's girlfriend, I'd never buy a painting from Izzy Reynolds. Where were her manners?

Reid elbowed me to move right, allowing him to slip away from her clutches. "Let's look at the smaller pictures over there. They would look good in the kitchen."

We walked to the far corner of the tent. I kept my voice low. "What wall do you mean?"

He leaned close and whispered into my left ear. "I have no idea. Just making something up to get some space between us and Izzy."

"I always knew you were smart."

Movement behind the tent drew my attention. It was France. She held a dark green bank bag and looked both ways. I motioned for Reid to watch.

We made a show of looking through stacks of pictures, but the entire time we kept our attention focused on France.

Izzy reappeared with an older woman and led her to the table beside us. "This new shipment of paintings from Jamaica would make a fun wedding gift for a young couple. The vibrant colors attract people. They can be framed or hung alone. The small size makes them perfect for placing in groupings. Best of all? They are originals from an artist in Kingston, Jamaica. You won't find these on everybody's walls like if you bought something from a box store."

The white-haired lady leaned on her cane. "They are bright, I'll give you that much."

I glanced at Reid. "What size do you think they are?"

"Twelve by sixteen. Why?"

"I'll tell you later."

I retrieved my sketch pad from my extra-large polka-dot tote and recorded the dimensions. Meanwhile, in the shadows of an enormous azalea bush, France greeted the tall man I'd seen her with the night of the concert. No wonder I was tired. I'd been staying up late, trying to prove Paul's innocence. The sight of these two stimulated me more than a double shot of espresso. With very little conversation, France passed the bag to the man in exchange

84

for a thick package. The length and width were close to the same size as the paintings from Jamaica.

The exchange was probably as innocent as it looked. Nothing nefarious unless you considered tax evasion or smuggling. France could also be trying to avoid paying a customs broker. Was it more cost-efficient to pay people to fly to Georgia with art? Was it quicker?

The two parted ways. France entered the tent, waved at us, then talked to Izzy before leaving.

"Reid, did you hear what they said?"

"France is heading to the art gallery to check in merchandise and will return later with lunch for them both."

It didn't sound suspicious, but what was the reality? "Should we follow France?"

"Why?"

"If the exchange I witnessed was as innocent as it appeared, why isn't she opening the paintings here?"

"Um, well, suppose they need to be framed. Or maybe she has to record them before displaying them." He shrugged. "Honestly, I don't see anything unusual in her action."

"Okay. Maybe I'm trying too hard to find something illegal."

"Could be. Although, Paul was suspicious of Fox Gallery and illegal activities." He reached for my hand as Izzy approached.

She gave us a dazzling smile. "Have you found anything?"

I said, "There's plenty of time for me to decide. How long do you think before I move in, Reid?"

"Once we make decisions on what we're doing, it should take eight to twelve weeks. You know, it's probably best to wait a bit. We may move walls, or you could decide to tile areas around the kitchen instead of hanging pictures."

I faced Izzy. "He's right, of course. I'll be in touch, though."

"Okay. You know where to find me." She turned to another customer.

Reid leaned close. "Let's follow France."

"Sounds good to me." In fact, it was exactly what I wanted to do.

Chapter Fifteen

The art gallery was closed, and the trip would've been a bust if we hadn't spotted Brandon Cross walking into The Sand Bar.

Reid parallel parked on the street. "Well, well, well. What do you know? Tom's not going to be happy to discover the pricey rehab he just paid for was money down the toilet."

"It's sad that Brandon can't kick his addiction."

"I agree. The kid is still in the denial phase. I'm going in to have a little chat with him. Will you please stay here?"

"Since you said please so nicely, sure. Let's hope he responds better to you than he did me." I lowered my window to catch a breeze and studied my notes.

Where was Brandon's mother? Had his parents divorced? I searched Facebook and other social media for any mention of his mom. "What am I doing? Bess will know for sure."

I dialed her number and doodled on my notes.

"Hello, Kate. I didn't see you in church."

"I went to the early service." Bashing her preacher wouldn't get me anywhere, so I didn't mention his rudeness. "How was your date?"

"He watched every woman in sight, then he got a little touchy-feely with me. It's a good thing I met him at the restaurant because I drove myself home."

Poor Bess. "I'm sorry to hear that."

"It's no big deal. I'm more comfortable being single than fighting off jerks. How's your investigation going?"

"Thanks for asking. I need a little more information on Tom Cross's wife."

Bess sighed. "It's a sad, sad story. She was an alcoholic. One year she was in Savannah celebrating St. Patrick's Day, and I do mean celebrating. Anyhow, she decided to drive home, but the woman was sloshed. She was driving a pickup truck with big tires. When she reached Harmon Bridge, she hit the concrete side and flipped over. The cops estimated she was going over ninety miles per hour and never hit the brakes. It was high tide, and she drowned in the marsh."

"Wow, that's terrible." Instead of judging Tom, I should show the man compassion. "It makes sense he'd be super protective of Brandon."

"Um, hmm. Tom has spent who knows how much money trying to set his son on the path of sobriety."

"Brandon's in The Sand Bar right now. Reid went inside to speak to him."

There was a sharp intake of breath from my friend. "Tom will be crushed. Just crushed. I should give him a call."

"Wait, Bess. Let's see what happens with Reid and the kid." I updated her on my informal investigation and kept talking until Reid returned. "Hold on, let me see what Reid learned."

Reid stood by my open window. "I think we can rule out Brandon."

"Bess is on the phone. Do you mind if I put her on speaker?"

He nodded. "Hi, Bess. We can take Brandon off Kate's suspect list. He finally admitted he was drinking Thursday night. The bartender confirmed his story."

"Reid, is he drinking now?"

"Afraid so."

"I'm going to call his daddy to pick him up. It'll break his heart, but it's the right thing to do." Bess ended the call without so much as a goodbye.

I lowered my sunglasses and met Reid's gaze. "Can we leave before Tom arrives?"

"Yeah." Reid circled the truck and pulled away before we crossed paths with the preacher. "What next?"

I scratched Brandon's name off my list with such a flourish it tore a hole in the page. Why didn't I feel better about eliminating one of the suspects? "Good question. I'm down to three persons of interest. Out of Tom, Anchorman, and France, who do you believe is most likely to be the killer?" My voice held an edge. I needed to calm down.

Reid did a double take, then pulled into Daniel's Deli. "As a kid, you never did well on an empty stomach or junk food. Let's get some protein in you and go visit Paul. We'll take him a couple of sandwiches and see how he's getting along."

"You amaze me, Reid. My husband never understood how my mood changed when I didn't eat. How did you remember?"

He backed his F-150 into a shady spot and laughed. "You lit into Paul and me a few times when we were kids. One day he joked about how cranky you got when you didn't eat. I made sure to always carry a snack when we were all together, especially if we went fishing and couldn't quickly get to food."

"So that's why you always had a package of orange peanut butter crackers." My face warmed.

"It was a small price to pay to stay on your good side. At the time, I never imagined hypoglycemia was a real condition and not just a quirk of yours."

I opened my purse and removed a pack of Lance peanut butter crackers. "Even today, when I get shaky, I crave these."

Reid laughed. "Nice. I'm glad you're taking care of yourself. Let's go inside and order something."

Once we were in the cool restaurant, I ordered the Danny Boy Special and sweet tea with mint and lemon. By the time our food was ready, I'd drained my tea and asked for a refill before we took off.

Three suspects on my list. I had something to work with, and once we fed Paul, I'd dig into why he didn't want me to visit the art gallery.

Chapter Sixteen

"Paul, why do you keep warning me away from Fox Island Art Gallery?"

The three of us sat on empty whiskey barrels on the back patio. Snowball had eaten crumbs from our sandwiches, then curled up at Paul's feet.

The earthy smell of low tide on the marsh wafted our way. Not the most pleasant smell, but a familiar scent and somewhat comforting.

My brother wadded up the paper wrapper of his roast beef on rye. "Why can't you take my word that it's not safe?"

"If we weren't suspected of murdering Carissa, I'd be more willing to stay away." I opened the sketchbook of my murder notes. "What's going on at the gallery?"

Paul glanced at Reid. "Help me out, man."

"You're on your own. I don't like getting in the middle of you two." He pointed his finger back and forth between us.

I said, "Here's what I know. Izzy sells paintings all over the world. Besides her local business, she ships them internationally. France is the manager of the gallery, which allows Izzy time to focus on her art, as well as flirt with Reid."

He growled. "Stop it."

I looked back at my notes and suppressed a grin. "This morning I witnessed France paying a man for paintings. At least that's what I suspect." I told my brother what I'd witnessed.

"Carissa worked at Fox Mart and also the art gallery. France paid her to help waitress at exhibitions or to mingle with potential customers. Marie works at the coffee shop, and she wasn't thrilled with the way France catered to Carissa's needs. Although, I don't have Marie on my suspect list. She's just a disgruntled coworker. As a matter of fact, Arden wasn't thrilled with Carissa's work ethic. Kyra Hodge liked Carissa, but they were both interested in artistic endeavors."

"Whoa, whoa, whoa." Paul ran his hands through his graying hair. "How do you know all this?"

"I intend to prove you're innocent. So, I go around and ask questions. It's my prerogative as a big sister to ignore your protests and protect you."

Paul's nostrils flared. "Not if it puts your life at risk. I can't just hide out while you track down the first killer in Fox Island in decades."

My brother and I hadn't argued in years, but we slipped into old patterns. At least with Paul, the root cause of our debates was due to our love for each other. "Officer Diaz told you to lay low from the press and allow him to work on the case."

"Did you hear yourself? Emerson Diaz is working on the case. He's been trained to investigate. You haven't."

"Time out, you two. Paul, take me through the house and show me what you've done. Kate, why don't you take Snowball for a short walk?"

I stood and snapped my fingers. "Come on, girl."

The Westie refused to come with me until Paul and Reid entered the house.

"You're stuck with me. Let's go, Snowball." The Westie followed me into the wooded area between the house and the marsh. "Thank you for taking care of my brother. When this is over, I think you need to stay with him. He needs you."

A squirrel darted across our path, and Snowball ran after the creature, barking along the way. I chased after the two of them. "Snowball, stop!"

The earth became mushier the farther we traveled. My cute tennis shoes would be destroyed, but I had to save the little dog.

The squirrel ran up a pine tree, and Snowball placed her front paws on the tree trunk and barked.

Leaning against another pine, I caught my breath. When my breathing evened out, I clapped my hands. "Enough. Stop barking."

She whimpered but returned to me.

"You need a bath." I picked her up, unwilling to risk another sprint through the woods. "You're so muddy; I'll probably have to toss this top too."

The dog had the nerve to lick my chin, as if it was a game.

"Silly girl." I'd always wondered if I was a dog person. Maybe cats would be my thing. Once I settled into my new, er old, home, I wanted a pet. "It's a good thing I ate, or else I wouldn't be able to carry you. How much do you weigh?" A better question was why hadn't I attached her leash.

Reid and Paul were on the patio when we returned.

"Oh, my goodness." Reid laughed. "What happened to you two?"

"Squirrel. Snowball needs a bath."

"Looks like you do too." Reid's assessment brought a smile to Paul's face. "Stay here."

I sat on the patio and removed Snowball's collar. "Paul, I don't mean to worry you."

"But you're a grown woman and so on and so forth. Reid just lectured me on trusting your instincts. He also mentioned you've ruled out Brandon Cross."

"Do we start by looking for Carissa's motive to frame you? Or should I start by looking for a killer who is trying to link you to the murder?"

"My gut tells me it's the same person."

"Why did you tell me to avoid the art gallery? Carissa worked there, so maybe it's the link. Did you give them a citation or something?"

Reid returned with a stack of towels, dish soap, and a large bucket. "Not the groomers, but it'll do in a pinch. I'll take Snowball. You two need to talk."

"Thanks, Reid." I smiled.

He took the dog and left Paul and me to finish our conversation.

"Sis, I haven't done anything to harm the gallery. However—"

My heart raced. He was going to share something good. Maybe it wouldn't be good, but it'd be juicy. "Yes?"

"We don't normally have many tourists in the winter. This year has been different. We've had more art festivals and events with artists. There have also been people, quite a few people, vacationing here from various Caribbean Islands. No crime there. But I started paying attention. I followed a tall, bald, Black man to the Valentine festival."

I held my hand up to stop him. "Since when did Fox Island start hosting a Valentine Festival?"

"See what I mean?" Paul raised his hands in a helpless gesture. "It doesn't make sense because it's not very warm. I was told that the merchants wanted to try holding the event to get them through the end of the slow season."

"Okay, then, I guess it makes sense. Go back to your story."

"The Black man attracted my attention because of his overstuffed back-pack. I mean, the thing was bulging, so I proceeded to trail him to the art booth. Izzy wasn't working the crowd, but France was there. The man handed her the backpack, and she passed a fanny pack to him."

"Then what?"

"This will sound horrible. I wanted to follow the stranger, knowing I could connect with France later."

"What's the horrible part?" I rolled the slick dog collar in between my fingers. It needed a good washing, or Snowball needed a replacement.

"A man had a heart attack, and I had to administer CPR until an ambulance arrived. By then, the stranger disappeared. I saved a life, but I lost the trail of whatever's going on. I hadn't noticed anything else until a week ago at the Spring to the Beach Fair."

Fox Island was well-known for holding fairs and festivals to attract all ages, but they usually began around Saint Patrick's Day. "Keep going."

"The stranger was back in town, and a woman was with him. I followed them but didn't want to do anything dangerous with the crowd. Once we left the fair, I lost their trail. Again. They're slippery."

"If this happened a couple of weeks ago, do you think they are the ones who paid Carissa to lie about you? If they're up to something illegal, it'd be a good motive. What do you think?"

"I'm honestly not sure."

"Okay, then, what do you suspect the man and France are exchanging?"

"The man could secretly be passing off artwork to avoid taxes, but would that pay for his flight and accommodations? I doubt it. I considered human trafficking. He takes money and gives France folders of victims and their specialties. It'd be profitable, but I've not seen victims."

"Tell me more."

"There are various types of human trafficking. Innocent people pay to come to America. They believe they'll have good-paying jobs waiting for them. Instead, they wash dishes and other menial labor, barely scraping by. Their bosses keep passports, making it impossible for them to leave even if they could save money."

"Do you believe the art gallery is involved in human trafficking?"

"I don't know everything happening on the island, but word would get out if this was going on."

Reid appeared with a clean dog and sat beside us without saying a word.

"Okay, Paul. Spit it out. What do you think they are doing?"

"Smuggling drugs."

Chapter Seventeen

"Drug smuggling? How?" I continued to twist the dog collar in my hands.

"It's connected to the artwork, but I don't know how."

"I've got the garbage from France's office. Should I give it to Officer Diaz?"

"You what?" A vein bulged in Paul's neck.

"I didn't steal it." I explained about remodeling France's office.

Paul said, "I'll text Emerson and ask him to meet you at…where's the safest place?"

Reid took the collar from me and placed it around Snowball's neck. "I'll handle the details with Emerson. Say, Katie, why don't you show the pictures on your phone to Paul. You know, the selfies."

"Oh, yeah. There's too much bouncing around my brain." I swiped through the photos, then handed my phone to Paul. "They're blurry, but maybe you can tell something."

Paul's eyes widened. "That's them. The guy with the backpack. The woman's the same one from the spring festival."

"Great. I'll show these to Emerson."

My brother fiddled with my phone. "I'm sending copies to myself."

"Okay, so it's possible these two are connected to Carissa. It'd most likely be through France."

"It's all a theory at this point. We have no evidence. Nothing worth even questioning them."

"Don't give up. We're making progress."

Reid handed me a faded T-shirt. "It's clean, if you'd like to wear it."

I glanced down at the mud covering my blouse. "Thanks. I need to clean up, but it won't take long."

An hour later, we met Emerson behind the old Dairy Barn burger place. We'd swung by my apartment and gathered the garbage bag and dust rags from France's office.

I shook his hand. "Thanks for meeting us. This might be nothing, or there could be a clue in here." I explained how it came to be in my possession. "I'm giving you the dirty dust rags in case this is related to drugs. Who knows?"

"Stranger things have happened." Emerson pulled on rubber gloves and took the potential evidence from me.

I glanced at Reid. "Using real cloth rags lessens my carbon footprint."

"Look at you being kind to our planet. Way to go." He smiled.

Emerson placed the items in his unofficial vehicle and closed the door. "We'll go through it, but to be clear, I'm handling the murder investigation."

"I know, but Paul is my brother. It would've been silly for me to throw this away if there was a possible clue in here."

"Right. Kate, you really, really, really need to be careful. If this case is related to drugs, we're looking at something more sinister than a crime of passion. If you keep sticking your nose into this, you might be the next victim."

I gulped. "I'll be extra cautious. One day I hope to see some grandbabies."

Emerson removed his fishing cap and adjusted one of the hooks in the thick outer band. "No, you're going to stay out of the investigation."

The man could not have been any clearer, but I didn't debate the issue with him. Again, it was pointless to argue an unwinnable case. We told him goodbye.

"Reid, thanks for all of your help this weekend. Why don't you take me home, and let's call it a day?" I yawned. "Maybe sleep will help me think clearly."

"You know yawns are contagious." He drove me home, humming on the way.

I rested my eyes, enjoying the peaceful moment.

"Katie, we're home."

I opened my eyes. "Sorry, I must've dozed off."

"You snored too."

"No way." I felt my face for drool. Dry. Thank goodness. "I appreciate the ride."

"Hey, you're not getting off that easy. I'll go inside and check for bogeymen."

We hopped out and walked to the door. I unlocked it and led Reid inside. "The place is so small. There's no way anybody could hide in here for long."

Reid checked every closet and even under the bed before moving to the front door. "Coast is clear. Lock up behind me."

"Yes, sir."

He stood there and looked into my eyes.

My heart skipped a beat.

This couldn't be happening. I forced myself to step back. "Goodnight, Reid."

"Night, Katie."

I locked and bolted the door before flopping onto the couch. Phone in hand, I searched social media for posts by Carissa, France, Brandon, Anchorman, and even Tom Cross. The preacher was a bust, so I focused on the others. Anything interesting got screenshot. When I finished, I sent these pictures to the nearest all-night pharmacy with the ability to print my pictures. Included in the order were the selfies at the concert and shots of France's office. A chain drug store on the other side of Harmon Bridge guaranteed the photos would be ready in an hour.

This would've been a good time for a guard dog, but making the trip alone was doable. It would've been less nerve-wracking if Emerson hadn't emphasized how dangerous it was for me to investigate. Still, I was a grown woman on a mission. I'd drive to the drugstore and return with the prints in hand.

Chapter Eighteen

To prove I wasn't careless, I texted Bess about my plan to pick up the photographs. My best friend was likely asleep, but if I didn't show up for work the next morning, at least she could sound the alarm. My text would give the authorities a place to begin the search. I shivered.

Yes, I could've alerted Reid, but it'd be cruel to keep pestering him with my problems. The man had a life of his own, even if I was his pretend girlfriend.

It didn't take long to drive to the store. There were a few customers, but it was easy to pick up and pay for the photos and a tri-fold board. I was a visual person, and these would help me put things into perspective. Much better than just writing notes.

Back in the dark parking lot, frogs croaked, and the humidity clung to me like a second skin.

A hand touched my shoulder. I turned and punched the stranger in the gut.

"Umf."

I raced back to the store. It'd be safe inside.

"Katie."

The voice stopped me in my tracks. Oh, no. "Reid?" Of course, it was Reid. Nobody had the same deep silky tone as he did when he uttered my name. I turned back. "What are you doing here?"

He winced as he straightened. "Seems like I should ask you the same thing. Less than two hours ago, you were settled in for the night."

"I'm sorry. How'd you know to look for me?"

"Bess called. She didn't want to worry Paul about your shenanigans."

"Shenanigans. Well, I'll be." I picked the packet of photos and the board up from the blacktop parking lot. "My brain won't shut down."

"If you don't get some rest, you'll miss clues, and there's also a risk you won't see the murderer coming after you."

My legs shook, and I leaned against the car. "You're not being completely fair. You snuck up on me."

"I guarantee the murderer won't announce his or her presence." Reid placed his hands on my shoulders. "Katie, I called out to you twice before touching you."

"I didn't hear you." Never before had I felt handicapped. The loss of hearing in my right ear had been a nuisance. I'd never considered it dangerous. "Reid, this means being deaf in one ear could be the difference between life and death."

"Not if you drop the investigation."

I nodded but didn't agree to anything.

Reid hugged me, and I clung to his strength. Held on for dear life.

All I Want for Christmas is My Two Front Teeth played on my phone. "That's going to be Bobby. He's been calling me for days."

"Answer it. I'll wait."

"You can listen." I swiped the screen. "Hi, Bobby. It's kinda late for you to be up."

"I'm at the clinic. Somebody broke into my dental practice."

"Did they steal drugs?"

"I don't keep drugs on site. If the culprits were looking for painkillers, they left disappointed. My guess is this has to do with our dear brother Paul."

I tried not to get aggravated with Bobby. "Who would come after you because of Paul?"

"Nobody can find him, so it makes sense they'll take it out on us. Whoever did it was chewing gum. They spit it out on my freshly waxed floor. It's also stuck on my new shoes."

Anybody who ever met Bobby knew he had zero tolerance for gum. "Why do you think this is connected to Paul?"

"I've never had trouble, and it can't be coincidental this occurred right after that girl announced the affair and got herself killed."

Tact wasn't a quality my brother possessed. "You can't believe Paul had an affair."

"He wouldn't be the first person to ignore their wedding vows."

Tears sprung to my eyes, and an awkward silence followed. Yes, he knew David had been unfaithful to me. I wouldn't allow myself to cry.

"Sorry, sis."

"Forget it." I took a deep breath. "Besides the gum, was there any other damage?"

"Nothing obvious."

"How can it be linked to Paul?"

"There were a lot of angry people posting he should be fired. This could be a sign the protestors are taking it to the next level." He sighed. "Susie had protestors and the press at her house. Lois convinced her to go visit her parents for a few days."

My sisters-in-law had been friends before marrying my brothers. In fact, Lois had introduced Susie to Paul. It made sense Susie would leave town if Lois suggested it. "That's one less thing for Paul to worry about."

"Where is he?"

Interesting to note Susie hadn't told them where Paul was hiding. "I'm sure he's fine."

"Hey, the cops are heading my way. Be careful." The call ended.

"Never easy with Bobby." One side of Reid's mouth quirked up. "Katie, the situation is escalating. I'm not sure if you're safe at your apartment."

I raised my hand to stop him. "It's as safe there as any other place on the island."

"Then go visit Ethan in Texas. Get out of town until the murderer is caught."

I shook my head. "No. This is my home, and I refuse to walk away from my business." I'd avoided so-called friends the last few years living in Lexington to get away from their gossip. My life at the beach would be different. I wouldn't hide from trouble.

"Would you consider staying with my mother?"

"No. Joy is probably asleep by now, and there's no reason to expose her to my family problems."

Reid walked away, then returned. "I'll follow you to your apartment."

"Thanks." I drove, comforted to see his headlights in my mirror. *Lord, protect us all.* Reid made a good point. Continuing to look into Carissa's murder could put my life in danger, but it was a necessary risk in order to save Paul.

Chapter Nineteen

Seagulls screeched, waking me up Monday morning. Six-thirty. I sat up, and the room spun. I wasn't a superhero who could solve crimes, but I was a worried sister. Sleep would be possible when Paul was proven innocent of his alleged crimes.

When the room quit spinning, I went through my morning routine of stretching, showering, and making the bed. Next came coffee. While eating a breakfast bar and savoring my first cup of coffee, I studied the pictures on my new evidence board.

Carissa's picture was in the middle, with photos of Anchorman, Tom, France, and a big fat question mark. It panicked me to know there were only three suspects on my list, so I added the possibility of a suspect I'd never heard of.

Officer Diaz wasn't going to share his investigation with me, so I needed to get more leads. Organizing my notes and this board were in my comfort zone. My husband had been a reporter. Oh my goodness. Reporters were hanging out at Paul's house. I left my coffee and hurried to get dressed.

Polka dots and my spoon ring were my signature trademark, but today was a day to avoid being recognized. I had a tote full of clothes I'd worn to cheer Ethan on at sporting events. In very little time, I'd dressed in white shorts, a blue Eagles T-shirt and pulled an Eagles ballcap over my ponytail. Bright blue Converse completed my sports mom ensemble.

I lingered long enough to swallow down my vitamin and drove to Paul's house.

"Yes." There were multiple vans along the road. I parked on the street and walked toward the crowd.

Mike Best, my favorite local news anchor, stood at the end of the driveway speaking to a cameraman. Mike was shorter than I expected. Even shorter than my five-foot-seven frame.

I stopped beside him and waited until we made eye contact. "Hi, Mike. I'm a big fan of yours. Are there any updates on the case?"

"Thank you. It's always nice to meet a fan." He tilted his head. "Have we met?"

"No."

He said, "We got word that Paul Wright's wife is going to make a statement this morning."

I gasped. Bobby thought she'd left town. What was going on?

"You seem surprised. Do you know Susie?"

So much for my poker face. This conversation was going south fast. Bess had challenged me not to lie to people even while trying to prove Paul's innocence. "Uh, we've met."

"Do you believe she'll stand by her husband?" He motioned to the cameraman.

I stepped away. "I'm not making any public statements."

"How do you feel about a conversation off the record?" He gave me a charming smile.

"Better than one on the record." Could I trust the reporter? On the news, he seemed like a man of integrity. It seemed worth the risk. "I'll share if you'll share."

He squinted his dark eyes. The sun highlighted a few gray hairs along his sideburns. "Are you trying to scoop me?"

"I'm not a reporter. You don't need to fear I'll scoop your story."

"And you're sure we haven't met?"

"Absolutely." I pushed my old aviator sunglasses up.

"Let's talk inside the van. I don't want to go off-site and risk missing Mrs. Wright's speech."

"Mike, I can almost guarantee—"

"Shh, wait til we're in the van."

Inside the back of the news van were monitors, keyboards, cables, and other mysterious items. "You're not going to secretly record me."

"I give you my word. No recordings unless you agree."

The space was tight, throwing us close together on our little swivel seats. Mike said, "You seem familiar to me. Are you a celebrity?"

"No. I've watched you on TV, just like thousands of other viewers. Who do you believe murdered Carissa Ruffalo?" I picked up a candy wrapper and dropped it into a small plastic trash can.

"The obvious answer is Paul Wright." He removed his dark suit jacket and loosened his black tie.

Despite my deceased husband's flaws, he always strove to unearth the truth. "You don't strike me as the kind of reporter who is satisfied with the obvious answer. Although, the fact you're standing in front of the Wrights' house tells me you might settle."

He chuckled. "Lady, I like your spunk. What's your name?"

"Not yet. Please tell me you'll dig deeper into this story. Wouldn't you like to be the reporter who doesn't take this story at face value. What if you solve the mystery and get some kind of award?"

The smile disappeared, and he leaned closer. "Seems like you've got a personal interest in this case. You believe the wife won't make a statement now, and you seem to think the cop is innocent. What's your angle, lady?"

My throat went dry, and I licked my lips. "Are we still off the record?"

"Yes." The sincerity in his eyes matched his tone.

"Paul Wright is an innocent man. He didn't have an affair with Carissa Ruffalo, and he didn't kill her."

"How do you know?"

"I'm Kate Sloan, Paul's sister. So, I beg you not to take this story at face value. Dig for the truth." My eyes watered, but crying wouldn't do any good.

He snapped his fingers. "I thought you looked familiar. I've studied your family, er Paul's family. I've seen a lot of pictures of you. Your husband was a reporter. David Sloan. I can't believe I didn't figure it out on my own."

"Do you believe me?"

"I won't fall for a pretty face. Why should I take your word for it that your brother is innocent?" He clicked a pen.

"Think about the victim. Carissa Ruffalo. Did you notice she didn't post much on social media before the alleged engagement to my brother?"

"Yep. Going to plays and the ballet were her main topics with the exception of a rapper boyfriend. Even then, she didn't post much about their relationship."

"Anchorman, aka Ryan Ford, was the boyfriend. She broke up with him before her death."

"Mind if I write that down?" He lifted his eyebrows.

"As long as you don't reveal your source." I sighed. "I don't mean to sound like a woman with trust issues, but hurting Paul is the last thing I want to do."

"I have a few trust issues of my own." Mike pulled a business card from his jacket and wrote on it. "This is my private number. How's that for mutual trust?"

I glanced at his slick business card. "I like it, but how will you know to answer if I call?"

"Mrs. Sloan, very few people get my personal number."

"Please, call me Kate. Do you have a list of suspects?"

"Nothing original, but I'll work on it. So, seriously, is Mrs. Wright not going to make a statement?"

"I've got it on good authority you're wasting your time here."

"Where do you believe I need to search for the killer? If the affair was a ruse and the murder was meant to frame Paul, this is some conspiracy theory."

"I'm not a reporter or a cop, and I won't tell you how to handle your investigation." I gave him my cell number. "Thanks for your time, Mike. I'm counting on you."

"I'll be in touch."

We exited the van, and I returned to my Bug. I hadn't learned anything from Mike Best, but he'd agreed to consider other options. I'd count that a victory.

Chapter Twenty

I entered Let's Get Organized carrying skinny lattes for Bess and me. "Good morning."

"Lawsy, girl. Whatcha wearing? You planning to go to a baseball game?"

"I decided to dress incognito, and I just met Mike Best."

"You met the newscaster?" She shook her head and tsked. "Dressed like that?"

I pushed her cup closer, hoping the caffeine would take the grouchy edge off my best friend. "Let me explain."

Bess removed the plastic lid and inhaled the vanilla coffee scent. "Go on."

"Should I start with last night or just fast forward to meeting Mike?"

"Tough question. May as well lay it all on me." She took a sip. "Why don't we sit, and if a customer comes in, you can skedaddle to the back room."

"I'll pretend you didn't just hurt my feelings." I settled in at our consultation table and pulled out my sketch pad. "Next time I investigate a murder, I'd like a journal. Reid gave this to me, and it works. But I like journals more."

"I don't want to hear about next time. Let's get you through this alive."

If Bess knew about the lecture Emerson had given me, she wouldn't be so calm. I replayed my actions since we'd last seen each other.

"Seems like you and Reid are getting mighty close."

"That's your analysis from all the clues I've gathered?"

Bess shrugged. "You've been a widow for over fifteen years. Did you date much in Lexington?"

"Never, and I'm not dating Reid. We're working together to prove Paul is innocent."

"Fine. We've got two ladies who'd like to meet you for a consultation. Can you squeeze them in?"

"Very funny. If they want to meet today, I'll only need to change clothes. Give me the basic details."

"Izzy Reynolds would like you to work on her office. She'll pay us to make it even more fabulous than France's office. It looks like your freebie is going to pay off. There's also Tessa Lawson, who'd like to convert a guest room into office space."

"So today's focus is going to be office space. If you call them, I'll go through our supplies." I walked into the back room.

"If I'm going to learn how to organize, I'd like to tag along." Her bangs were parted in the middle, and the rest of her hair was pulled into a sleek ponytail.

"Sure, but I thought you were more interested in the business aspects."

"Yeah, I am, but I think organizing spaces will be fun. I liked what we did for France."

"Working together will be so enjoyable." I pointed out office supplies that might work for Izzy. "With her artistic abilities, we'll need to order pieces appropriate to her talents."

"Her art is colorful. Do you think she'll prefer neutrals in her office or bold color pieces?"

"We'll make a copy of my interview questions. Once we discuss them with our clients, we'll know what direction to go." I straightened a stack of clear shoebox totes. "I really thought closet spaces would be what people needed organized."

Bess said, "Most people don't need winter clothes here, and we're more casual than residents in Savannah. With more people working from home these days, I understand why dedicated office spaces are popular."

I took notes on what Izzy might need, then closed my notepad. "I'll change and be back in thirty minutes."

"See you soon."

A news van was parked across the street. Coincidence? Doubtful. Instead of walking straight to my apartment, I took the long way around. A man dressed in khakis and a red polo shirt followed me.

I darted into Fox Mart.

Kyra stood at the register. "Good morning. Oh, it's you."

"Hi, Kyra. How are you today?" I glanced out the window.

The man in the polo sat on a concrete bench, looking at his phone.

"How can I help you?"

"See that man?" I pointed him out.

"In the red shirt?"

"Yes, he's following me. Is there a back way to slip outside? I don't want him to follow me home."

"If he's a stalker, you need to call the police."

"It's worse than that. I'm worried he's a reporter."

Kyra bit her lower lip and looked from me to the man. "I thought a lot about what you said. If your brother didn't kill Carissa, we could all be in danger. I want justice for my friend, so I'll help you get away from that guy."

"Thanks, Kyra."

She led me past the employees' room and opened the door to a storage area. Boxes were stacked against one wall. On a rickety table was an open cardboard box of white T-shirts. Plastic bags littered the concrete floor.

I picked a few up and threw them in the large trash can on the way to the exit.

Kyra opened the door, and sunshine flooded the dimly lit space. "Be safe."

"You have no idea how much I appreciate this." I jogged down the street to my apartment. Lucky for me I still wore sneakers. Whether living on the coast or solving a murder led to more running, it was probably time to invest in better sneakers. If I had to run from danger, I needed good running shoes.

Chapter Twenty-One

A while later, Bess and I stood in Izzy's large office. The place was even worse than France's had been before we tackled it.

Izzy sat in her desk chair and waved her hand in a circular motion. "Well? What do you think?"

No way I'd let this opportunity pass us by. "Of course, we can organize it for you. What's your favorite color?"

"Lime green."

"Fun. Do you want this place saturated in color, or do you prefer pops of green?"

"Lime green."

"Right. We'll make sure there's plenty of lime green in here." My face warmed, and I walked around the space.

Bess said, "I don't believe you answered the question. We want to make sure you love this office when we're finished."

Izzy leaned back and propped her feet on the scarred black desk, then crossed her slim ankles. Gorgeous black Valentino T-strapped lace pumps adorned her feet. "Pops of color will be more to my liking."

She was going to be a challenge if she wouldn't be more specific the first time we asked a question. I circled around to her. Business must be extremely good for her to afford Valentino shoes. Or else there was more to the gallery than selling art. "I love your shoes."

"Me too. I wear them every chance I get." She moved her foot back and forth.

Bess nodded. "I prefer flats, but I can appreciate what you're wearing.

We've all got to dance our own dance."

There was a knock on the door, and France entered. "Oh, sorry. Izzy, I didn't know you had people with you."

"That's okay. What do you need?" Izzy remained stretched out. She was either completely relaxed in her surroundings or trying to look powerful.

"We need to discuss a new shipment when you have time."

I pulled a tape measure from my bag. "I can take measurements if you two want to talk."

France shook her head. "It can wait."

"Don't be ridiculous." Izzy stood. "I'll come with you. Kate, to answer your question, a neutral background is my preference."

"Thanks."

Izzy and France left us alone.

"Bess, why don't you follow them and eavesdrop? It could be a shipment of you-know-what."

"You must be off your rocker. They might catch me."

I pulled cash from my wallet. "Say you're getting us something to drink from the café."

Her muttered response didn't faze me because I couldn't distinguish the words. Measuring the window and walls kept me from obsessing on what Bess would learn.

If Paul's hunch was right, and the gallery was connected to drug smuggling, this could be an important clue.

One of Izzy's shelves held art supplies. Paint, brushes, rags, and open packages of chewing gum. I snapped a picture of the packets of gum and sent it to Bobby with a text message. *Is this possibly the same gum you found in your office?*

His reply was immediate. *Maybe.*

So much for that clue.

A pretty cabinet would be a nice way to hide painting materials. I pictured a fun antique china hutch. It could be painted lime green and placed against the neutral wall.

Izzy's updated office required more attention than France's space. We'd declutter, paint, buy pieces to store her supplies and organize. I opened drawers and cabinets to get a feel for storage containers. For a normal person, I'd allow one container for pens, pencils, and other writing utensils. Did an artist need more containers for these supplies? I made a note to ask Izzy. The system we created would need to be functional for the artist.

In the corner was a three-drawer file cabinet. I tried to open the top drawer. It was locked. The other two couldn't be opened either. I would ask if she wanted to keep it in her office.

Izzy's space confused me. Did she create art here, or was this a business space? It seemed like she'd have a studio for when she wanted to paint. Or maybe she'd take an easel outside for inspiration. It'd be sad to think of her working in this uninspiring room when she painted.

Bess returned carrying two cups of coffee and shut the door with her foot. "Sister, you're not going to believe what I heard."

I took one cup from her hand and leaned close. "What?"

She whispered. "France has another meeting tonight with someone called Jason Nesbitt. He must be from out of town, because he's returning to his home island at the end of the week."

"What island?"

"I don't know, but didn't you say Izzy sells artwork in Jamaica?" Bess took a sip of coffee. "Aw, I needed this."

I couldn't help but smile at my dear friend. "Yes, and she also sells works from Caribbean artists."

"Okay. Let's think about how you can smuggle drugs into our country with artwork."

I sipped my coffee. "Mocha latte. Nice."

"I know what you like." She gave me a saucy wink.

I paced around the office and noted the bare walls. "Reckon why she doesn't have paintings or any wall art?"

"Kate, you're sounding more like Georgia than Lexington. To answer your question, we really need to find out the purpose of this space."

"I couldn't agree more, and don't forget, Georgia is my home." I reached for my list and passed it to Bess. "There's an inventory of items I believe we need. I included issues we need to discuss with Izzy."

She read over it while sipping her coffee. "Looks good. Why don't we find her and get some answers?"

I walked into the hall with the staff offices and spotted Izzy. "Hey, when you have a minute, we'd like to nail down a few things."

She strode to me with purpose. Click. Click. Click. Her heels tapped on the wood floor. "What would you like to know?"

"Where do you paint?" We entered her office.

"I have a she-shed area in my backyard. It's temperature controlled to protect my paintings."

"Why do you have so many art supplies in your office?"

"Hmm. Probably because I have items shipped here. I don't want to risk packages being stolen from my porch." Once again, her answer didn't match my question. Maybe she was also hearing impaired.

Bess said, "We need to create a system for getting your art supplies from here to your studio so they're not cluttering up your office. What do you do in here?"

"Business."

Her comment wasn't helpful. "Like do you meet with people in here?"

"I deal with email, research artists who reach out to me, and pay the bills. Other times, I have appointments with people."

At last, we were getting somewhere. "Would a small sitting area be helpful? A few chairs around a coffee table, or maybe a loveseat and a couple of chairs?"

Izzy smiled. "How about a couch? Sometimes I get headaches and wish I could lie down for a few minutes."

Bess scribbled on my notepad. "A couch it is. We'll box up your paints, markers, and color pencils for you to take to your studio. Would you like clear containers, or should we put them in cardboard boxes for you to transport?"

"Clear containers. I might even have you girls work on my art studio, if I'm pleased with how the office turns out."

Girls? We were both in our early fifties. Oh, well. "Moving on. What about your file cabinet? Would you like something fancier? Or do you even need it?"

Izzy's eyes widened, and she hurried over and pulled on the drawers. When they didn't open for her, she relaxed her shoulders. "I definitely need it."

"Would you like it if I could find a lime green cabinet?"

"That would be fabulous." She patted the dented gray cabinet. "I will need to be able to lock the drawers, though."

"No problem." I noticed Bess continued to take notes. "Can we decorate your walls?"

She looked around the room as if with fresh eyes. "This is my business area. Maybe hanging some of my art will encourage others to want to buy some. Let's do it."

We continued discussing suitable ideas with Izzy until her phone buzzed. She pulled it out and looked at the screen.

I stood across from her. One of my secret skills was being able to read upside down. When my son Ethan did homework, he had never wanted me to look over his shoulder. I learned to read sitting across the table from him. It'd helped me to decide if he was on the right track or not.

Today I was able to read her message until she stepped away and turned her back on me.

Izzy said, "I need to go. Are you two through here?"

I picked up my purse and coffee. "We're done for now. We'll draw up a plan and meet with you later in the week. We'll have estimates on the cost as well."

"Good. I'm sure you've heard about starving artists. There will be a budget for this."

Bess gathered her things. "That's good to know. We'll give you some options. How do you feel about second-hand furniture?"

The artist motioned for us to walk ahead of her. "If it's in good shape, I'm agreeable."

We said our goodbyes, but at the gallery's door, I stopped. "Bess, I want to speak to the barista who made this wonderful drink." I spoke loudly in case anyone was watching.

"I gave her a tip. Oh yeah, here's your change." Bess handed me a smooth dollar bill and a few coins.

"That's not why I'm going. You go on, and I'll walk to the store."

Bess whispered in my ear. "I don't know what you're up to, but I am aware you probably read the text message Izzy received."

"I'll tell you as soon as I can. See you in a few minutes." I turned on my toe and entered the coffee shop. "Hi, Marie."

"Oh, hi. Was your latte okay?"

"It was perfect. I'd like to order some cookies to serve at a business meeting."

Her face lit up. "I've got your traditional chocolate chip, peanut butter, and sugar cookies. I also have peach drop cookies and gluten-free chocolate mudslide cookies."

"Oh, your specialty cookies sound delightful. I'll take a dozen of the peach drop today."

"Coming right up." The barista placed them in a white box, then met me at the register.

"Marie, have you heard of any developments on Carissa's murder?"

She told me the price, ignoring my question.

I handed her a credit card. A chill danced up my spine, and I looked around. A few customers sat at tables. Some were in conversations, and others sat alone. "Marie, do people come here just for your coffee? Like, they don't just drop in after viewing the gallery."

"Yes, ma'am. There are a few locals who come in frequently." She returned my credit card and receipt. "I hope you enjoy the cookies."

"Thanks. You have a good day." I walked through the lobby.

France stood at the information desk by herself. She stared at me until our eyes met. "Kate, I like what you did to my office. I think your organization scheme will help me be more productive."

"I'm glad to hear that, France. See you later." I hurried outside and down the street. Had she listened to my conversation with Marie? Was she the reason Marie had ignored my question?

I succumbed to the frightening sensation of being observed and walked faster. If it hadn't been for the cookies, I might have broken into a run. By the time I entered Let's Get Organized, I was huffing from my fast walk and fear. Had my imagination played tricks on me, or had someone truly been watching me?

Chapter Twenty-Two

Inside the store, Bess was giving price quotes on the phone. It allowed me time to collect myself until Bess ended her call and looked at me. "Kate, you need to get in shape. It's not that long of a walk between here and the art gallery."

I nodded. "You're right."

She narrowed her eyes. "Hmph. Tell me about Izzy's text message."

"The other person mentioned meeting her at the band's trailer at the lighthouse tonight."

"You got a time?"

"She turned around before I could read more." I walked to my desk and found the sketch pad with my notes on Carissa.

"You know, I'm really surprised the fair is lasting so long. In the past, we had weekend festivals. Even in the summer, when we had lots of tourists, the events didn't last all week."

I moved the unused storage containers from the front counter to a shelf in our workroom. "Do you think the longer events bring in more tourists?"

Bess plopped down at her desk and turned on her computer. "I don't know, but let's see who's in charge of this week's event."

"While you do that, I'll see what's on social media." My breathing had returned to normal, and I settled in front of my computer. It didn't take long to find tributes to Carissa and negative comments about Paul. Ugh. I switched to Mike Best's TV station. There was a short clip of him reporting on Carissa's murder. He ended the piece by questioning who else may have had a motive to harm Carissa. "Well done."

"What are you talking about?"

"It's Mike Best. He ended his segment by suggesting there could be other suspects. Isn't that nice?"

"You were due for someone to give you a break."

"True. Did you learn anything?"

Her eyes widened. "I sure did. Fox Island Art Gallery is sponsoring the fair. I looked at the applications to have a booth, and the prices are dirt cheap. They don't even require you to sell art. I mean, I'd get it if you want to sell pottery, wood carvings, wind chimes, stained glass, and items in the realm of the art world. But there don't appear to be any restrictions."

"Interesting. You know, I saw people selling fancy extra virgin olive oil."

"My point exactly."

"Hey, Bess, do you think you could arrange for Pastor Cross to meet with me?"

"Why? Do you plan on apologizing for accusing him and his son of killing Carissa?"

"Well, I didn't exactly accuse Brandon of murder."

"When you ask a man for his alibi during the time of a murder, you're pretty much accusing him. What you did was even worse. You virtually accused the pastor's son of murder."

"Yeah." If your best friend couldn't acknowledge your bad behavior, who could? "I should have found a different way to get the information. So, will you please convince Tom to meet me?"

"I don't know, Kate. He's my friend and my pastor. You're putting me in a bad position."

"Fox Island is too small of a community to live on someone's bad side. I'll be on my best behavior."

She sighed. "I'll see what I can do, but there won't be any shenanigans. You can't discuss the murder or Brandon. Apologize. That's all."

"I reiterate. I'll behave."

She sighed. "Okay. I trust you."

"It's time to change the subject. Do you want to look at the consignment shops for a couch, or should I?"

"There are some nice places in Savannah. I'll handle it. We're going with neutrals and pops of lime green."

"That's my understanding." Izzy had been evasive during our meeting. "When we present our final plan, she'll have to sign off on it. We won't let her claim the final product isn't what she expected."

Bess crossed her arms. "Yeah. Sometimes rich people are worse about wanting their money back than the poor people."

"Don't you know it."

We made plans to divide and conquer. After Bess left, I sat at my desk to record my cookie purchase. There was writing on the back of the receipt. *Meet me at dark behind the dental office.*

Ah ha. She did know more than she'd been telling me. I read the note again. She wasn't asking me to meet her. She was telling me. No way would I miss my opportunity. Fox Island only had one dentist, and it was my brother, Bobby Wright. He would be furious if he found out about this rendezvous. Not because I might be in danger, but because it would reflect badly on him if I was caught.

I was also smart enough not to go alone in case it was a trap. I needed to create a plan to hear Marie's information, stay safe in the process, and keep Bobby from finding out.

Chapter Twenty-Three

I closed the shop early and walked home to change clothes. On the way, I had a quick phone conversation with my son. Ethan was busy, and most of our talks were short.

When I entered the apartment, a moment of joy filled me. In a few short months, I'd have my forever home. This apartment worked for now because it was inexpensive, and I was able to rent it for a month at a time. I enjoyed how close it was to the action of Fox Island, but I'd be more comfortable in the quieter area where my new home was located.

I opened the refrigerator. Not much to choose from, and Reid had agreed to accompany me tonight. I removed a container of Greek yogurt and some bowls of fresh fruit. It was my standard meal when I was in a hurry or too tired to cook. I tossed blueberries and strawberry slices into the creamy white yogurt and returned the containers to the refrigerator.

Taking a seat at my little table, I looked through the photos I'd taken and developed relating to the murder. There had been various pill bottles at Carissa's place. It didn't make sense to have so many vials when she was clean. Had the murderer staged it to make the police suspect a drug overdose? Drugs had shown up in her bloodwork, but that didn't mean she'd taken them willingly.

The next picture was from Carissa's kitchen. Wine and uneaten brownies. The authorities must have also tested them. Too bad I couldn't find out the results.

People cooked marijuana in brownies. Maybe the killer intended to drug Carissa. Ballet dancers ate healthy foods and watched their weight. It seemed reasonable to assume she'd refuse to eat the sweet treat. Maybe that led to a fight, and what? Had she been forced to get in the tub so the killer would drown her? It'd take too long to fill it with water, and there were no obvious signs of a struggle.

The next photo was of Reid and me at the concert. A selfie with the tall bald man and small woman in the background. Their faces were fuzzy, but I'd recognize them if we crossed paths again.

There was a knock at my door. I shoved the pictures back in their envelope and went to look through the peephole. Reid stood there, and I opened the door.

"Good evening."

"Come in." I stepped to the side and closed the door when he was in my apartment. I studied my door. "Reid, there's no protective chain here."

He rubbed his fingers along the doorframe. "My guess is there used to be one. During a remodel of this place, a builder probably decided it wasn't necessary. Deadbolts are safer, and most people have some kind of security system these days for protection. Why? Do you want a safety chain at your new place?"

I inhaled his fresh woodsy scent. "No. Did I tell you that Carissa had a chain on her door? It was open as far as the chain allowed, but the door had been locked."

Reid frowned. "Was there a deadbolt option?"

I tried to remember. "Yeah, but it wasn't engaged. How did the killer get out of the apartment with the chain in place?"

"That's the big question. It's probably why they considered suicide in the beginning." He rubbed his chin. "Is there only one point of entry into Carissa's apartment?"

"No, she also has a sliding glass door leading to a small balcony. Her apartment is on the fifth floor." I opened my package of photos and found the pictures of Carissa's sliding door. "These are a tad blurry. I tried to take them discreetly after the police arrived."

"Are these the photos you had printed at the drugstore?" He shifted his focus from the picture to me.

"Yeah. I'm a visual person."

He flipped through all the pictures. "Are the originals on your phone?"

"Yes. Why?"

"My eyes aren't the best. Can we make the picture bigger? I'd like to examine the balcony door."

I reached for my phone and located the picture before handing it to him. "In case you're wondering, there was nothing in the sliding door track to prevent it from opening. But there was a metal security bar lying to the side. See?"

Reid squinted.

I pointed to the object.

"Oh. I see what you mean. In conclusion, it was possible for the killer to leave by the balcony if, and it's a big if, they are athletic. Plus, they risked getting caught scaling down the building."

"I've thought about the escape. The person could've used rappelling equipment, or it might have been as simple as dropping from one balcony down to the next. Repeat the process until you reach the ground, then run."

"I'd say it's possible for a strong and maybe a tall person. You'd need to swing a leg over the rail and land on the balcony below you."

"Do you think the police searched for rappelling ropes? Honestly, I've never rappelled, so I don't really know what all is involved."

"Yeah, I don't know either."

"It's getting dark. We should go meet Marie."

"Okay." I moved my bowl to the sink, grabbed my crossover purse, and we left.

"Where are we meeting her?" He opened the truck's passenger door for me.

"You won't believe this. She said Bobby's office. I'm sure it'll be deserted, and that's probably why she chose it."

Reid laughed. "Bobby won't be happy if he catches wind of it, but I'm sure Marie plans to stick to the shadows if she's going to share sensitive information." He motioned for me to get in.

I opened the notes app on my phone and buckled the seatbelt.

"Whatcha doing there?" Reid pulled away from the curb and drove to Bobby's office.

"I want to take notes during our conversation."

"I imagine it'll scare her away. Let's pay attention, and you can write it all down after she leaves."

"Then I should've brought my sketch pad, but you're right."

Sirens sounded, and blue lights flashed. Reid pulled over, and three police cars zoomed past us.

Reid eased the truck back onto the road. "Let's hope Marie doesn't get spooked by the sirens."

Chapter Twenty-Four

We sat in Reid's truck behind Bobby's dental office, waiting for Marie to show. My palms grew damp. "I hope she's okay. This was her idea."

"I know. A lot of things could've happened to delay her, or it could be a simple case of nerves. Maybe she got scared and changed her mind."

"What if she's in danger? I'd hate for something bad to happen to her, especially if it's because of me."

"Try to stay calm."

"Easy for you to say." My shoulders slumped. "Sorry. That sounded mean."

Reid laughed. "You've said meaner things to me in the past, but apology accepted."

Ouch. His comment hurt.

Minutes ticked by.

A van pulled into the parking lot and came to a stop near us.

"Game time." I jumped out of the truck and walked to the driver's side. "Marie?"

The window lowered. "Who is with you?"

"That's Reid Barrett. He's harmless."

"Oh, yeah. Izzy has a huge crush on him." She white-knuckled the steering wheel.

"What did you want to tell me?"

Reid joined us. "Evening, Marie."

"Hi." She looked straight ahead. "There's something hinky going on at the gallery."

"Like what?" I kept my voice calm and soft.

"There have been a lot more deliveries the past few months. One day I had a shipment of supplies come in at the same time that Izzy received a package. Well, to be fair, it could've been a package for France. I didn't realize it, and I was expecting new menus. When I saw the box, I assumed it was for me." Her voice faded away.

"What happened?" I inched closer to hear her words better.

"I used my box cutter, but I'd only started down one side when France appeared. She jerked it out of my hands so fast I cut her hand. I had to grab a towel to stop the bleeding. France claimed the box contained a picture from a new artist they wanted to feature."

"Did you believe her?"

Marie looked in both directions, still clutching the steering wheel. "I've accidentally opened a piece of art before, and I didn't damage it. So, what was the big deal?"

Reid said, "It does sound suspicious. Is it possible France was just having a bad day?"

"The gallery used to only feature paintings by Izzy and pottery by local artists. In the past, Izzy was all about supporting our local community. Now we display paintings by artists from Jamaica and Trinidad. It doesn't match our mission statement. You know what I mean?"

I described the people I'd seen France with at the concert. "Do you know who I'm talking about?"

Marie nodded. "Yeah, but I don't have much interaction with them. I'm usually the first one to open the gallery because of locals who want coffee. There's a door that slides across and locks the gallery entrance. It's not noticeable unless you're looking for it. Anyway, one morning, the door was open halfway."

"Did you see anyone?" Reid's smooth voice had a calming effect.

She shook her head. "No, but Izzy came in before France that day. She grilled me about the open door. I told her I don't know the security code and I don't have a key. There was no reason to blame me."

I said, "To enter the gallery, you need a key and a code?"

123

"Yes." She dropped her head onto the backs of her hands. "That's all I know. It's nothing really, but you asked questions. Maybe you can fit these weird episodes with your pieces of the puzzle and discover what's going on."

Reid said, "What do you think is going on?"

Marie sat straight and looked at us. "I don't know. Art smuggling? Or some kind of insurance fraud scam? I need to get out of there before something happens to me like it did Carissa."

I gasped. "Do you believe Carissa died because of something happening at the art gallery?"

"Carissa was focused on making money to move to Atlanta for her career. Anytime France asked her to work, she agreed. I'm scared she saw or heard something dangerous." She paused. "On the day Carissa died, she had an argument—"

A car pulled into the parking lot with bright lights shining on the three of us.

Marie screamed. "They found me."

Chapter Twenty-Five

A sleek BMW squealed to a stop in front of us. Bobby jumped out. "Kate, what are you doing here?"

"How'd you know where to find us?"

He pointed to the security cameras.

"I'm out of here." Marie drove off in her van, leaving Reid and me to face my angry brother. Smart girl.

"Bobby, I can explain." I walked to him.

"It's bad enough our brother is being accused of an affair, there's also gossip about the murder, and now you're having clandestine meetings in my back parking lot. How's this going to look? I'll tell you how it looks. If anybody drove by and saw you three, they'd think it was a drug deal going down. You and Paul are going to destroy my practice. Reid, how'd you get roped into this?" Bobby's arms flailed, and his voice grew stronger with each word.

"Calm down, man. Your brother is innocent. You believe that." There was an uncomfortable pause. "Don't you?"

Bobby groaned. He was a year younger than me, but he often acted like the oldest child. Other times, he acted like the middle child. "I know he's innocent, but his actions affect my business. I've got a family to support."

I said, "Bobby, Paul is the victim, and he needs our support."

He turned on me. "What specifically are you doing here?"

"I'm doing everything I can to prove our brother is innocent. The young lady you scared off had some potential information that could help Paul."

"But why'd you have to meet her here?" His voice grew loud again.

"She picked the place." I shrugged. "It's a coincidence, and I couldn't talk her out of it because she slipped me a note."

Reid crossed his arms. "Bobby, do you know anything about a drug smuggling operation in Fox Island?"

He shook his head. "No. Of course I have drug seekers who want me to pull a tooth and give them a prescription for pain meds. I know how to weed them out, but I don't have a clue about illegal drugs."

I'd have been shocked if he had a clue. "Sorry we upset you."

"By the way, where is Paul?"

His question caught me off guard. "He's staying—"

Reid held his hand up to stop me from answering. "Bobby, do you really want to know? We're keeping his location a secret. If we share it, you can't tell the police or anyone else."

Bobby nodded and paced in front of his Beemer. "Keep it to yourself then. I don't plan on going to jail."

I stood in front of my brother and touched his arms. "I'm sorry we upset you tonight. I love you." I gave him a hug. It lasted a while, but I didn't let go until he hugged me back.

After the hug ended, Bobby laughed. "You give the best hugs, sis. Be careful."

"You too."

"I've got to skedaddle. See you later." Bobby shook Reid's hand. "Take care of her for me."

"Yep."

Bobby drove away, and Reid turned to me, scratching his head. "Are you certain Bobby is your biological brother? Not switched at birth?"

I laughed all the way to the truck. "He's nothing like us, but he's my brother."

"I'm starved. Why don't we grab a bite?"

There was no way I could refuse him after the scene with Bobby. "Sure. You pick the place."

"I'm feeling like BBQ Stampede."

In a few minutes, we were in the dark establishment. Dark wood booths and log walls gave the restaurant a Western feel. After we ordered, my phone vibrated. Paul's face appeared, and I answered. "Hey, Paul. What's up?"

"Susie is ready to talk to you. She's been to your apartment, but nobody answered the door. Where are you?"

"BBQ Stampede."

"Would you order her a pulled pork sandwich and Brunswick Stew? I believe she'll wear some kind of disguise."

"You got it." We ended the call, and I motioned for the waitress. The perky brunette returned, and I placed the additional order.

"I'll bring everything out at the same time." She glanced at our glasses. "I'll also refill your drinks."

"Thanks." Reid waited until she ambled away. "Is Paul going to join us?"

"No, but Susie is. She has some information."

Reid drummed his fingers on the table. "Do we agree that Susie didn't murder Carissa in a jealous rage?"

I pictured my lithe sister-in-law with her long dark hair. "She has the sweetest disposition. She rarely gets angry. The rumors that Carissa spread about Paul hurt Susie, but surely, she doesn't believe them."

A woman wearing sunglasses and a ball cap pulled low slid into my side of the booth, and hip-bumped me. The cap covered shoulder-length blond hair.

I did a double-take. "Susie? Are you wearing a wig?"

"Yeah. Remember when my sister had cancer? She lived with us for a few months because her doctor was in Savannah. I found the wig in the guest room and decided to wear it."

Reid said, "The sunglasses might be overkill."

She yanked them off. "I didn't want the press to follow me. One of my loyal neighbors loaned me her car. It's been shocking how many people believe the lies."

Our waitress carried a tray and placed our food on the table. "Can I get you anything else?"

She'd forgotten to refill our drinks, but I wanted to talk to Susie without interruptions. "I think we're good. Thanks."

Reid picked up his fork and dug into a mound of barbecue pork.

Susie stared at her plate. "Thank y'all for meeting me."

"What do you want to discuss?"

"Thursday night." She reached for her water glass and gulped it dry.

I patted her shoulder. "We're on your side. You can tell us anything."

She glanced around the restaurant. "Thursday evening, I went to Carissa's apartment. Much to my surprise, she invited me inside. I spilled my guts to her. I was a big blubbery mess. I begged Carissa to tell the truth. She listened to me go on and on about what a good man Paul was. By the end of the conversation, she agreed it was wrong to spread lies about Paul."

"Then what?"

"She said they paid her to spread the rumors, and she'd already spent the money to get an apartment in Atlanta. Carissa had big plans to go back to the ballet, and Atlanta was going to be her fresh start."

Reid wiped his mouth. "They? Who did she mean?"

Susie turned her hands over. "She never told me. Whoever it is paid her a lot of money. She didn't know why they wanted to ruin Paul's reputation, but she thought it was an easy way to get ahead financially."

I pulled my sketch pad and pen from my crossover bag and began taking notes. "You met with Carissa. She felt bad. Someone paid her."

Susie picked up her sandwich. "Yeah, she promised to call the bad guys and tell them she wanted out."

I added that to my notes. "What was Carissa wearing when you arrived?"

"A black leotard. She turned off the music when I came inside. She'd been doing stretches and whatever ballerinas do."

"What time was this?"

"Eight-thirty." She bit into the sandwich, closed her eyes, and rolled her head back.

"I don't guess you took her brownies and wine."

"No. That seems like a friendly gesture, and I planned on a confrontation."

"Right."

I made a note to question Ian about the argument he overheard. Was it possible he'd seen the killer and not even realized it? The question needed to be asked.

The three of us finished our meal with very little discussion. Susie ducked out before we did, and I picked up the tab.

Reid said, "What do you think?"

"First, I hope nobody saw Susie enter the apartment. Second, I want to ask Ian what time he heard the argument between Carissa and a woman."

"Yeah, it doesn't sound like they got into a fight." He stood and reached for my hand. "I think it's time to call it a day."

"You're right." I took his hand and stood. Funny thing, though, he held it all the way to the truck.

Chapter Twenty-Six

Tuesday morning, I met Izzy at Fox Island Art Gallery to review the plans for her office update. She signed off on everything.

I wandered through the gallery and admired the paintings by the featured Jamaican artist. Bright blues, greens, and yellows. I much preferred this art to Izzy's modern paintings. On my way out, I stopped in the coffee shop section.

"Hi, Marie. I'd like an iced mint mocha latte."

"Coming right up." Her strained smile didn't reach her eyes.

I paid her with cash. "Keep the change. I'll be at the table over there."

"Okay." She turned around.

I didn't recognize any of the patrons and chose a table in back to watch for a possible clue.

In the welcome area between the gallery and the coffee shop, Izzy and France had a quiet conversation. They stood close together with their heads bent over a piece of paper.

"Here you go. Have a nice day." Marie set my drink on the table and returned to the counter.

"Thanks." I left and drove to the apartment complex where Carissa had lived with the intention of questioning Ian.

I sipped on my drink and role-played how the conversation would go on the drive over. When I reached his door, I took a deep breath, then knocked.

Ian opened the door wearing a shirt and tie and athletic shorts. He frowned but waved me inside without speaking.

He walked to his standing desk and looked at the computer screen. "Yes, sir. I'll have my suggestions ready for you by four o'clock." Ian paused. "Yes, sir. Thank you, sir."

The other man's face disappeared, and Ian removed his computer headset with a little microphone. "Sorry, I forgot your name."

"Kate Sloan."

"Right. How can I help you?"

"I won't take much of your time. Do you remember what time you heard the argument between Carissa and the other woman?"

He rolled his head. "I'd finished watching a college basketball game and had started catching up on some research on cryptocurrency for a client. It was probably around ten."

"Did you see anything unusual Thursday? It may not have seemed important at the time, but it could be a clue."

"Ms. Sloan, why are you asking me these questions?"

I shrugged. "She accused my brother of some bad things. My only goal is to prove he's innocent."

"Nothing stands out as unusual. If you'll excuse me, I need to get back to work."

"Okay. Thanks for your time, Ian." I pulled a business card out of my purse. "If you think of anything, will you call me?"

He looked at my card. "Fine. See you around."

I left with one thought nagging me. Who had Carissa argued with around ten o'clock Thursday night?

* * *

Bess and I gathered supplies and met at the gallery. She'd purchased an off-white couch with tiny lime green stripes, and we expected it to arrive soon. It wouldn't help Izzy's organization, but it provided a landing spot for client gatherings or a nice place to rest if struck by a headache.

Bess organized normal office supplies while I began sanding the file cabinet with 400-grit sandpaper. I hadn't been able to find an affordable one, so my only option was to paint the cabinet in front of me. I covered my face with a scarf, because I've been known to breathe in the dust, and that was never a pleasant experience.

"I've got the art supplies in clear totes and labeled. Will you help me move them to the hallway?"

"Perfect timing. I just finished sanding and cleaning this bad boy off. Helping you will give me time to let it air dry before I apply the metal primer." I put my supplies on a stool and picked up one of the boxes.

Bess said, "The guys should be here with the couch soon."

"Who did you hire?" I placed one box on top of another.

She propped her hands on her slim hips. "You best behave. Brandon is bringing it here with a friend."

"I'll be good." I looked up at the sound of male voices. "Bess, here they are." Two large bodies filled the hall.

Bess stepped in front of me. "Hi, guys."

"Hey, Ms. Bess." Brandon smiled and pointed to the other guy. "This is a friend of mine, Ryan."

"Nice to meet you. Let me show you guys where the couch is going." She turned and entered the office with the young men, leaving me standing alone in the hall.

I followed the three and said, "Hi, Brandon. Hi, Ryan, or do you prefer Anchorman?"

His cornrows swung as he turned to face me. "Hi, there. You're the lady who asked me about Carissa."

"Yes, I'm Kate Sloan. It's good to see you. I appreciate you and Brandon helping us."

He nodded. "Ain't no thing."

"Thanks anyway, and Brandon, thanks to you too."

Brandon mumbled, "Welcome."

"Ryan, do you have any concerts coming up?"

"Yes, ma'am. I'm playing every night at the fair this week, and I'm playing at the pier Saturday night. Besides that, I don't have many gigs lined up. I have to find other ways to make money because of down times."

"That's too bad. I'd be happy to take down your contact information for little jobs like this."

"Cool." He gave me his phone number.

"Thanks." I nodded at Bess. "I'll finish the cabinet."

She directed them to place the couch in the middle of the room so we could cover it when the painters arrived. Bess even charmed the guys into loading Izzy's supplies into her van. They wouldn't be too heavy for us to unload by ourselves, but I imagined there'd be plenty of opportunities to pay the guys to work.

Two ladies arrived in Izzy's office and began prepping the walls. They spoke in Spanish to each other, and one even hummed as they painted.

Later, Izzy popped into the office. "How's it going?"

Bess said, "Good. Real good. We should have it complete by tomorrow night."

"Perfect. I've locked the art gallery. If you two are ready to go, I'll set the alarm."

"Oh, I lost track of the time. Can you give us a few more minutes?"

"I need to get to the festival." Izzy twisted her long gold link necklace with a pointer finger to the point I thought it would break. "You know, if it's not ready by tomorrow night, it's okay. I really need to go now."

I looked from Izzy to the painters. "Okay. I'll tell them we need to leave."

"You've got five minutes to clear out of here."

"Yes, ma'am." Bess and I explained the situation to the painters, even though we didn't really understand what was happening. In less than five minutes, we were all driving away from the art gallery.

Chapter Twenty-Seven

I drove to Danny's Deli and ordered sandwiches. I studied the busy parking lot. People filled their vehicles with gas at the connecting service station. There were little boys wearing baseball uniforms, and I remembered the days of picking Ethan up at school, feeding him, and rushing to a ballgame or practice. It wasn't a surprise he'd chosen a career related to sports. I sent him a short text, telling him how proud I was of him while waiting on my order.

Nothing inside the deli or in the parking lot appeared suspicious to me, then again, would I know what was suspicious? Once my food was ready, I pulled my Beetle Bug out and drove to a nearby neighborhood. Nobody appeared to follow, so I worked my way to the back road leading to Paul's hideout on the marsh.

To my surprise, Reid's truck was there. I parked and gathered the food. After a quick look at my reflection and adding lipstick, I strode into the house.

Snowball barked a sweet greeting.

"Hiya, girl. How are you doing?" I loved on the Westie with my free hand.

Paul appeared. "Sis, whatcha doing here?"

"Surprise." I hugged him. "I've got sandwiches. Thought you could use some company."

He kept me in his arms longer than usual. "Thanks." His voice sounded emotional, and he stepped away. "Do you have enough food for Reid?"

I followed Paul to the back deck. Snowball shadowed my brother. "Yeah. I ordered an extra for your lunch tomorrow. If you don't mind, he can eat it."

"Perfect. Have a seat, and I'll get him." Paul ran down the steps, and I picked the dog up.

I held her close to my body and walked the length of the raised deck. "How do you like living off the grid? Are you a city girl, or do you prefer it out here?" The house was surrounded by trees, and there was a creek dock with a floater on the creek. I imagined Carissa had pampered the little dog.

The sun and clouds played, casting shadows over the yard.

Paul and Reid appeared.

"Hi Reid, I brought supper."

Paul said, "The dock's coming along. I added benches. Do you two want to eat there?"

I looked from him to the dog. "Will Snowball run away?"

"Nah, but we can put her harness and leash on if it will make you feel better."

I didn't relish the thought of chasing her through the woods again.

Reid spoke up, "May as well play it safe."

In a very short time, we were all sitting on the dock with sandwiches, veggie sticks, and insulated tumblers of sweet iced tea.

Paul said, "Fill me in on Mike Best."

I crossed my legs. "He was at your house yesterday morning with other reporters. When he finished updating the station, I talked to him. We ended up in his TV van for a private, off-the-record conversation. I finally confessed who I was and begged him to look at other potential suspects."

"Sounds like you challenged him. What do you think, Reid?"

"Oh, she definitely challenged his manhood and his claim to being an investigative reporter." Reid chuckled. "Seems like she challenged us a time or two when we were growing up."

"If it was only a time or two, you got off easy, man. My estimate is she challenged me on a daily basis to be better or do something more challenging."

"Hey, I'm right here, guys." I waved a carrot stick in the air.

Reid's smile disappeared. "Yes, you are. It sounds like you did real good,

Katie."

I met his gaze. "Thanks. Mike agreed to look at Carissa's background and draw his own conclusions to possible suspects."

Paul was sitting next to me, and he elbowed me. "I appreciate what you're doing, but I'm also concerned. When we were only trying to convince Carissa to confess to lying, it was all good. The murder elevated the risks."

"I won't push too far." I bit into my sandwich.

Reid sat to my left, making it easier for me to hear him. "We believe this entire thing started because of your belief there's a drug smuggling ring on Fox Island."

Paul said, "Right. I was watching some suspicious activity. There have been more drug overdoses in the area. My hunch is the Fox Island Art Gallery is involved."

"Do you think Izzy is part of the ring, or France?" I wished my sketch pad was with me with the notes, but I opened my phone and the note app on it.

Reid wadded the wax paper wrapper into a ball with a crinkle noise. "France is the business manager. My guess is she's involved. Paul, what about Izzy? After all, the gallery is her business."

He finished chewing a bite of his turkey sub. "I've studied her earnings. The woman makes enough for a comfortable living with her artwork. Some pieces go for thousands of dollars."

I nodded. "If I liked her modern art, I couldn't afford them. She drives a Volvo, wears nice clothes, and owns an amazing house with an art studio in the backyard. Is she living on her salary, or has she overextended to the point she's gotten into dealing with drugs?"

Paul stared off into the distance. "All good questions to which we don't have the answers."

"Where does that leave us?"

Paul shrugged. "I haven't come across evidence to point to her."

I wrapped the remainder of my sandwich to save for another time. "Then we don't know if she's involved at this point. We believe France is part of the drug smuggling operation. Has anyone looked into Jason Nesbitt?"

"Who's that?" Reid stood and did some cross-body arm stretches.

Paul reached for my sandwich. "I'll finish this off, if you don't mind."

"Go for it." I passed it to him.

Paul said, "Jason Nesbitt is the featured artist at Fox Gallery for a few days. Wi-Fi is spotty here, and I haven't learned much more."

I said, "I viewed his work, but his name wasn't displayed prominently. I'll see what I can learn tonight."

Reid rolled his head. "How did you get so good at investigating people, Katie?"

My face warmed, but this wasn't the time for holding back information. "Years ago, before my husband died, I suspected him of having an affair. I did a deep dive into our finances, and I learned how to track his phone. It wasn't as easy back then as it is now. I was obsessed with finding the truth, and it was not healthy. When my doctor discovered the acoustic neuroma, I shifted to dealing with my brain tumor and forgot about proving David was guilty. Scratch that. He was guilty, but I quit trying to find the other woman." One day I might share how she'd appeared on my doorstep after David's death, claiming to be the mother of his daughter. I shook the memory off.

Reid patted my hand. "I'm so sorry, Katie. That must have been rough."

Tears sprung to my eyes, and I swiped at them. I couldn't reflect on my past when trying to help Paul in the present. "One good thing is I learned some investigating tricks."

Reid nodded. "Okay. We'll let you handle Jason Nesbitt. I may have a lead myself."

"Who? Or what did you find?"

"We have a riverboat pilot in the area. He helps cargo ships get into the port in Savannah. He's a friend, and I thought we might ask him if drugs are ever smuggled in on the ships."

Paul groaned. "Drugs definitely come into port. The Coast Guard, Homeland Security, the United States Customs and Border Control will all get involved if the drugs are seized from a cargo carrier. Reid, what pilot do you know?"

"Jimmy Morgan."

"Oh, yeah. He's a great guy." Paul bit into my leftover veggie sandwich.

My gaze shifted from Paul to Reid. "Do you think he's willing to talk to us?"

"You betcha. I've been remodeling his mother's house. She's very particular and prone to changing her mind. Jimmy has told me more than once that he owes me. Big time."

"Can I join you when you meet with him?"

"Sure. Let me text him."

Snowball gobbled up bites of food my brother tossed to him.

"Is that okay for her to eat?"

"Don't see why not." He tossed her another bite.

It wasn't worth debating. A breeze blew my hair into my face, and I pulled it back into a ponytail. Moving to the beach had taught me to always carry bands for such occasions.

Reid stood. "Good news. He can meet us now."

I hopped up. "Great. Should I follow you?"

"Yeah. I'll keep you in my rearview mirror, but just in case, here's the address." He texted me the address and gave me verbal directions to the riverboat pilot's home.

With Snowball at his side, Paul walked us to our vehicles. "I appreciate you two and all you're doing for me."

I gave my brother a long hug. "Hang in there. The truth will set you free, and we're going to discover the truth soon."

"Thanks. I don't relish spending the remainder of my life behind bars." He picked up the Westie and held him close.

"Shh. Don't think like that." On the way to Jimmy Morgan's house, I wondered about bringing Susie out to see Paul. The way the press followed her, it'd be a risk. If it would help Paul's mood, though, it might be a risk worth taking.

Chapter Twenty-Eight

Jimmy was as nice a person as I could've hoped to meet. His thick black and white hair, fat moustache, and goatee complemented his tan skin with a smattering of freckles. Despite numerous wrinkles, I guessed him to be maybe ten years older than me.

The three of us sat in his family room with large windows exposing a fabulous view of the creek. The furnishings were comfortable, and the space was warm and inviting. It was obvious he was a Georgia Bulldog fan, because he had little statues of bulldogs and other sports memorabilia scattered throughout the room.

"So, how can I help you two?" Jimmy kicked back in his brown leather recliner.

Reid and I sat on a loveseat, and he was to my right. He looked at the riverboat pilot. "Jimmy, Kate is Paul Wright's sister."

Jimmy nodded. "Our chief of police. I hear he's in a bit of a pickle."

Reid said, "Yes, sir. We're trying to help prove he's innocent of everything, including the affair."

"I wish you luck. How is it you think I can help you?"

Reid leaned forward, forearms on his thighs. "We believe the trouble began when Paul started investigating a possible drug smuggling group. He noticed suspicious events at a local fair—"

I interrupted. "It was a book fair, I believe."

"Right, but we're wondering if the smuggling is linked to the art gallery. Just because there's a book fair, it doesn't mean there weren't booths devoted to art or coffee or what have ya."

Jimmy stroked his white goatee. "Seems to me that Fox Island is having a whole lot more fairs and festivals than we did in the old days. By old days, I mean even a couple of years ago."

Reid slapped his thigh. "We were thinking the same thing. Then we started wondering if the events are linked to drug smuggling."

We hadn't solved the question of how the drugs were arriving in Fox Island. "Jimmy, what are your thoughts? If there's a drug smuggling ring here, is it coming from the container ships or another way?"

Jimmy continued to stroke his beard. "There have been instances of containers with items hiding cocaine and heroin. For instance, there was a shipment of sports equipment and the footballs were stuffed with little plastic bags full of drugs."

I leaned closer to the man. While he sat on the side of my good ear, he was soft-spoken. "Do you remember if it came from one of the Caribbean Islands?"

"I can't rightly remember. Savannah is the fourth largest port in the United States. There have been multiple occurrences of smuggling. People will smuggle anything they can make a buck on. Nothing worse than human smuggling, in my opinion. I'm trying to wrap my brain around how the art dealers would send pieces over to be distributed. Then there's also the question of how are the drugs snuck into or onto the artwork."

My heart leapt. "That's a great question. Izzy's primary focus is paintings."

Reid nudged me. "Didn't you say she's broadening?"

"Kinda, but I don't know about how far she's branching out. Although I saw a metal donkey on a shelf in France's office. Maybe it was a sample of the new kind of art they want to sell at the gallery."

Reid shrugged. "Or it could've been a gift."

"True."

Jimmy rested his hands on his belly. "Mind you, I'm not saying you can't smuggle drugs in picture frames, but what if your artist has a talent for recycled art. You know what I mean? They take trash and turn it into treasures. Suppose a fella has old bicycle parts in a shed. Take it a step further, he's an artist. He might find more pieces like wrenches, screwdrivers, lanterns, pots and pans. You following me?"

I nodded.

"He could make a sculpture out of them. If he made a sea turtle, a flamingo, a jellyfish, or anything suited to the beach, he could sell his creation. Most likely, these are odd-shaped pieces. Now this would be a perfect way to smuggle drugs into the country."

Reid straightened his legs. "You've given us a lot to consider, and it makes sense."

"Glad to help ya, and I hate to bust your bubble, but most illegal drugs enter the states through Mexico."

My shoulders slumped. "That's disappointing."

"It seems to me instead of focusing on the big dog and working your way down, you should flip it. Catch the locals and work your way up the chain."

"Your theory makes sense, except we're trying to catch Carissa Ruffalo's killer, and I don't know where that person fits on the chain of command."

We chatted a few minutes, then thanked Jimmy profusely. He walked us to the door, and I said, "Thanks again."

"Anytime. Go Dawgs."

I smiled. "Yes, sir. Go Dawgs."

Reid saluted the pilot and walked me to my car. "Are you too tired to swing by the art fair?"

"You are speaking my language, Reid Barrett. Let's go."

"I'll follow you."

I took off with a smile. It was so good to be back at Fox Island, where my true friends lived. They had my back, and I'd do anything for them. Tonight was a perfect example of Reid putting Paul's needs ahead of his. Once my brother was in the clear, I'd make it up to Reid.

Until then, my focus remained on proving Paul was innocent.

Chapter Twenty-Nine

Reid and I walked toward the booths. He leaned near me. "It's not near as crowded tonight. Will you continue to be my pretend girlfriend if we cross paths with Izzy?"

I reached for his calloused hand and ran my thumb over his knuckles. "Sure thing, honey."

He winked at me. "Thanks, sweetie pie."

"I'll tell you one thing. Izzy was in a sure-fire hurry to get here today. She all but ran us out of her office. Oh." I stopped and faced Reid. "Ryan, er Anchorman, is performing tonight. He was very nice to me earlier today."

"How'd you manage to cross paths with Ryan?"

"Bess asked Brandon to move a couch into Izzy's office for us. He brought Ryan to help."

He stopped walking and faced me. "Interesting. How'd that go?"

"Brandon was aloof, but Ryan was friendly. I behaved myself, or else Bess might have dissolved our work relationship. Honestly, it might have ruined our friendship too. She's awful protective of Pastor Cross."

"She worked for Tom for years at the church. I imagine part of her job description was to protect the preacher. You know, guard his time from petty distractions."

I thought about his assessment. "Good point."

"Where to first?"

"The first time I heard Anchorman perform was also the first time I witnessed France passing something to the strangers. How about if we wander over to the stage?"

142

"Sounds like a good plan." Reid squeezed my hand, and we walked to the performance area. A poster announcing the show revealed we were thirty minutes early. "I dread suggesting this, but should we swing by the Fox Island Art Gallery booth?"

"You're a good sport. Let's go." I headed to the designated area and stopped at the sight of Izzy talking to the tall man who'd aroused my suspicions. "Reid, do you see what I see?"

"Sure do. Close your mouth." He chuckled. "It's gaping open."

I did and frowned. "Should we still go over there?"

"I didn't take you for a coward." He tugged on my hand and made a straight path to Izzy.

Izzy did a double-take when she noticed Reid. "Darling, how are you tonight?" Her silky voice made the hair on my neck stand to attention. Yuck.

Redness appeared on Reid's jaw. "Good. We're doing real good. Kate ran into Ryan at your gallery this afternoon. We decided to come see his performance."

Her chin lifted. "It's a little too hard rock for my taste, but to each his own."

Reid looked at the man beside Izzy and stuck his hand out. "Hi there. I'm Reid Barrett."

The muscular man shook Reid's hand. "Jason Nesbitt. You can find my art at Izzy's gallery."

That was my cue. "Oh, I love your paintings. They are fun and colorful."

"Thank you, thank you." His deep voice carried a joyful note. "I was very happy when Izzy offered to feature me."

I turned to Izzy. "You should make Jason's name more prominent. I liked the art, but I had no idea who the artist was. The only things I knew for sure was the artist was Jamaican, and I liked the paintings."

"That was the plan. I want you to buy Jason's art from me and not somebody else." Izzy's voice grew shrill.

Jason raised both hands, palms out. "It's no worry. Nobody else sells my artwork."

Izzy smiled at the Black man, and her posture relaxed. "Soon, my dear. Soon, everyone will want to buy your paintings."

With Jimmy's words fresh on my mind, I wondered about Jason's artistic abilities. "Do you only paint? What about sculpture or pottery?"

"I only paint, but my cousin, Deshane Palmer, is in Georgia trying to find a buyer for her sculptures." His teeth were so white, it made me wonder if he'd ever drunk a cup of coffee.

Sculptures? Ding, ding, ding. Had I found the connection between Izzy and the drug smugglers? Although Jason seemed so nice. I didn't want him to be involved in drug smuggling. "Where are her pieces sold?"

In the distance, music began.

Izzy said, "You two should go if you don't want to miss the concert."

I looked at Jason. "Good luck with your art career. I'm already a fan."

"Thank you. Thank you."

Reid motioned with his head for me to get moving, and we left Izzy and her artist.

We retraced our steps to the stage in time to witness France take the stage.

She beamed at the audience. "How's everyone tonight? Are you ready to rock?"

I clapped along with the cheering crowd.

France waved her arms. "Give it up for Anchorman and The Freak Band." She left the stage, and Ryan appeared.

Notes loud enough to scare the sharks in the ocean rang out. I covered my left ear, wanting to protect the only one that worked.

Reid tapped my shoulder and pointed to the back of the crowd. "Maybe it's not as loud back there."

I turned and weaved my way through the fans until I made it to the back row. It wasn't much better, but in the distance, I spotted France, and she was with Jason Nesbitt and the woman I now believed to be Deshane Palmer.

I'd left Officer Diaz's business card at home, so I texted Paul and asked him to reach out to the cop. Emerson needed to be here in case something went down.

The threesome broke up and went in different directions before I noticed any law enforcement. Another missed opportunity. How had that happened?

"Let's get out of here before you blow a gasket." Reid took my hand in his, and we left the concert.

I stayed alert on the walk to the parking lot. My good ear rang, challenging me to hear much of anything. When we reached my VW, I glanced at Reid. "How'd you know I was mad?"

"Your eyebrows came down, and the corners of your mouth narrowed. Your skin also turned red."

His words confirmed I needed to develop a poker face. "I can't believe you noticed any of that."

"Oh, Katie. I've been reading your moods for years. I looked over your shoulder when you texted Paul. You were worried then. Later, the three potential suspects took off before help arrived. That's when you shifted into anger. Take a deep breath. We'll start fresh tomorrow morning."

I sighed. "Do you know how frustrating it is when you are the voice of reason?"

He laughed. "Good night, Katie."

I drove to my apartment with Reid following. It would've been a waste of breath to tell him not to. In all honesty, I felt safer knowing he had my back.

Reid was right. Tomorrow would be soon enough for a fresh start.

Chapter Thirty

I overslept Wednesday morning and hurried to get ready. A quick glance at my schedule showed I was supposed to be back at Izzy's office. I texted the artist to confirm. When she acknowledged she'd be prepared for me, I sent a message to the painters.

A dancing ringtone sounded, and I answered Bess's call. "Good morning."

"Where are you?"

"Sorry. I'm about to leave. Are you at the art gallery?"

"Yes, but there's no way I'll enter without you. Oh, wait a second. I see Tom Cross. I bet he's going into the coffee shop. I should be safe with him around."

Was my best friend interested in the pastor for romantic reasons? I seriously needed to dig into her feelings about the local pastor. I had doubts about a man who tried to get me to attend another church.

"Kate, did you hear me?"

"Stay with Tom." I pulled on my good sneakers. "I'll be there soon."

The call ended, and I gathered the items to take with me. After locking the apartment, I jogged to my Beetle. It wouldn't take long to reach the gallery.

I opened the car door and moved my foot to get inside. A snake hissed. It was in my driver's seat.

I screamed.

Oh, no. The creature stretched out from my seat to the passenger seat, and who knew where his tail was? Unsure of specific body parts, I only knew there was more to that thing.

Again, he hissed at me.

I screamed and fell to the ground on my backside.

The long snake with the triangular head and beady eyes slid his yellow-gray body toward the door opening.

Heavy footsteps thudded on the sidewalk.

A young cop appeared. "Lady, what's wrong?"

I pointed to the car. "Snake."

He turned and let out a manly scream, then slammed the door. He whipped around and faced me. "What are you doing with a rattlesnake?"

"Are you kidding? It's not mine." My heart raced.

"It's venomous. We need to call for backup." He held out his hand and helped me to my feet. "I'll call the Department of Natural Resource people. They'll come get it out safely."

"Is there any such thing as safely removing a snake from a car?" I held my purse against my chest like a shield. "What if there are more snakes?"

"When the snake catchers show up, they'll inspect the entire car." He made the call to the appropriate authorities.

When he finished, I looked at his nametag. "Officer Collins, I don't suppose you'd be interested in buying a good VW Beetle? I've taken great care of it over the years. It's not even that old."

He laughed and held up a hand to stop me from talking. "Ma'am, it's going to be okay. Any, and all, snakes will be removed."

"All?" My heart raced, and a headache formed behind my eyes. "Are you going to stay with me until the DNR arrive?"

"As long as there's not an emergency, I'll stay with you. But if I have to take off, you'll be safe."

Across the street was Island Perk Coffee Shop. "Do you suppose we have time to grab a cup of coffee?"

"I should stay here, but you go ahead."

"Be right back." I went to the appropriate crosswalk and waited for the signal. It'd be a crying shame if Officer Collins had to write me a ticket for jaywalking.

The environmental people still hadn't arrived when I returned. I passed a paper cup to the young policeman. "I asked them to add cream and sugar, but not too much."

"Thank you, ma'am."

"You're welcome. By the way, I'm Kate Sloan."

He nodded. "Chief Wright is your brother."

I studied the young man with the crew cut, trim physique, and tanned skin. "How'd you know?"

He shrugged. "It's a small town."

"You can say that again." I sipped my coffee. "Should I ask if you're friend or foe?"

He pointed to a wood bench under a store awning. "Why don't we have a seat?"

"Sounds good, but you didn't answer my question." I walked over and sat in such a way as to have my good ear to him. I didn't want to miss his answer.

"To be honest, the department is kinda divided. Your brother is a stickler for following the rules. There are a few of us who think the bottom line is the only thing that matters. Chief Wright doesn't just want to get thugs off the street; he wants them convicted at trial." Officer Collins looked up and down the sidewalk. "I believe your brother is innocent."

"That's good to know, because Paul isn't guilty. He didn't have an affair, and he didn't murder Carissa Ruffalo."

He turned the cup in his hands. "How'd you get a snake in your car?"

I met his gaze and thought about the answer. Had it happened when I'd been visiting Paul? "I was at the concert near the lighthouse last night. But surely, I would've seen a snake slither into the car."

"Did you leave the windows open?"

I shook my head. "No. I have allergies and usually keep the windows shut in the spring."

"I hear ya. I get allergy shots every week, but fall is my worst season." He sighed. "We still don't know how the snake got into your car. Living in the middle of town like you do, it's possible kids did it for a prank. Do you always lock your car doors?"

"Almost always, but I got home late last night, and I was bushed. It's possible I forgot to lock them."

A government truck parked along the street, and a man and woman walked toward us. The man said, "Are you the owner of the car?"

"Yes, I'm Kate Sloan."

The four of us talked for a few minutes, then the environmental people did their thing. Two snakes were removed. Both were venomous.

Officer Collins remained with me through the entire removal process and until the environmental people left.

"Do you feel safe to drive your car?" His expression was earnest, not condescending.

"I'm not sure I'll ever feel safe driving it again. It looks like it's time to put my big girl pants on and pretend like I'm brave."

"Hey, you are brave, Ms. Sloan. Officer Diaz told us that you're trying to prove your brother is innocent. He thinks you should leave the investigation to us, but if you find yourself in a bind or anything, give me a call." He handed me a card with his contact information. "I want to prove your brother is innocent, too."

"Thank you."

"Stay safe. I don't believe it's an accident two venomous snakes found their way into your car. I plan to file a report. This is also more than a teenage prank. It may be a warning to back away from the murder investigation."

I gulped. He'd spoken the words I'd been too afraid to say.

With a wave, I got into my little car and drove to the art gallery. I stayed alert to more potential danger.

How far would Carissa's killer go to stop me? Did they want to prevent me from catching them, or were they trying to stop me from exposing a potential drug ring?

Chapter Thirty-One

"Where have you been? I was about to call the cops to find you." Bess shook her finger at me in the art gallery's entry.

"I ran into a little trouble. Scratch that. It was big trouble in the form of snakes." I told her what happened.

"Oh, my goodness. Snakes!"

"Shh. Where is the pastor?"

"He had to visit a parishioner, but snakes?"

"Let's go to Izzy's office, where we can talk."

Bess stuck to my side as we walked to the office. "Have you told your brother?"

"Not yet. I came straight here." I knocked on the door.

"Come in." Izzy was locking her desk drawer with a key. "I expected you earlier."

I said, "It's my fault. I had a little trouble starting my car."

Izzy strode away from us. "I'll be around today. I have some meetings in France's office if you need to find me."

Bess nodded. "The painters are coming to finish the walls today, and Kate will finish your file cabinet. When everything is dry, we've got rugs to add. Do you want a new desk?"

"It serves its purpose." Izzy glanced at her desk before disappearing down the hall.

"It makes my life easier." Bess unloaded a bookshelf.

I started to work on the file cabinet. "How was your time with Tom?"

"It's always so easy to spend time with him. We have a lot in common, and he has a huge heart for the poor."

I kept my thoughts to myself on his behavior toward me.

"Oh, girl. I can hear your wheels spinning. The man lost his wife, and Brandon is all he has when it comes to family. You went after his only child. How would you feel if he'd gone after Ethan?"

"Point taken." I slid open the bottom drawer of the cabinet and painted the front lime green.

"But?" Bess stacked the books in totes for Izzy to go through later and guide us on what to keep and discard.

"Brandon's alibi for Thursday is being at The Sand Bar. Come to think of it, how solid is the timeline of his alibi?"

Thud. Books landed in another tote. "Kate, you removed him from your list of suspects. Don't be putting him back on there."

I dipped my brush into the paint and stroked it on the next drawer. "I'm not."

"Who else is on your list?"

"Nobody I want to mention while we're here."

"Hola." The taller of the two women spoke. "Are you ready for us?"

"Yes." Bess scooted the bookshelf to the middle of the room. "Let's hope today is productive with no interruptions."

The women had taped the baseboard trim the day before and soon began painting. Cantina music played from a paint-splattered boombox. One lady hummed, and the other focused on painting.

Bess said, "Kate, will you help me move this credenza away from the wall? It's heavier than it looks."

"Sure." I put my brush down and picked up one side of the modern white credenza. "Is this staying or going?"

"It doesn't fit the ambience of the room, and there were no papers on it. My guess is we're tossing the thing." Bess lifted her side, and we moved to the center of the room next to the bookshelf.

Bess jerked her head to the empty spot and pointed. "Look."

A little white camera with a red light blinked at us.

Chapter Thirty-Two

Bess and I stood in the parking lot a few minutes later. Bess's eyes were wide. "That was a security camera."

I nodded. "Yeah. Do you think Izzy was recording us? What did she hear?"

"Today, we talked about the office and Brandon."

"What a relief I didn't share my ideas on other suspects." Butterflies fluttered deep in my gut.

"What do we do now?" Bess wrung her hands.

"We're assuming she's spying on us, but what if someone is spying on Izzy?"

"Go on."

I paced a minute, then returned to Bess. "We believe someone at the art gallery may be involved in the drug smuggling. The thing we don't know is who."

"Or how many." Bess pinched her lip with her fingers.

"True. Izzy and France could both be part of the ring, or it could only be one of them. Marie said packages were coming into the gallery, and France got angry at her when she started opening one."

"Okay, I hear ya."

"The way I see it, if Izzy is innocent, then France may have planted the camera to learn if Izzy is suspicious."

"Or even double-crossing her." Bess leaned against her blue minivan. "What if Izzy is part of the ring?"

"Good question. Let's say France is innocent and suspects Izzy of doing something wrong."

"In both of your scenarios, France is the one who planted the camera. What if someone else did it?"

I paced again in front of Bess. "What if the drug smugglers are using the gallery, but Izzy and France don't realize what's going on? Maybe the smugglers get the artwork into the gallery, and their Fox Island Connection buys the art without anyone being the wiser about the drug ring."

"No, there's a flaw in that logic. So far, the only artist besides Izzy is the Jamaican."

I stopped. "You're right. Jason Nesbitt. I met him last night, and he's very nice. I really don't want him to be involved."

"Yeah, well, I don't want Brandon to be an alcoholic." Bess sighed. "What do you suggest we do?"

"We're going to call Izzy to the office and ask about the credenza. While she's in there, we'll ask where she'd like to put the camera. Gauge her reaction. Did she know about it or not?"

"Okay, it sounds like a plan, but we need to let Paul and Reid know." She pulled her phone out of her jeans pocket.

I held up my hand to stop her. "Only Reid, please. I'll tell Paul when we know more."

"It's a deal." Bess shot off the text message, and she returned to the office while I tracked down Izzy.

The artist was in the gallery with France. They were in a deep discussion about where to place a new painting.

I cleared my throat. "Sorry to interrupt, but when you have a chance can you come answer a couple of questions for us, Izzy?"

She glanced at France. "Handle this however you want, but we need to take some of Deshane's pieces to the art fair tonight."

"What about Jason's art?"

Izzy pinched the bridge of her nose. "One painting only. Let's not forget the gallery is supposed to be primarily focused on me."

"Right."

Izzy joined me. "What do you need to ask me about?"

I motioned for her to follow. "There's a piece we're not sure is being utilized. Everything needs to have a function, or else we need to get rid of it. We want to make efficient use of your space, so the office works for you."

"What piece do you mean?" Izzy entered the office and kicked off her high heels.

Bess turned down the music and smiled at the painters.

Like a game show host, I stood beside the credenza and waved my hands in dramatic fashion. "There wasn't anything on this. It's great if you use it, but if not, we can find something that works better for you."

Izzy's face softened. "I often lay photos or small paintings on this to get a feel for the piece."

I said, "Then it should stay. Do you want us to put the camera back on it?"

"What camera?" Izzy tilted her perfectly made-up face.

Bess held the item up for Izzy to inspect. "This is what we found."

"That's not mine. I'd never stoop so low as to secretly film a meeting between myself and a client."

"Oh, Izzy, we weren't accusing you of doing anything wrong. Isn't it here for security purposes? To alert you if someone breaks into your office." Her frown worried me, and I wasn't sure how to recover from my snafu. "If you didn't know it was here, maybe France placed it on the credenza to catch someone trying to steal items from your office."

"I'll get to the bottom of this." Izzy gripped the small security camera and fled from the room.

One of the painters hummed an unfamiliar song, and I turned the music back up for them.

Bess crossed her arms. "Well, that was uncomfortable. What now?"

"I'll get more coffee, and you continue in here."

"I'd never turn away from more coffee, but I think in this situation, it's code for snoop."

"Be right back." I shrugged and grabbed my wallet. This little errand might only be about coffee, but it was possible I'd overhear something juicy.

Chapter Thirty-Three

"Good morning, Kate." Marie gave me a crooked smile as if afraid I'd say something about her confession in the dental office parking lot a couple of nights earlier. "I have fresh raspberry scones."

Shouldn't she trust me by now? Oh well, I'd play along. "Yummy. I'll take four." The painters could probably use a break. "And four coffees."

"You're my best customer when you work here. I hope they keep hiring you."

"Me too, but the place isn't that big. I'll still come by for coffee even when not working at the gallery."

"Thanks. It won't take me long to prepare your order."

"Take your time. I'll mosey over to the art gallery." I left her and headed for the exhibits.

Izzy's art still didn't do much for me. I could appreciate the fact others liked her style, but Jason Nesbitt's art appealed to my love of the beach.

I'd traveled the States while married to David, and it'd been fun to learn how others lived. Lexington, Kentucky, had been a good fit for raising my son, and I appreciated the beauty of the area. But every day that I woke up in Fox Island, it felt more like home. I'd grown up here, and except for Ethan, my family lived here, my closest friends were here, and it was where I was free to be my true self. Jason's pictures touched something inside me.

France appeared. "He has a unique talent, don't you think?"

"Absolutely, but I don't see any prices. Are these for show only?"

"Jason and Izzy are tweaking the details before we can sell his pieces."

I wasn't sure what she meant. "Can I commission Jason to paint something

155

for my home?"

France lifted her chin. "He might take advantage of you financially. All sales should go through us."

I didn't like her haughty tone. Maybe France and Izzy were taking advantage of Jason since she was so quick to suggest I wouldn't be fair with the Jamaican artist. "Has he signed a contract with your gallery?"

"Honestly, it's not any of your business."

"It is my business if I want to buy one of his paintings." I'd spent years holding my own, raising a son, learning to live with hearing loss, and making a living as a widow. Standing up to France should be no different.

"I'll discuss it with Izzy, and we'll let you know." The young woman turned and left me standing in front of a painting with blues, yellows, greens, and splashes of red. Boats were anchored near the shore and bobbing in a cove.

Marie tapped my shoulder. "Kate, your order is ready."

I must not have heard her call my name if she'd felt the need to touch me. I tore myself away from the artwork. "Great. We're in Izzy's office today, but it'll take me two trips if I don't want to spill coffee."

"I'll help. It's a slow morning."

We gathered the drinks and scones and walked to the hallway leading to the offices. "Do you lease the coffee shop, or do you work for Izzy?"

"I work for them."

"Do you dream of starting your own place like Island Perk Coffee Shop?" I entered the room ahead of Marie, and we set the snack on the credenza.

She said, "We can discuss my dreams another time. Do these ladies speak English?"

"Some."

"I'm fluent in Spanish. Do you want me to tell them it's time for a break or anything?"

"That would be wonderful."

Marie's announcement was received with big smiles and movement to the coffee and scones. They thanked us and doctored up their coffee before sitting on the floor with their food and drink.

Marie said, "I best get back to work."

"Please call me. I'd like to discuss placing an order later, but I need to put some thought into it. Here's my contact information." In case anyone was spying on us, I wanted to make it appear as if Marie and I hadn't been together outside of the gallery.

She took my business card and nodded as if understanding my unspoken message. "Thanks. I'll be in touch."

Bess said, "If you're okay here by yourself, I've reached a stopping point until the room is painted and dry. We've been contacted by a couple who are both working from home. They need to organize space for them to work efficiently without getting on each other's nerves. I'd like to run by their home and see the space in question."

I laughed. "There are definitely challenges when people work from home. Call me if you need me. I'll apply the last coat of paint to the cabinet and stay until the walls are finished."

Bess took off, leaving me to my task and to think about the happenings at Fox Island Art Gallery. Was it possible drugs were being sold in addition to the art?

Chapter Thirty-Four

I knew better than to meet Marie at my brother's dental office. So on Wednesday evening, we met at my apartment.

She entered the small space and looked around. "Where's your bodyguard?"

"My what? Oh, you mean Reid? He's my friend."

"I wouldn't want to get crossways with him if he thought you were in danger."

"Oh, that's kinda sweet." My face warmed. "Have a seat."

She sat on the wicker chair with blue striped cushions. "I parked in the public beach parking lot and don't think anyone was watching me."

I settled in a wicker chair across from her. "Yeah, we need to be cautious until Carissa's killer is caught."

"What do you want to discuss?" She pulled the hood of her sweatshirt off, and her long blond hair spilled forward.

"I'd like to order some muffins, a loaf of homemade bread, and do you have any sandwich spreads?"

A big smile lit her face. "People love my pimento cheese, and I make a good country ham salad. How much are you talking about?"

This is where it would get dicey. I didn't want to reveal it was for Paul. "It's for a shut-in. How about six muffins, one loaf of bread, a container of the pimento cheese, and one of the ham salad?"

She took notes on her phone. "When do you need it?"

"As soon as possible. Can I pay you directly, or does the gallery get a cut?"

"Oh, you can pay me. I didn't sign a contract with Izzy, even though

France pushed for it. I was catering small events before I worked at the gallery. There's no way I'd give them part of the money."

I leaned forward to hear Marie better. "But they tried to get you to sign something."

"Yes. I almost had to walk away from the job with them, but they gave in at last."

"You know the Jamaican painter?"

"Jason Nesbitt. I know who he is, but he doesn't talk to me much." She shrugged. "It's probably not his fault, though. France shadows his every move when he enters the building. He probably couldn't order a cup of coffee if he wanted to."

"That's weird. I quizzed France earlier today about wanting to buy one of Jason's paintings. She wouldn't tell me a price or how to buy something from him."

Marie looked up from her phone. "Do you think it's because he's not an American?"

"I'll look into it, but it felt more like a control issue."

Marie nodded. "I can see France wanting to be in charge of his money. She'll probably convince him the only way to sell his artwork is to use the gallery. If he doesn't believe her, she'll throw his cousin into the mix."

"I bet you mean the pretty young girl."

"She's not that young, but she is pretty. She does sculptures with recycled items. Izzy doesn't see it as competition like Jason's work."

"I guess that makes sense, but Izzy's paintings are almost like a different genre. Does art come in genres like books? Modern versus beachy?"

"I'm a barista and baker, but I'm learning more about art every day. I believe the genres of art are more like painting, sculpture, literature, music, and that sort of thing. I feel like you're thinking more about expressionism, surrealism, and that kind of stuff."

"You're right. It's been a long day."

Marie stood. "I'll swing by tomorrow morning with your order. Is six o'clock too early?"

"I'll be awake." I started to walk her to the door, but she detoured to my little kitchen table. "What is this?"

My face grew hot. She'd found my murder board. "Oh, Marie. Please don't mention this to anyone. For your own safety as well as mine."

Her eyes widened as she stared at my notes and pictures. "I'm in the background right there." She pointed to the fuzzy photo of Paul and Carissa.

"Did you ever see them together?" I watched for signs of deception.

"Individually, I saw each one. Carissa was in the gallery quite a bit, but I only remember seeing your brother once. He was alone and on duty." Marie shivered and crossed her arms. "This isn't real."

I wanted to cheer but remained quiet while she studied the different photographs.

"You may have heard Carissa helped cater social events at the gallery, but she mostly mingled and flirted with the rich men."

As much as I wanted to push Marie for more clues, it wasn't fair to put her in danger. "Thanks for sharing that with me. Do you have family here to watch out for you? A boyfriend, maybe?"

"No, my mother and I had a huge fight years ago. My parents pretty much disowned me, and I haven't seen them in forever."

"Why don't I follow you home? No, that could put you in more danger. Will you text me when you get home?"

She met my gaze, and a tear trailed down her cheek. "It's been a long, long time since anyone cared enough to make sure I was safe. Thanks. I'll text you."

I walked her to the door, and she pulled up her hood before running outside.

I added what I'd learned to the sketch pad of notes. Even if Izzy and France weren't involved in drug smuggling, they didn't seem to be fair to others. In big fat letters, I wrote the word greedy.

How far would their greediness take them?

Chapter Thirty-Five

Thursday morning. One week from Paul's discovery of Carissa's lying posts online. One week from our lives spiraling out of control. Six days from our discovery of Carissa's dead body.

A desperate sense of urgency propelled me from the bed. I got ready in record time. Marie delivered my order for Paul before six, and I was ready when Reid arrived.

"Good morning." I hopped into the passenger seat before he shut off his truck.

"Morning. Are you in a hurry?"

I placed the food on the backseat and fastened my seatbelt. "Yes. Why hasn't the killer been caught? And even when the person is arrested, how will we prove there was never an extramarital relationship between Carissa and Paul?"

"Slow down." He didn't move the truck. "We're going to see your brother, and we'll come up with a game plan."

"You're right. Hey, maybe Anchorman, um Ryan, can shed light on why Carissa claimed to have an affair with Paul."

"Didn't Susie say the bad people paid Carissa to spread lies about the fake relationship?"

I opened the sketch pad and reviewed my notes. "You're right. Carissa told Susie that the night of the murder. There's also the possibility Kyra knows more than she admitted. She was so busy defending Carissa, and I don't think she even considered other possibilities."

"Remind me who Kyra is."

"She works at Fox Mart and was friends with Carissa. I think she's a musician, but I could be remembering it wrong." I'd already made one mistake this morning.

Reid ran a hand over his face. "I'm in desperate need of coffee. Let's run into Island Perk." He pointed at the coffee shop across the street.

"Sounds good."

The coffee shop wasn't crowded. To be fair, it was six o'clock in the morning, and they were just opening when we arrived. We ordered fun lattes, because why not? I was living life in the oh-so-serious lane at the moment, and I'd take fun wherever I could find it.

My hands shook a bit as I sipped my drink. "It might be time to cut back on my caffeine consumption."

Reid drove with one hand on the steering wheel, and he held the caramel latte in his other hand. "Really?"

"Yeah. I've been drinking way too much since returning to the island. I don't know if it's to be sociable with Bess or because of the stress of Paul's problems. Either way, once we prove he's innocent, I'll cut back. In the meantime, it's been enjoyable discovering so many different types and flavors."

"You do you, Katie. I usually enjoy a morning cup of Joe, and the rest of the day, I drink sports drinks and water."

The light of the rising sun dimmed as we drove through a stand of pine trees. "How do you think Paul is? Truthfully?"

Reid sipped his drink before replying. "He's frustrated. He believes he's protecting Susie and the family by laying low, but he'd rather work the case."

"I wish I could find something tangible to help us catch the real killer."

Reid said, "You need to stop operating under the false narrative that you need to protect the world."

"But Paul's my little brother."

"It's true that he's your younger brother, but he's a grown man, and he's a cop. I know he appreciates your help. You asked me to be honest. Paul is worried about you. The cops will catch the killer."

I pointed at Reid. "They won't find the murderer if they're only looking at Paul, Susie, and me. It scares me that they'll ignore clues pointing to the culprit. Listen to what I learned yesterday." I updated him about Jason Nesbitt and the proposition Marie received when she went to work at the gallery.

"Marie was smart not to sign the contract."

"What about Jason? He's in unfamiliar territory. What if he's a trusting person and signs a contract with Izzy?"

Reid held up two fingers. "False narrative."

I remained quiet during the rest of the drive. I'd show him false narrative. The cops had to consider all possibilities, including my brother. There was no need for me to waste time considering Paul, Susie, or myself were guilty of the murder. I was free to track down the true killer. I wouldn't back down from proving Paul was innocent, and if I could protect Jason Nesbitt, I would.

We surprised Paul with the goodies and visited for a few minutes. Snowball sniffed around for crumbs.

Paul said, "That reporter, Mike Best, set up an interview with Susie for this morning. Kate, he said you suggested he keep an open mind. Do you have time to be at the house with her during the interview?"

"You bet. I'll check with Susie for more details."

His shoulders slumped. "Thanks. I should be there to protect her, but my presence would add chaos to the interview."

Reid said, "I hate to end this, but I need to meet an electrician at one of my work sites."

We said our goodbyes, and Reid drove me to Let's Get Organized. He walked me to the front door. "Katie, I sense you're mad at me, but I'm scared about your safety. Please, be careful."

"Reid, I've been taking care of myself for years." I was starting to sound like a broken record. I held my hand up to stop his reply. "I know what you're going to say. There's a killer on the loose—"

"And you're the one stirring the pot."

I smiled. "You couldn't help yourself."

"What?" He placed a hand on his chest and gave me an innocent look.

"Trying to get the last word in. I'll be careful."

His gaze met mine. "Why don't we go see Officer Diaz this afternoon? If you can make an appointment, I'll free up the time."

I squeezed his hand. "Thanks, Reid. I'll do that."

As soon as he took off, I entered the building and called the police department. They gave me an appointment to see the cop, then I called Susie. We agreed on a time for me to arrive at her house.

With specific plans to move forward on my murder investigation, I sat at my desk to check the work calendar.

My estimated time for the walls to dry had been wrong, thanks to the humidity. Surely by now, Izzy's office walls would be dry. When Bess arrived at work, we would have time to go finish putting the office together and reveal it to Izzy.

Besides meeting with Emerson Diaz, I wanted to speak to Jason Nesbitt. The Fox Island Lighthouse Art Festival had ended. Did that mean Jason and Deshane had returned to Jamaica?

If I could locate Jason, my excuse would be I wanted to buy a painting for my new home. It'd be true. His art appealed to me. I also planned to find out more about his cousin.

"Good morning." Bess entered the shop. "You're here mighty early."

"Good morning. I thought we could finish Izzy's office and hopefully get paid."

Bess looked at our schedule. "I believe that should work, but we need to hustle. You're signed up to meet a family with three teenage girls who share one bathroom."

I laughed. "Something tells me it's going to be a challenge."

Bess winked. "It seems like you don't mind a challenge. If it wasn't for an appointment with Beach Hair, I'd help you out. The salon hired another stylist, and they need to make space for her without crowding everyone."

"It sounds like business is good despite my being distracted with Carissa's murder. I promise to make it up to you soon."

"Don't you worry a bit." She gave me a one-armed hug.

I wasn't sure if worry was a big enough word to cover my concern for

Paul. Until he was free, I'd continue to look for any possible clues to prove he was innocent.

Chapter Thirty-Six

"Tada!" Bess opened the door for Izzy to enter her new office space. Izzy surprised me with a little squeal. "The color is perfect, and the space is fresh and inviting."

Bess showed the artist all the improvements we'd made. She patiently explained the organization system.

Izzy sat in her office chair and sighed. "Ladies, thank you so much. I'd always rather be painting. Working the business angle is a such a bore, but you've made it so I won't dread coming to work."

I'd stood back to allow Bess to take charge of the big reveal, but it was time for me to speak. "Izzy, here's your invoice. If you find something doesn't work for you, let us know. We'd be glad to return and tweak this or design a different system for you."

"I can't imagine it won't work." She put on her glasses, studied the invoice, and wrote a check. "Here you go. Our next project together will be my art studio."

"We're looking forward to it." I took the check and placed it in my purse.

After saying our goodbyes, Bess dropped me at my apartment. "Will I see you at the office later?"

"Yeah, but I need to support Susie after I handle the bathroom crisis job. Mike Best is going to interview her. I also plan to speak to Officer Diaz this afternoon. After that, I can deal with our messages."

"Ain't no thang. Whoever gets to the office first can handle the messages." Bess waved and drove off.

In the distance, waves pounded on the shore. Five pelicans flew over me single file. A gentle breeze lifted my hair off my shoulders. I began to relax, but this wasn't a vacation. I was in Fox Island for everyday life, and I felt blessed.

Inside the apartment, I filled a tumbler with ice-cold water and drove to the house where the three teenage girls lived. It turned out the girls were in school, and their mom showed me the bathroom in question. She basically told me the space was out of control and she'd pay me to get it organized.

No problem. I made notes of systems that would work and mentioned them to the woman. She agreed to all my suggestions because she claimed she was exhausted from the arguments every morning. "I'll get an estimate to you, and if it's acceptable, we'll schedule a time to return."

"Thank you so very much." She walked me to the door and waved. "I'm counting on you to restore my sanity, or at least add peaceful mornings to my life."

I laughed with her, then glanced at my watch. It was later than expected, and I hightailed it to Susie and Paul's house. The news van sat in the driveway. Rats. I parked behind it and jogged to the back door. It was unlocked, and I let myself inside. "Susie?"

My sister-in-law appeared. She wore a blue blouse over black slacks. "I was worried you wouldn't make it. Come on."

I followed her into the living room. A cameraman stood in a corner with his gear already set up.

Mike walked to me with an outstretched hand. "So, we meet again, Ms. Sloan."

I shook his hand. "Please, call me Kate."

"Kate, it is. Any chance we can interview you too?"

I glanced down at my blue and white polka dot top over faded blue jeans. It'd been a long morning, and I hadn't checked my appearance in hours. Plus, I wanted him focused on Susie. "I'm only here for moral support. Maybe another time, and thanks for looking at other potential suspects."

"You're off the hook this morning, but you did promise an interview when the killer is arrested."

"Okay." Had I made a promise? I'd take his word for it, because I clearly didn't remember. Too much was happening.

Mike took charge, and I moved to the shadows.

The interview began. "Mrs. Wright, did you ever meet Carissa Ruffalo?"

"We crossed paths at the art gallery once, and another time we had a conversation." Susie clasped her hands on her lap. Her shoulder-length hair had been curled under at her shoulders, and her bangs were brushed to the side.

Throughout the conversation between Mike and Susie, my sister-in-law kept her composure.

Ten minutes passed with Susie answering questions about Paul. She always made a point of sharing how dedicated Paul was to our community.

Mike said, "One last thing, Mrs. Wright. Do you believe your husband was in a relationship with Carissa Ruffalo?"

"No. Paul and I take our marriage vows seriously. He's always been faithful. People alter photos every day, and that's what this young lady did. I don't know why she targeted my husband, and I am sorry for her family's loss. But Paul was not involved with her, and he didn't murder her either."

"If your husband is innocent, did you murder Carissa?"

"No, because she was not a threat to my marriage. I had no motive to do her harm."

Mike said a few words to the camera, and the interview came to an end.

I hugged Susie. "You did great."

"Thanks. I'll be right back." She walked up the stairs.

I looked at Mike. "Do you have any leads for me?"

He handed the microphone equipment to the cameraman. "I'm looking into the drug angle."

"Have you noticed Fox Island is having more events to bring in tourists? At least that's what I keep hearing around town."

"I've noticed the increase myself. It seems like an easy way to launder money or sell drugs. Maybe both. In fact, there's another music festival here this weekend. It starts tomorrow night and ends Sunday afternoon."

"You don't say. I'll have to check it out." I'd attended more community events in the last week than some years in the past.

"Then I'll probably see you there."

"Please be sure to give yourself time to investigate the vendors."

The cameraman spoke to Mike, then left the house.

Mike smiled. "Any specific vendor?"

Oh, how I wanted to point out Fox Island Art Gallery. "I'd focus on art vendors. I don't want to sway you, but see what you come up with."

"Kate, you're causing me to lose sleep. Not in a good way, either. Maybe when your brother is cleared, we can go out together."

"You believe he's innocent?" My heart leapt then fell. Wait a second. Had he asked me out on a date?

"Let's say I know you believe he's innocent, and you're very persuasive."

Susie reappeared, and our conversation ended. Susie and I hugged again, then I followed Mike outside because I'd blocked his TV van.

I'd learned Fox Island was about to host a music festival but nothing else. It'd been a boost to my spirits to know Mike Best was pursuing the truth. It'd also been nice to maybe get asked out on a date. I wasn't positive of his age, but he appeared to be too young for me. If I was completely honest, I couldn't go out on a date with anyone when my heart seemed to be set on another man. I'd made that mistake once, and it wouldn't happen again.

There'd be time later to consider my love life. I needed to grab a quick bite and meet Reid so we could be on time for our appointment with Officer Diaz.

Chapter Thirty-Seven

I drove to the police station and met Reid in the parking lot. He opened my car door. "You ready for this?"

I took a deep breath and stepped out. Perspiration beaded along my hairline, and I pulled my hair into a ponytail and secured it with an elastic hair band. "It depends on what he tells us."

"Suppose it's bad news. Or say he wants to speak to Paul again. How will you respond?"

"I don't think Paul wants me to obstruct justice, but I also won't turn him in. However, I can take a message to my brother. If he turns himself in, it'll be different." I removed my sunglasses and looked at Reid. "This is going to be harder than I expected."

"How do you want the conversation to go?"

"I'd like to tell Emerson what I've learned the last day or so. Do you think he'll believe me?"

"Yeah, I do. Emerson has worked with Paul for years. His wife teaches at the same school as Susie, and they're friends."

Friendship didn't mean the woman was on our side. "I'd bet Mrs. Diaz believes Paul is guilty."

"Her name is Amelia, and why do you think that?"

"If Amelia and Susie are friends, she'll want to defend Susie. Hence, she is against Paul."

Reid shook his head. "Not necessarily. She could stick up for Paul, and that's what we want. Emerson needs to hear that his wife believes Paul is innocent."

"Oh, Reid. I saw a comment from her a few days ago. I think she called Paul a scumbag." I pressed my lips together.

"That's unfortunate, but one thing at a time. Let's talk to Emerson, then if we need to deal with Amelia, we will." He touched my shoulder and nodded toward the police station. "Ready?"

"Yes." I lifted my chin and walked into Fox Island Police Station.

We were led to Emerson Diaz's office, and he stood when we entered. "Have a seat, please. I assume you're here to discuss the murder of Carissa Ruffalo. I don't have much time, so let's get down to it. You, Paul, and Susie are moving down the suspect list."

I sank back into my seat. "We're still on your list?"

"To be fair, I can't completely rule you three out, no matter how I personally feel about the situation."

"Okay. Have you investigated the art gallery? I discovered a security camera in Izzy Reynolds's office. Do you—"

"Whoa, whoa, whoa. Did you break into the gallery?" Officer Diaz's voice grew loud.

"No way. I was there for work. Bess King and I were organizing Izzy's office. We just happened to find the camera while moving a piece of furniture. We mentioned it to Izzy, and she acted like she had no clue how it got there. So, if she is telling the truth, why would someone spy on Izzy? Do you know about Jason Nesbitt and Deshane Palmer?"

He pulled a digital voice recorder out of his top drawer, pushed a button, and placed it on the desk. "Do you mind?"

"I'm happy you're taking me seriously. Record away." My heart felt a tad lighter.

"Tell me about the two people."

I repeated their names and shared about the artists from Jamaica. "One odd thing is that Jason keeps popping up, but Izzy doesn't seem to be selling his artwork. Trust me, I know. I asked for a price on one of his paintings, and nobody would tell me. They also acted weird when I said it was fine by me to pay Jason directly. So, why does she have a few of his pieces on display at the gallery? Oh, and—"

Reid patted my hand. "Take a breath."

My heart raced, and I did slow down. "There have been some exchanges between France Granger and Jason." I described what I'd witnessed.

Reid said, "I've seen it myself. It reminded me of a drug deal you see on TV."

"Can you be more specific?"

I motioned for Reid to continue. He looked to the officer. "They stood close. Packages were exchanged, then they left in opposite directions."

Despite the recorder being on, Officer Diaz jotted something in his little notebook. "What did you think was in the packages?"

"Jason gave France the bigger package, and she gave him something smaller. In my mind, it was an envelope of cash."

I butted into the conversation. "Our theory is Jason gave France artwork and drugs in exchange for the cash. I thought maybe Izzy only displayed his paintings so nobody would suspect there was a drug deal going down. It also explains why she wouldn't sell me one of his paintings."

"If you think this Jason Nesbitt smuggled drugs into the country from Jamaica, why is he hanging around?" The cop speared me with his gaze.

"I don't know, but I promise there's something bad going on."

"Do you believe the artist murdered Carissa?"

I shook my head. "I hope not, because he seems like a nice guy who maybe got in over his head."

"Anything else?" Officer Diaz frowned.

My heart beat hard. "Um, I don't mean to offend you or anything, but I saw a comment on social media from your wife. I understand she's a lovely person, and I know she and Susie are friends. In fact, she probably believes she's defending Susie. There are a lot of cruel people in the world."

Officer Diaz glared at me. "What's your point?"

"I need to find a way to ask her to remove her comment. My goal is to have Susie introduce me to your wife. I don't want to go behind your back and make you mad, though."

"Thanks for the warning, but let me handle it." He clicked off the recorder and stood.

CHAPTER THIRTY-SEVEN

Reid said, "Emerson, we appreciate your time and hard work on this case."

I reached out and shook his hand. "Yes. Thank you very much."

"It's my job. You two take care."

We walked to the parking lot and stopped at Reid's truck. "What else do you plan to tackle today?"

"I'd really like to find Jason Nesbitt."

Reid groaned. "Where should we start?"

Chapter Thirty-Eight

I t was so different hanging out with Reid than it'd been with my husband before he died. Reid had a confident yet comfortable air about him. I felt safe, like he'd protect me from harm, and maybe more important, he wouldn't hurt me.

He pulled into the parking lot of the art gallery. "If you don't mind, I need to return a couple of calls while you look for Jason."

I looked around the parking lot. "Izzy's Volvo is here, so you probably should keep a low profile. Too bad we don't know what Jason drives."

"For all we know, he's not driving."

"Good point. I'll hurry." I opened the truck door and stepped onto the sandy blacktop.

Reid gave me a two-finger salute. "Be safe."

Once inside, I did a quick tour of the gallery. No sign of the artist, so I headed to the coffee area. "Hey, Marie. Have you seen Jason Nesbitt?"

Her eyes grew wide. "He's not in here."

I studied her pained expression. "Are you okay?"

Her eyes darted from me to the patio door. "Yes. How are you, Ms. Sloan?"

Were we being watched? I played along. "I'm good. Is it too late to order two coffees?"

"No, ma'am. I'm open for a few more hours. What would you like?" Her smile lacked warmth. Something was definitely off.

"I'd like a lavender latte and a cold fruity drink. Anything you have will work."

Marie gave me my total, and I paid her.

"It won't take long. Who's with you?"

"Reid Barrett."

"Your bodyguard. Good." She turned her back on me. "Would you like to take this outside?"

"Sure." I headed out and sat at a table, texting Reid that there might be trouble brewing.

An emoji flashed with a thumbs up.

A young couple sat in the sun, and there were two older women, sipping coffee and chatting.

In the shadows, sitting under a crepe myrtle, was Jason. He was a big guy, and he looked uncomfortable at the little white and blue bistro table. He couldn't even fit his legs under the table.

France swept through the outdoor eating area, and she joined Jason.

One of my coping mechanisms for limited hearing was the ability to partially read lips. I removed my phone, texted Reid, then switched to camera mode. I tapped the video button and zoomed in on France and Jason. My goal was to focus on their mouths while appearing to check my messages.

"Whatcha doing there?" Reid's voice carried an amused tone.

"Shh. Sit down." I propped my phone on the table, leaning it between the napkin holder and a salt shaker.

"Are you okay?" He sat beside me.

"Yeah, thanks for coming."

Marie approached us. "A lavender latte and an iced strawberry green tea."

"Thanks." I pointed to my phone and hoped she understood I was watching the two across the room.

"Enjoy." She nodded and left us alone.

Reid leaned close to my left ear. "Seriously, what are we doing?"

I whispered, "We can't hear what they're saying, but maybe I can read their lips later."

"Well aren't you just the fanciest thing since whipped butter?"

I busted out laughing. "Whipped butter? Hunh."

The door opened from the coffee shop, and Tom Cross walked over to us.

"May I?"

Reid jumped up and shook the man's hand. "Pastor Cross. Please, have a seat."

I smiled at him. "Yes, please do."

The tall man took the seat on the side of the table, away from my cell phone. "I need to apologize for the way I treated you on Sunday. I'm a single parent and tend to be overprotective, even though my boy is a grown man. I'm sorry."

His apology impressed me. "I'm a single parent myself, and I know it's challenging."

His eyes almost sparkled, and he smiled. "I can assure you that while Brandon has many problems, he didn't murder that young lady."

I'd already ruled him out, but I didn't want the preacher to know about my investigation.

Reid came to my rescue. "Pastor, did Brandon know Carissa?"

He removed his sunglasses and rubbed his eyes. "Yes. They both attended a support group at church. It includes alcoholics and people who struggle with substance abuse. It's a twelve-step program based on other successful groups. Fox Island is a small community, and we combined the groups. Savannah is a short drive, but many of these people have lost their licenses. Those who are still legally allowed to drive may give in to the temptation of bars along the road to the city. The church felt the need to help our locals, and that's why we started our support group."

The urge to mention Brandon's relapse was great. Instead, I reached for my latte and sipped it.

Reid said, "Were you the leader?"

Pastor Cross shook his head. "No. It's led by a man with training in that field. We also think the people will feel free to open up to a person who's not in the ministry. I don't judge people, because we all have a cross to bear. But if even one person felt intimidated by my profession, it'd be a shame. Therefore, we hired Tony Shepherd to lead the group."

Reid scratched his chin. "I don't believe I know him."

Movement caught my attention. France and Jason stood and left in different directions. I covered my phone with my hand. France zipped past us, and she looked perturbed. Jason moved slower toward the gate leading to the parking lot.

"Excuse me for a minute." I hurried after him. Away from the others, I called out, "Jason, wait a second."

He turned on me with a frown, and my knees shook. He didn't look happy, and I didn't want him to take his anger out on me.

Chapter Thirty-Nine

"Oh, it's you." Jason Nesbitt's voice was deep, and I stepped closer to hear him better.

"Yes, I'm Kate Sloan. I'd like to buy one of your paintings, but the gallery is not making it easy."

Jason looked right and left. "I can't talk to you here."

"Okay. How about meeting me at my business? It's just down the street. We can give you a ride."

"No. We shouldn't be seen together."

That was scary. "Will you go to my store? It's Let's Get Organized."

"Yes. I've got pictures on my phone of my paintings. I will show you. How about twenty minutes?" His voice was deep and almost lyrical.

"I'll be there." I returned to the table where Reid and Pastor Cross were talking. "I'm so sorry for my rudeness."

Tom Cross patted my hand. "If you are trying to catch the killer, you'll see my son is innocent. I'll pray for the truth to be revealed."

"Then you'll understand we have to run. I've got a lead to track down."

Reid lifted his eyebrows. His gaze drifted from Tom's hand on mine to my eyes. "I guess we'll roll then. See you Sunday, Pastor."

"You two should call me Tom." His eyes locked with mine.

I moved my hand from his and grabbed my latte and purse. "Bye, Tom."

Reid stalked to the truck and slammed his door. Anger rolled off him.

I hopped in, wondering if I'd misspoken to his pastor. No, it was worse. I'd been rude and run away. "Do I need to apologize for running after Jason while Tom was talking to us?"

He two-fisted the steering wheel and pulled onto Ocean Boulevard. "Kate, I plan to see this so-called investigation through with you. Paul has always been a good friend, but after we prove he's innocent, we might need to avoid each other. I can help you find a different contractor."

He'd called me Kate, not Katie. It felt like I'd been sucker punched. I grabbed a hold of his arm. "No, Reid. Why would you suggest that? I want you."

"You want me to what? To help your investigation? To fix your house?" His tone shifted from anger to hurt.

What in the world was happening? We'd been fine before the art gallery. Yikes. Was he upset about Tom touching me? Could he possibly be jealous? The preacher hadn't meant anything. "Um, Reid, can you pull over for a minute? Jason is walking to my store, and I think we need to talk before we meet up with him."

Reid muttered under his breath, but he pulled into the library parking lot. The truck idled. "What?"

"I'm not used to baring my soul. Are you ready for this?" I rubbed my hands on my jeans.

He let out a big sigh. "I'm a grown man. Just lay it on me. You want to date Tom Cross. Is that it?"

I gasped. "No way."

"We knew each other growing up, but I'm too old, and frankly too tired, for high school games. Just because we were pretending to date each other, it's understandable you didn't take it seriously. I know it wasn't real."

I unfastened my seatbelt and twisted my body to face him. I propped my elbows on the console and took Reid's face in my hands. "Reid Barret, listen and listen good. Life threw us some curve balls. I made a poor choice marrying David, but I can't regret it because of Ethan. However, I loved you in high school. Somehow in my mixed-up teenage mind, I didn't think we could date because Paul was your best friend."

Reid took my hands in his and smiled. "I was crazy about you, Katie. Like you, I didn't think we could date because of Paul."

"Did you have a happy marriage?"

179

His smile disappeared. "Jill and I were good friends. She had ovarian cancer but no insurance. I married her to get her on my insurance plan. It was a hard fight, but in the end, cancer won."

"Why didn't you remarry?"

"Oh, Katie. You stole my heart years ago. It wouldn't have been fair to anyone else to get married. It was always you that I loved." He leaned forward, and our lips touched. At that moment, I knew what home meant for me. It wasn't Fox Island. Home was Reid Barrett.

Chapter Forty

Reid and I entered Let's Get Organized a few minutes later. Bess was talking to Jason, and she quirked an eyebrow at me. I felt a warm glow from the kiss, the mind-blowing kiss. Make that the life-changing kiss. Could Bess see a difference in me?

I said, "Jason, thanks for waiting."

"Yes. Yes. You said you want to buy one of my paintings?"

I glanced at Reid. "You're my contractor. Do you want to look with me?"

"We'll make anything you pick work."

I turned to face Jason, who was tapping on his phone. "Let's see what you have for sale."

He handed the device to me. "This is a waterfall near my home. Here's Treasure Beach." All his paintings involved water, and he used bright colors.

"You are so talented. I think my favorite is the rowboat on the deserted beach. Is it for sale?"

"Yes."

"Are you sure you won't get in trouble with Izzy or France? Did they try to convince you to sign a contract with them?"

He stepped back. "I must go now."

"Wait, Jason. I want to help. Are you in any kind of trouble?"

He shook his head. "I cannot discuss it with you. It is not safe."

I couldn't promise to protect the young man. "I don't believe you should do business with the gallery."

"No. I must go." He left the building. I ran after him, but he'd disappeared.

Reid stood on the sidewalk with his arms crossed. "You know, for days we've suspected there could be drug smuggling connected to the art gallery. I hope there's nothing worse going on."

"Like what?"

"Jason was scared. I'm sure of it." Reid frowned. "I bet it takes a lot to shake him. Do you think it's possible he's being blackmailed by Izzy or France?"

I considered Reid's words. "You're right. He's a big guy, and I just didn't think he might be fearful of someone else."

Reid paced. "It's possible he's not anxious for his own safety. What about the cousin?"

"Deshane Palmer is petite, and she seems younger than her cousin. He was excited about selling a painting to me right up until the moment I mentioned Izzy and France."

"Katie, neither one of us is trained to investigate the gallery, drug smuggling, or human trafficking. Let's keep our focus on proving Paul is innocent and hope the other pieces fall into place."

"You're right. I had hoped Jason might provide a clue to what is happening with France and Izzy. France seems to be the one doing the secret handoffs, and Marie said France got mad at her when she almost opened a package." I waved to get Reid's attention.

His mouth hung open, and his gaze appeared to follow a white sedan driving up the street.

"Reid. What's wrong?"

He ran a hand over his face. "Don't worry about it."

I touched his arm. "You're doing so much for Paul and me. If there's something wrong, I want to support you."

"It's nothing."

"Reid, if we're going to have a relationship, you need to trust me." I pressed my lips together. It'd be a crying shame for us to lose a chance at a real relationship after all these years.

"My mother just drove past us." Red splotches appeared on his tan face. "And?"

"There was a man in the passenger seat, and I'm pretty sure it was my father."

Oh, no. Sam Barrett had left his family years ago. Joy and Reid woke up one morning, and the man was nowhere to be found. The police had looked for him. Joy had hired a private investigator. Nobody had seen the man for decades.

What would possess him to show up today?

Chapter Forty-One

Reid huffed. "That's plain ridiculous. No way my old man turned up out of the blue. He left divorce papers when he disappeared. Mom signed them and pretended to get on with her life. She dated and even remarried."

"Three more times, right?" In my mind, nobody had ever compared to her first husband. It made more sense why Reid had never married anyone except for Jill.

"Yes, she's been married a total of four times."

A couple walked by with a stroller. A small boy smiled and waved at me. "Hi."

"Hi there, sweetie."

The parents continued their walk, and I reached for Reid's hand. "Let's go inside where we can have a bit of privacy."

"I should check on my mother."

"Why don't you text or call? I'm not sure you're ready to face your dad if they are together."

"If Mom has to deal with him, I should be on her side."

I didn't agree at all with his statement. Talk about false narrative. Or did I understand the meaning behind the phrase? Maybe Reid was downright delusional. Whatever the problem was, he didn't need to confront his runaway dad. "Reid, I just don't feel like it's a good idea."

"You're probably right, but I'm her only child. I'll see you later." He kissed my forehead and left me standing on the sidewalk.

With feet of lead, I entered the store. "You'll never guess who just showed up in town."

"Who?"

"Sam Barrett."

"Oh my goodness. That can't be good."

"To make matters worse, he's with Joy. Even worse, Reid has gone to stand by his mom's side."

"What do you think Mr. Barrett wants? Is he dying? Does he need money? What in the world possessed him to come to Fox Island after all these years?"

"A lot of very good questions, Bess." My phone vibrated. "Maybe that's Reid."

"If you're lucky."

I snatched up the phone. "Hello."

"Kate Sloan?"

"Yes, who is this?"

"Ian Wilson. Carissa's neighbor."

I sat at my desk and reached for a pen and paper. "I remember you. How can I help you?"

"I can't quit thinking about Carissa. The sight of her dead body haunts my dreams."

"Ian, do you have someone to talk to? Or would you like to meet me for coffee? I know we're not close, but we experienced the same thing."

"Thanks, but I'm taking off for a few days. This weekend, I plan to head to Atlanta and crash with my folks. My mom is really worried about me."

"I understand." Boy, did I get it.

"Anyway, I kept thinking about last Thursday. I have replayed the day over and over in my mind and just remembered seeing a strange woman in the apartment parking lot the night of the murder. She carried a paper bag, and she wore all black. It was like athletic apparel and some kind of cross-trainer shoes."

"Have you told the police?"

"Nah. I thought they might laugh at me. It's probably nothing, but I've not seen her around here, before or after the night of the murder."

"Please, Ian, tell the cops what you know. Do you want me to meet you at the police station? How about I pick you up?"

"You don't think they'll blow me off?"

"No. If it's not important, they'll rule it out. But it could be a clue."

"Okay. Can you meet me now?"

"On the way." I disconnected.

Bess had her hands on her hip and cocked her head. She would've been a terrifying mother. "Now what?"

"Ian remembers seeing a woman in black at the apartments last Thursday night. We're meeting at the police station for him to report it."

She flicked her hand at me. "Go on then."

I hugged her. "Thanks for understanding, Bess. I promise to make it up to you."

"Yes, you will." Her giggle assured me she wasn't mad.

"Oh, wait. My car is still there. Can you give me a lift?"

"What are friends for? Come on." Bess drove me to the station and dropped me off, where we saw Ian waiting.

Ian and I went inside and caught Officer Diaz in his office. Ian told him the same story he'd told me. It was short but consistent.

We were thanked and escorted out. I smiled at Ian. "Thanks for reporting your story."

"I hope it helps. You've got my number if you need me."

"And if you remember anything else, let me know." I gave him a motherly hug.

"Will do. Take care of yourself." He sauntered away.

I missed my son and sent him a quick text. We were overdue for a long mother-son chat.

Next, I texted Reid, but he didn't reply. After a quick inspection of the interior of my Beetle, I slid into the driver's seat. Would I recover from the memory of the snakes in my car? It was probably a good thing life was so hectic.

In a few hours, it would be a week since Carissa had been murdered. I was no closer to clearing Paul's name. I'd ruled out Tom Cross from my original list of suspects. Brandon had been in The Sand Bar that night. Even if he'd left in time to commit the murder, it didn't seem like he'd be steady enough to make sure she drowned and escape by using the balcony. That left France Granger, Izzy Reynolds, and Ryan Ford, aka Anchorman, the rock star and Carissa's ex-boyfriend.

Were the Jamaicans involved in the murder? It seemed more likely they were connected to a drug smuggling ring.

If I could determine the motive for Carissa's murder, it'd be much easier to figure out the killer. Also, how did her lies figure into the murder? If Ryan had killed her, the motive might have been jealousy.

I studied the police station. I was here because Ian had seen a woman in black. If she was connected to the murder, it may have been Izzy, France, or even my sister-in-law Susie. Ugh. Which one, though?

Officer Diaz exited the police station. I jumped out of my car and took off to intercept him. He was bound to have more answers. Maybe I could persuade him to share.

Chapter Forty-Two

"Officer Diaz. May I speak to you?" I caught up with him on the sidewalk in front of the police station.

He didn't slow his stride. "Ms. Sloan, my wife would like me to make it home for dinner once in a while."

"I know, but I'm so confused. When Ian told me about the woman, I suggested he needed to report the incident."

"You did the right thing bringing him in to talk to me. So, what's the problem?"

"Should I focus on a female killer?"

He stepped down onto the blacktop parking lot and paused by an official Fox Island Police truck. The officer was a big man with a commanding presence. "No. You should not look for the killer, whether it's male or female. Do you understand? I'm tired of having the same conversation."

I met his dark-eyed gaze. "I apologize. It's not my intention to get on your last nerve."

"But you're worried about your brother. It's understandable. Off the record, you know I believe Chief Wright is innocent. Officially though, I need to explore every lead."

His words lifted my spirits a fraction. "Thank you. I hope you have a pleasant evening with your family."

He smiled and shook his finger at me. "Stay out of trouble. I don't want to hear about any more venomous snakes appearing in your car."

"That was pretty terrifying, but Officer Collins was great. I'll see you later." I hurried to my car and hopped in. Surely nobody would put more snakes in it while the police chief was talking to me. Still, I glanced around. I couldn't help myself.

When I was certain the car was snake free, I drove to the store. Bess had left for the night, but I went inside and worked on the plan for the teenage girls' bathroom.

An hour drifted by, and I checked for a message from Reid. Nothing. I was too restless to go home, so I worked on some preliminary ideas for Izzy's art studio.

Too bad I'd never seen her home. Could I call her this late? It was going on eight. I'd seen Izzy at the art fair later than that. What was the worst she could do? I looked up her contact information and called.

"Hello."

"Hi, Izzy. This is Kate Sloan. I've started working on ideas for your personal art studio. Would it be possible for me to run over tonight and check it out?"

"Sure, darling. I'm a night owl. When should I expect you?"

I checked her address. It was off the island, but not by far. She probably lived on the marsh or one of the many creeks around Fox Island. "How about twenty minutes?"

"The gate will be open and the lights on. Come to the front door."

"Okay. See you soon." I gathered my work sketch pad, not the one for murder notes, and headed to my car. Before driving off, I texted Reid and Bess. I knew better than to go off alone without telling anyone my destination.

It'd been a long, tiring day. No real questions came to mind to tie Izzy to Carissa's murder. I'd treat this visit like a real client meeting. If anything dawned on me, it'd be icing on the cake.

* * *

Izzy led me through her shabby chic home. The design gave the appearance of being comfortable. To my trained eye, I knew a lot of money had been invested in achieving this look. "Your home is beautiful, Izzy."

"Thank you." She led me through the family room to a sunroom and out the door. "My art studio is a separate building. Follow me."

We walked along a stone path until we reached a structure bigger than the apartment where I currently resided. Floodlights came on when we approached. There were two steps leading up to the door, and Izzy inserted a key into a sliding glass door. "Welcome to my little slice of heaven."

Windows lined the front wall. There were painted canvases on easels. Because I didn't understand Izzy's art, I wasn't certain if they were complete or not. The largest painting was dark. Black, gray, purple, and blue swirled together in a depressing way. Was it a boat in a storm? I stepped away so Izzy wouldn't catch me frowning at the painting.

In the back corner of the room was a kitchenette. High on the wall was a large open space, like a cave, filled with canvases. A pretty ladder was bracketed to a metal pole leading to the open space. It'd be easy to climb up and move around the area.

"Izzy, this is amazing." The studio was full of potential, and I was excited to show her how it could function better.

"As you can see, it's disorganized. I need a system to keep my supplies nice and orderly. It's important for me to keep paint, brushes, palettes, sponges, and painting knives at each station."

"We can do that. Maybe something like a library cart. Each station can have its own cart, but if you want to move the easel, then you can easily roll the cart to your new spot."

"Perfect. It's also important to keep this space neat and clear, so I don't trip over things."

I walked around the room and took notes. We discussed how she used the kitchenette so I could improve the efficiency. "What's back here?"

"That's a bathroom. I also have a little sitting room and a small bedroom. Some nights when I finish a project, I'm too exhausted to walk to the main house."

Interesting. "Do you need me to organize those spaces?"

"No. They're just fine." She practically shooed me away.

Okay then. "Kitchenette and the main area are the only spaces I will organize. Correct?"

"Exactly."

"How about colors? Do you want us to paint the room lime green? It's very soothing as it is, though."

"You're right, and I don't want any bold colors to distract from my painting."

I nodded. "Do you mind if I walk around?"

"Take your time." She sat on a barstool and watched me.

"How about the tables? You've got three. Do you need them all?"

"I like the bistro table, and the farmhouse table is important to me. If you leave a couple of chairs in here, the rest can go."

I made notes on her requests. "Do you have a storage building for them?"

"No. You can haul them away."

"Okay. I may donate them to the veterans center."

"Splendid."

I measured the space and sketched a possible design.

There was a thud. I couldn't decipher the direction of the sound, but Izzy hadn't knocked over anything. "What was that?"

"Nothing to worry about, I'm sure." She crossed the room to where I stood. "Are you finished?"

"Oh, sure. I'll create an organization design and present it to you either tomorrow or the first of next week."

With her hand clutching my elbow, Izzy ushered me out of the building. "It'll have to be next week. I'm fully booked tomorrow."

"I'll be in touch. Are you going to have a booth at the music festival this weekend?"

"Yes. Even though it's only a weekend festival, I believe it's important to keep presenting my work to the public."

"That makes sense. You don't have snakes here, do you?"

"The island has snakes, but most won't bother you." She snickered. "As long as you don't bother them."

I grabbed my phone and turned on the flashlight. "Are you selling Jason's paintings?"

"I had planned to do that very thing, but he's a stubborn man. Negotiations broke down, and I won't be selling his paintings."

"That's too bad." I rounded the house and felt a little relief at the beams coming from the front porch lights. "Okay. I'll talk to you next week."

"Take care." Izzy was on her phone before I had even started my Beetle.

I drove past a black Volvo in the driveway. What had the suspicious noise been in the studio? An object wouldn't randomly fall. So, what had caused the thud?

Chapter Forty-Three

"I'm at your house, and I've got a few questions for you. Can you come over?" The sound of Reid's voice comforted me after my meeting with Izzy.

"Yes. I'm about to the bridge. See you soon." The call ended.

Moving into my own place would be good. Living in an apartment with so many sounds from town and traffic noise wasn't my favorite thing.

Headlights grew larger in my rearview mirror.

I glanced at my speedometer. I wasn't driving too slowly, but I mashed the gas pedal to get the driver off my rear fender.

The vehicle moved closer.

I tightened my grip on the steering wheel. No wonder Reid didn't enjoy riding in little cars. I pressed harder with my foot and sped up.

The image of the truck's front grill filled my mirror.

I increased my speed and crossed from the concrete bridge onto Ocean Boulevard.

The truck rammed me, and I lost control. The Beetle spun around. My life flashed before my eyes. My childhood, the angst of my teen years, the bad marriage, my son, and all the way up to tonight. Stomping on the brakes didn't slow my speed.

My little car careened off the highway, landing on the edge of the marsh.

I'd been run off the road.

Deliberately.

My heart raced. I glanced down at my body. No apparent broken bones. Good. I tried to calm my ragged breathing and dialed 9-1-1 with shaky fingers. I informed the operator I'd intentionally been run off the road, then I hung up and called Reid.

"Are you almost here?"

"No, I've been in an accident. I'm on this side of the bridge, but a truck pushed me into the marsh."

"Get out of the car, Katie. It could sink or flood. The tide's coming in." His footsteps pounded on what I imagined were the outside steps of my future home.

"I don't like the sound of that."

"Stay on the line." His truck door slammed, and his vehicle roared to life.

"Okay, but I'll put it in my pocket."

"I'm on the way."

"Thanks." I stuffed the phone into my pocket and grabbed my belongings. No, I didn't need everything. I left my travel mug, sweater, and phone charger, then climbed out of the car with my work bag and drawings. Right away, my feet sank into the pluff mud. What had I been thinking? I knew better than to forcefully step into the gooey, soft mud. With one hand, I steadied myself against the car before trying to take another step.

My slip-on tennis shoe was stuck, but my foot escaped. Now what?

"Hey, lady. Do you need some help?" A young man called out.

"Yes!" My reply was more of a hysterical scream than a normal response.

"My girlfriend's on the phone with the police. We saw that monster truck ram into you."

I balanced on the foot that was stuck in the muck. "I got one foot loose, but my shoe's still in the mud."

"It's best to move around as much as you can, but whatever you do, don't try to yank your feet out."

Yanking was the very thing I'd been doing. The rich, earthy scent that was usually the smell welcoming me home, now made my stomach clench. "I'm closer to the car than the road. Should I go back to it?" Even though Reid had told me to get out, at the moment, it seemed like the safest option.

"No, don't get back in your car. The tide's rising. Can you toss me your stuff?"

"Are you sure you'll catch it?"

"Ma'am, you don't have a lot of options. The lighter you are, the better."

I stuffed my papers and sketch pad into my work bag and zipped it up. "Ready?"

"Yes."

I threw the bag to him. The motion threw me off balance, and my other foot splatted into the muck.

"Got it."

Yay for my bag being safe, but I was terrified. "What about me? What should I do next?"

"Be right back."

I fought the urge to cry. The kid didn't need a hysterical woman when he returned. If he returned. *Oh, Lord, please let him come back for me.*

Before long, he reappeared. "I'm a golfer. My dad might kill me for trying this, but you grab the head of my driver, and I'll try to pull you out."

It was worth a shot, and I didn't have a better idea.

He held the club out to me, and I latched onto the cold metal head. Titanium if I remembered correctly from conversations I'd had with my son. "Got it."

"Now, nice and easy, try to lift a foot."

This time my shoe stayed on, but my ankle wasn't happy with the motion. With the young man pulling, and me trying to slog through the pluff mud, I finally made it free. "Thank you, thank you. You probably saved my life."

"Anyone would've done the same thing."

"I doubt it. What's your name?"

"Liam Deloach."

"I'm Kate Sloan, and if you ever need a favor, look me up."

A police car appeared. Blue lights flickered in the night's darkness, and the siren blared.

Officer Collins soon arrived and placed a warm blanket over my shoulders. "Fancy meeting you again. First the snakes and now the muck. Who did you rub the wrong way?"

I looked at him. "You believe me?"

"Yes, ma'am. You also have two witnesses, and they have a partial license plate number for me. We may not catch the person who left the snakes, but we'll catch the jerk who ran you off the road. Luckily, he didn't bump you off the bridge. The marsh water is much deeper there."

I shivered.

"Kate!" Reid's voice cut through the sirens and all the other voices.

"Reid, I'm over here."

He ran over and swooped me up in his strong arms. "You liked to have scared me to death."

I clung tight to him, and the blanket fell to the ground. "I was so scared." The sobs I'd been holding back erupted.

"Honey, I'm not letting you out of my sight again."

He carried me to his truck and opened the door.

I balked. "No, I'm caked with mud."

"I don't mind, but I know you won't want to make a mess. How about my tailgate?"

"Perfect."

He lowered the gate with his free hand, then he placed me on the tailgate. "Just one second."

I looked at the commotion all around us. Cops had blocked both lanes so a tow truck could try to pull my car out of the marsh.

Reid appeared with another blanket and wrapped it around my shoulders. "I think you've got a friend in Officer Collins."

I smiled. "He and I have been through a lot in a very short time."

An official police truck appeared, then stopped, leaving the lights pointed at the crime scene. "I knew it was too much to expect a night off. By the way, I called your brother. He's on the way." There was a note of amusement in Officer Diaz's tone.

I glared at him. "You shouldn't have done that."

"We've cleared him of the murder. In fact, we've cleared you too."

"How? Why?" I tried to read his expression.

"Without going into too much detail, one of our tech experts was able to prove the pictures of Paul and Ms. Ruffalo were phony. A security camera across the street shows you and your brother entering the apartment, but you don't leave until the next day. We were also able to prove his phone was at your place and in use. It's a good thing he made calls and sent text messages that night. That's all you need to know at this juncture."

"And me?"

"You and Paul alibied each other, and we're able to prove his whereabouts. So, you're safe."

"What about Susie?"

"We've got a reliable witness. One of the backyard neighbor kids had a campout in the yard, and the parents were running back and forth with food. They saw her on the back deck and through the kitchen window during the timeline for the window of the murder. We need Chief Wright on the case, and we need you off. You were lucky tonight." His voice turned serious. "I'm just glad we're not calling the coroner."

"That makes two of us." I leaned into Reid.

"Make that three." Reid tightened his hold on me.

Chapter Forty-Four

Ethan woke me up with a phone call the next morning. Bess had told him what I'd been up to. Boy, could that kid give a lecture. After hanging up, I showered and prepared for the day.

I met Reid at my soon-to-be-new house. A meeting had been scheduled with the closing attorney, and Reid had gotten permission to go onto the property if he didn't physically change anything. We stood in the middle of the kitchen, and he smiled. "It's good to see you this morning. How'd you get here?"

"Paul brought me over. I'll either need you to drive me to work, or I can walk." I shrugged. "It's not that far."

"I don't mind dropping you off. When will you find out about your car?"

"As much as I enjoy my Beetle, it's not fair to make Bess always use her van for work. I might look into an SUV or something with more room."

"A bigger vehicle? You don't say." His eyes twinkled. "The reason I asked you to come over is to get your opinion on the cabinets. They're in good shape, but I don't feel like they're your style. We can either replace them or reface them."

I touched the door of one of the maple cabinets. "It's a little sticky."

"Yeah. Years of cooking can sometimes leave a buildup."

"Can they be cleaned and painted to look nice? Or would it be easier to replace them?"

Reid crossed his arms. "In my opinion, if you need more space, go for new cabinets. If you can make do with these cabinets, it'll save money to reface them."

"How much money? Is it worth putting you to all that trouble?"

"It's a significant savings. On the average, refacing is one-fifth the cost of buying new cabinets. You can still put your touch on the kitchen, and you'll have the satisfaction of not adding waste to the landfills."

"Okay, you've convinced me. We'll use these cabinets."

"Nice. I think it's a good decision. Let's look at your main bathroom. In my opinion, it needs a major overhaul."

"Reid, if you think it needs to be gutted, I'll agree. You're the expert on what to save and what to toss."

He chuckled. "Hey, you're the organizer. It sounds like we've got something in common."

I smiled. "You're exactly right."

We went through a few rooms and discussed what needed to be done. Reid rubbed his hands together. "I can't wait to get started."

"I'm ready to settle down. The last couple of months have been hectic."

"I imagine that's right. Do you have time to stop for a cup of coffee?"

"Absolutely. By the way, Paul read me the riot act about the accident last night, and Ethan got onto me this morning."

Reid's blue eyes zoomed in on me. "That doesn't surprise me."

"Yeah, well, I'm to leave the murder investigation alone. Paul is working with Officer Diaz, but I still don't know the exact reason we were cleared." I walked out the door and waited for Reid to lock the house. "You know what gets me?"

"What?" He held my hand as we walked down the stairs.

"I know more than Paul does at this point. He's got to catch up before he can really investigate."

"Katie, your brother is trained to solve crimes."

"I know, but still." Yikes. I sounded like a pouty teenager. "Sorry for my bad attitude. Can we go to the Fox Island Art Gallery Coffee Shop?"

"It depends on if you are going in order to snoop or to support Marie." He opened the truck door for me.

I leaned against his shoulder. "How about half and half?"

He laughed. "I'm only agreeing because you'll probably go alone later."

The morning sun filtered through the pine trees. Spanish moss hanging on an oak tree filtered the sun's rays. A garbage truck rumbled on a nearby street. Thud. Roar. Crunch.

"Reid, I think there was someone hiding in Izzy's art studio last night. I heard a noise in a back room, and Izzy hurried me out of the building. Then instead of taking me back through her house, she walked me around the dark side yard to the driveway in front. It was creepy."

"What do you think?"

I paced in the driveway. "With human smuggling, or modern-day slavery, is it possible to only have one or two people under your power? On the news, you always see a truckload of people crammed together. It makes sense the bad people have to disperse the victims. Right?"

He leaned against the truck and crossed his feet. "I really don't know. I've had guys work for me, and I've assumed they were here from Mexico to make a different life for themselves. I've treated them to meals because often they send money home to their families. They have told me this. I've never had someone say they are being held against their will. Of course, victims of human smuggling are probably scared. We need to discuss this with Paul."

"Jason disappeared yesterday when I mentioned Izzy and France. Do you think it's possible Jason was the person I heard? The art studio is nice, but if he's being held against his will, it's still a prison."

Reid pushed off the truck. "We need to tell Paul."

"You're right." I punched his number into my phone.

"Kate, what's wrong?" Paul's voice sounded anxious.

"I'm fine, but there's something from last night I forgot to mention. We need to meet."

"Your new house?"

"Fine. We'll be there in five."

Chapter Forty-Five

Paul stood on the sidewalk when we pulled up to my future home. "Good morning."

I hugged him. "Morning. What'd you do with Snowball?"

"He's at the house with Susie. You know how much she loves dogs, and it scored me some brownie points. Tell me whatcha got."

"Last night, I was so frightened about the truck and the wreck that I completely forgot to tell you about Izzy's studio." I went into detail about my meeting right down to the unexplained noise.

"Are you sure it was in the building? It might have been a limb falling outside."

"I know my hearing loss sometimes can be confusing, but at the time, I was standing with my left ear toward the back rooms. I heard a sound. Izzy rushed me out of there like she was worried I'd look behind closed doors. Do you think she called someone to hurt me on my drive home?"

"It's possible, and your wreck was no accident. You're getting too close to the truth, and the thugs need to remove you." He pinched his bottom lip.

Reid said, "Paul, your trouble began when you thought drugs were being brought to Fox Island via the art gallery."

"Yes."

I looked at my brother. "Carissa sometimes worked at the gallery. Carissa posted about a relationship with you, and the next day she's murdered. I'm with Izzy at night, and on the way home, I'm run off the road. It just seems like the art gallery must be involved."

Reid said, "Didn't Marie tell you that Carissa was at the gallery the day of the murder? Did she have an argument with someone?"

"Yes, with France."

Paul pulled his phone out. "I need to record everything, then check my notes. I don't like feeling at a disadvantage during an investigation."

My hands began to tremble. "I haven't had breakfast, and we need to warn Marie. I don't want her to be the next victim in whatever's going on."

"I'll talk to the young lady."

I shook my head. "If you show up and talk to Marie, it could put her in danger. Let us go."

"Sis, I need to talk to her myself."

"Fine, but please meet her at a neutral place."

"Like Bobby's dental office?" Paul shook his head. "I would've loved to have seen his expression."

"No, you wouldn't. It wasn't pretty." Reid twirled his keys on his forefinger. "How about we go see Marie and order breakfast? It'll look normal, but we'll warn her of the danger. If she agrees to leave and meet you, we'll text you the location."

"You also need to text me if she refuses. In that case, I'll go to the gallery to speak to her."

I rubbed my brother's shoulder. "We'll be in touch."

Reid and I jumped into his truck, and he drove us to the gallery. On the way, we discussed scenarios of how to approach Marie. We reached our destination with a game plan and entered the building.

France and Izzy stood at the entry desk. Izzy was shaking a finger at the younger woman. Both turned to greet us. Izzy's eyes grew wide. She ran her hands down her black linen tunic. "Kate, I didn't expect to, er, see you so soon. Did you stay up all night working on plans for my art studio?"

"No, you said not to bring them to you until next week."

"Why are you here then?"

"I'm hungry, and Reid hasn't eaten either. We decided to get muffins from your coffee shop." I tilted my head and strove to produce an innocent smile. "Funny thing happened on my way home from your place last night. A big truck—"

Reid placed a hand on my shoulder. "It was a monster truck, according to the witnesses."

"You're right, sweetie." I gave Reid a legitimate smile. "As I was saying, this big monster truck ran me off the road. Lucky for me, I'd made it across the bridge before being forced into the marsh. Double lucky that there were witnesses to come to my rescue."

France stepped closer. "You say there were witnesses?"

"Quite a few, actually. The cops took statements and hope to catch the creep. Of course, I didn't see anything except for lights in my rearview mirror."

Izzy's complexion paled. "I'm glad you're safe. If you'll excuse us, we need to discuss tonight's event."

"See you later." I watched them head for the hallway of offices before leaning close to Reid. "They have hidden security cameras. We need to be cautious in case they watch our exchange with Marie."

"I hear ya."

The shop was hopping, but I didn't see any of the regulars. Maybe the people were tourists. We waited in a short line before greeting Marie. I said, "Good morning. We'd like to order some breakfast."

Reid was studying the display of baked items. "Can I get a blueberry muffin and black coffee?"

I did a doubletake. "You don't want a latte?"

He patted his trim midsection. "At my age, you gotta watch the calories."

Hmph. The man didn't have an ounce of fat on him. Maybe it was because he made healthy choices when it came to food.

"How about you, Kate?" Marie lifted her eyebrows.

"Can you make a skinny mocha latte? And I'd like a strawberry muffin."

"It'll only take a few minutes." She wrote down our order, and I paid her. "Keep the change. We'll sit outside while we wait." I took the paper receipt with me.

Reid and I chose a table in the shadows, and I began writing a note to Marie.

He touched my hand. "If they see the note, she could be in more danger.

Shoot, it could put you in danger too."

My hopes faded. "How do we tell her without being obvious?"

"Trust me. I've got a plan."

"Okay." I dropped the pen and paper into my purse. "What's on your agenda today?"

"I want to go to the house where Paul was holed up. He said he tackled some of the projects to avoid boredom. I want to look it over and verify his work will pass inspection. What about you?"

"After we make sure Marie is safe, I better check in with Bess. She's liable to end our partnership if I don't show up for work."

"Last night was work when you went to see Izzy."

"True. Although, if she's behind Carissa's death, we won't be able to organize her art studio."

Marie appeared, carrying a tray with our order. "Here you go." She handed us the muffins first. Next, she passed the latte to me, and she handed Reid a mug of coffee.

He sloshed some of the hot liquid over the rim, and it splashed onto the table.

Marie gasped. "Oh, no. I'm so sorry."

He lifted his hands like trying to calm her down. "Marie, we think you're in danger. How soon can you leave this place?"

Her eyes grew wide at his comment.

I reached for paper napkins and began to blot up the mess. "Marie, act like you're helping. I was forced off the road and into the marsh while driving home last night right after seeing Izzy. If she's behind Carissa's death, you may be her next target. The bad guys might think you know something about their business."

Marie pulled a towel out of her apron pocket, and she blotted away without saying a word.

"Did you hear me?" I kept my voice low.

"Yes, but I don't know where to hide. Izzy and France know where I live." She picked up the half-empty mug. "I should refill this. It'll give me a moment to think."

"It's going to be okay. We just need to stay one step ahead of the bad guys." I tried to make eye contact, but she scampered away.

In the large entryway of the building, Mayor Washington spoke to a group of people.

"Quit staring." Reid pointed to my muffin. "We should eat like there's nothing unusual going on."

"You're right." I bit into my strawberry muffin. It was moist, sweet, and delicious. "Yum."

Reid took a bite of his, and Marie returned.

"I put it in a to-go cup to make sure I didn't spill it a second time." Her voice was louder than necessary.

Reid matched her volume. "It was my fault, but thanks for the lid."

Marie handed me an empty paper cup and top. "I thought you might like one too."

"Thanks. If you don't mind, would you pour it in there for me?"

"It'll be my pleasure." She bent down to reach for my mug. "I can leave now, but where should I go?"

Reid leaned forward and picked up his coffee. "I've got just the place in mind. How soon can you get away?"

"Fifteen minutes."

"Perfect. Hopefully, they won't think we're together."

Marie transferred my coffee and placed the lid on the cup. "Kate, will you call me and act like my friend has been in an accident or something?"

"Yes. Why don't we meet behind the community church and leave your car there? We can drive you to your hiding place."

"Okay. I'll wait for your call." She straightened up. "You two have a nice day."

We went through the motions of eating, then left through the patio's gate. Once we were in the truck, I texted Paul. Our plan to save Marie was in motion. I just wished there was a way to protect Jason Nesbitt. Deep in my heart, I believed if he was involved, he'd been coerced.

Chapter Forty-Six

Paul met Marie, Reid, and me at the same house where he'd spent the last week. The four of us sat at a new rustic wood patio table, and it seemed odd not to have Snowball with us.

Paul turned on his recording device. "Okay, Marie. Let's review the day of the murder. Think hard about what you overheard."

"Remember, I wasn't all that close to them. However, I did hear part of the conversation." Marie crossed her arms. "Carissa told France that she wanted out. She had a new job opportunity in Atlanta, and she had to leave Fox Island if she ever hoped to dance again. France said something about the job not being finished. Then Carissa said she never meant to hurt anyone. She tried to leave, then France grabbed her arm. She said something about being foolish and that she'd regret walking away. But Carissa left despite the threat."

Paul tapped the table. "Why didn't your report this after Carissa's murder?"

Marie slumped back into the chair. "I was petrified of getting myself killed too."

I patted her arm. "Take it easy on her, Paul. She's telling you now."

He frowned at me, and I probably shouldn't have interrupted his interrogation.

Marie said, "Chief Wright, I'm sorry. As you can see, I don't really have family to count on. I tried to provide some information about the mysterious order."

"Tell me more about that incident."

I listened as Marie told Paul the same story she'd shared with me.

"Do you think the gallery is part of a drug smuggling ring?"

"Today, I do. Before this, I had my doubts. After Kate called me this morning, pretending I needed to go to the hospital, France declared I couldn't leave. I told her that friends come before work, and I took off before she could physically stop me. Thank goodness the mayor was taking a group of dignitaries through the gallery." She pointed to me. "You probably saw them in the coffee shop when you were there."

"I don't know Mayor Washington personally, but I did see him with a group of people inside."

"If those people hadn't been there, I might not have gotten away." Her expression crumpled. "Will I be safe here? I don't want to be by myself. Who will hear me scream if they find me?"

"Shh. It's going to be okay." I patted her hand. "Who are you the most scared of?"

"France, I think. Although, Izzy could be the boss and make France do the scary stuff."

Paul said, "I can put you in an official safe house with guards, but I'll need you to testify when we catch the killer."

"Then what? Do I have to change my identity?" She zeroed her gaze on Paul

"It depends on who the enemy is. Worst case scenario, we might have to enroll you in the Witness Security Program. How would you feel about that?"

"I guess if it's the only way to stay alive, I'll do it."

"Good to know. For now, I'll arrange to get you in a local safe house." Paul left us.

Reid stood. "This seems like a good time to check the progress on this place."

Then it was only Marie and me.

She flattened her hands on the table. "This is crazy, isn't it? I'm a simple barista with a desire to start a bakery. How can I know anything worth changing my identity?"

"Remember what Paul said. His main goal is to keep you safe."

Marie nodded. "I appreciate that, but I don't have any clothes or books or cooking supplies."

"Let me talk to Paul when he's finished. Maybe he'll let me pick up your clothes and toiletries."

"Oh, yeah. I don't even have a hairbrush with me." She began to cry.

"Oh, sweetie. It's going to be okay."

She sniffed. "France and Carissa argued the day she died. I hope my argument with France doesn't mean I'll die today."

"You've got us to protect you. Carissa was alone, and she probably still trusted France. Although Izzy may have murdered her."

"I bet those two are in cahoots." She brushed away tears. "Are we for sure it wasn't her ex-boyfriend?"

"No, but Ryan seems like such a nice guy." I remembered how pleasant he'd been helping us move furniture at the art gallery.

"He's got a dark side. He can be controlling, and he sometimes said mean things to Carissa. You know, now that I think about it, moving to Atlanta could've been about more than advancing her dance career."

"What do you mean?"

"He didn't take the breakup well. I wouldn't say Ryan stalked Carissa, but he sent her plenty of text messages. He promised to change. At least Carissa was smart enough not to fall for him again."

"France said Ryan is her boyfriend, but he denied it. What do you think?"

Marie shrugged. "Their relationship isn't serious. My guess is he can't control France, so he's not that into her."

Paul joined us. "We've got a plan. Two agents will be here in a few hours. Until then, we're not going to leave you alone."

I said, "Can I go to her place and pick up some clothes?"

"Too dangerous. Give me your address, Marie. I'll send one of my guys over to gather some belongings."

She told him where she lived. "Is there any chance you can send a female agent? I believe they'll be more in tune to what I might need."

"Not a problem."

"Paul, wait." I moved to stand by him. "What's going on? Are you back at work?"

His eyes sparkled. "Yes, ma'am."

"Good." I gave him a quick hug.

He walked into the house, leaving me alone with Marie again.

"You're doing the right thing. For safety reasons, I don't know if we'll be able to talk for a while, but I'll pray for you."

"Thanks."

Frogs croaked, and animals scrambled in the wooded area behind us. We talked about baking and general stuff.

A female cop arrived with two big suitcases and a duffle full of Marie's stuff. "I didn't know what you needed, so I gathered as much as possible. Good luck." Her red ponytail swung back and forth as she walked away.

Marie stood. "Does this place have a kitchen? I need to make coffee and fix us something to eat. Waiting for my protective team is making me a nervous wreck."

"Paul's been here for a few days, and I'm certain there's a coffee pot somewhere. Let's see what we can find." If working with food helped Marie deal with the stress, I was all for it.

Reid and Paul joined us in the kitchen, and we drank coffee and snacked on cheese and crackers.

Paul said, "It's important you don't contact anyone until the killer is caught. We're getting closer, but we need to see how many layers there are to the crime ring."

I zoned out of the conversation at that point. Layers? Could it be Jason was a low-level employee or drug smuggler? Or were the people on the street at the lowest level? Did Jason get recruited by France or Izzy? Had they tricked him with promises of selling his art? The poor guy wanted to sell his paintings, so what, or who, was stopping him? Was he trying to protect his young cousin? Or was I bumbling down the wrong path? Was Jason really the brains behind a drug smuggling ring in Fox Island?

Chapter Forty-Seven

Reid was driving me to my apartment. It was dark, but we both decided we weren't hungry after the snack Marie had prepared.

"I can't believe I missed an entire day of work." I removed the ponytail holder and rubbed my head.

"If you're helping put an end to a drug smuggling ring, Bess should understand. She's a smart woman."

"I'm ready for everyone to know the truth about Paul's relationship with Carissa."

"Don't you mean his non-relationship?"

"Yeah, you're right. Then I can focus on Let's Get Organized."

He turned onto Ocean Boulevard. "Why don't you?"

I sank into the seat. "Maybe because it's personal. These people targeted Paul, killed Carissa, and made an attempt on my life. I can't walk away. You know what I mean?"

"It doesn't get much more personal than that."

"Paul didn't mention if they've found out who ran me off the road."

Reid stopped at the crosswalk to allow a family with young children to walk across the road. "My guess is the truck was stolen. Have you decided what to do about your car?"

"I'm replacing it. Can you take me to Bobby's house? He could loan me a car for now. I'll text and see if he's home." I typed and sent my brother a message.

"No problem." The people reached the other sidewalk, and Reid drove up the road.

My phone vibrated. "He's home."

"Do you really think he'll loan you something to drive?"

"He may complain about Paul and me, but when it comes down to it, he's always on our side."

Reid turned and wound his way to my brother's neighborhood.

Bobby met us in the driveway and hugged me when I hopped out of the truck. It was the longest hug he'd given me in years. "What's going on?"

I stepped back and made eye contact. "Paul's been unofficially cleared of murder. Unofficial because he was never charged."

"Okay, but tell me about your crash into the marsh."

"Here's what happened." I explained the situation. "Can I borrow something to drive for a few days?"

"Why don't you take Lois's Jeep Cherokee? She and I can share my car, or she can drive the truck." Bobby motioned for us to follow him. He tapped his phone, and the garage door rose. "Kate, are you sure you're okay?"

"Yeah. I just need some wheels."

"Do you want to stay with Lois and me? We've got plenty of room. It might be safer for you here."

I choked up over Bobby's concern. "No. I'll be fine at the apartment."

"If you need me, call."

"I will." I gave him another hug. "Thanks. I love you."

"Love you too, sis."

Reid cleared his throat. "I'll follow Katie home and make sure she's safe."

"Thanks, man." Bobby shook Reid's hand.

I backed out of the drive and drove to my apartment. The reflection of Reid's headlights in my mirror gave me comfort, unlike the sense of terror I'd experienced the night before. I reached Chatham Street and parked near my apartment.

Reid met me on the sidewalk. "Let's check inside."

"Sounds good." We entered my apartment and looked in closets and under the bed. "All clear."

"Would you feel better if I crashed on the couch tonight?"

"How about maybe staying for a bit and we can play cards or watch a movie?"

"How about rummy? I'm afraid a movie might put me to sleep."

"Have a seat." I opened the drawer where I kept office supplies and a few games and reached for a deck of cards, a pencil, and scratch paper."

Reid said, "Would you like me to shuffle?"

"Sure." I handed him the deck, then turned on some music. "You never mentioned your dad. Was that him riding with your mom yesterday?"

"Yes, it was." He clenched his jaw.

"Do you want to talk about it?"

He met my gaze. "One day, just not yet. I'm beat."

"Okay." I respected his decision. Raising a son, I'd learned not to push certain issues. This fit the category of waiting until Reid was ready to share about the father who'd abandoned him and his mom all those years ago.

We played cards with the sound of waves in the background and a mixture of music on my app. I'd never been scared in a home alone, but tonight, I was afraid. Reid had been kind to sense my fear. I was more than ready for the killer to be caught so life could return to normal.

Reid scratched his head. "I think you're cheating, but I can't figure out how."

"I'm not cheating." I laughed.

"How do you keep beating me? I've never played this bad. Look at our score."

I tried not to smile. "Just lucky, I guess."

"I don't think so." He yawned.

"You should go home and get some rest."

"Are you sure you don't want me to stay?"

"Absolutely." I gathered the cards and put them neatly away.

Reid walked to the door but took my hands in his before stepping outside. "Call me if you need anything. I don't want you to be frightened."

"I'll call." I leaned close and kissed his cheek. "Goodnight, Reid."

"Night, Katie." He gave me a quick kiss and left.

I walked over to my murder board. Marie was safe with law enforcement. Paul was free and working on the investigation. Carissa was dead. I'd ruled out Tom and Brandon. I'd been run off the road after visiting Izzy. Coincidence or direct link to the artist?

Izzy, France, and Ryan were my top three suspects at this point. As much as I wanted to rule out Jason Nesbitt, I wouldn't.

With a yawn, I opened my laptop on the kitchen counter and watched a couple of rappelling videos. They confirmed it was possible for the killer to have left the apartment by using a rope.

I moved to the living area and sat on the slip-covered couch, and reviewed my notes. Ian had seen a woman dressed in black the night of the murder. He'd also overheard Carissa argue with a woman. If I could only find one piece of concrete evidence, I'd be much closer to finding the killer.

What clue did I need to find?

Chapter Forty-Eight

I woke up on the couch the next morning with a kink in my neck. After a hot shower, I dressed in a red-and-black polka dot top and jeans and walked across the street to buy coffee.

It was eight-thirty, and I was on a mission before heading to work. After buying two coffees, I drove Bobby's Jeep to Pelican Shores Apartments, where Carissa had lived.

I took the elevator up to the fifth floor and knocked on Ian Wilson's door. When he didn't answer, I knocked again. He'd mentioned leaving town this weekend. Had I missed him?

The door whipped open. A frowning Ian stood there bare-chested and wearing sweatpants.

"Good morning. I brought you some coffee."

"How do you know I like coffee?" His voice sounded froggy, like he'd just rolled out of bed.

"I decided to risk it." I held the paper cup out to him, and he took it.

"Thanks, but I doubt you came all this way to serve me coffee."

I shot him my best smile. "True. Would you mind letting me stand on your patio?"

"Why?"

"Whoever murdered Carissa must have left via the balcony."

"You're probably right because the chain was on the door." He stepped back and waved me into his apartment. "You may as well come in. Let's see what we can figure out."

"Thanks, Ian."

He removed a security bar from the sliding glass door track. "It seems silly to have one of these when I live so far up. But after Carissa's death, it made sense to buy one, and they're not expensive. So, why not?"

"I think you made a smart decision."

He slid open the patio door, and we stepped out. He sat on a bar-height Adirondack chair and sipped on his coffee.

I gripped the balcony rail and looked toward the ground. "Oh, that's a long way down." My stomach lurched. I glanced next door toward Carissa's apartment.

"I doubt anyone will rent that place after the murder."

"Have the police released it?" I tried to get a better look, but the rail moved a little.

Ian gasped. "Watch it. That's not the most secure thing. We don't need another dead body."

I moved away from the rail and looked toward the parking lot at a man who seemed to be staring up at us. "Ian, do you know who that is?"

"Where?" He stood beside me.

"That guy down there. White male, dark hair, and tall."

The figure turned and ran in the opposite direction.

"I can't say for sure."

"Do you have a guess?"

The person jogged to a path leading to the beach and disappeared from view.

He sighed. "There was some dude pestering Carissa for her stash of drugs. He was aware that she'd gotten clean, and he wanted to buy anything she might have squirreled away. He was tall and dark-haired, but I didn't get a good look at his face."

"That's too bad. Don't addicts usually get rid of their drugs when they go to rehab?" I remembered the prescription vials in the bathroom where she'd drowned. Had the killer known about the drugs and somehow forced her to take them? If the medicine had belonged to someone else, their name would've been on the label.

"I think she was afraid she'd get hurt again and wanted them just in case.

Know what I mean?"

"I guess. Let's switch gears. Say you got trapped on your balcony with no cell phone. How would you physically leave?"

"The building only has seven stories." Ian touched the rail and looked up. "I might move the chair to the rail so I'd be steadier when I put my feet on it. I'd hold on here—nope. I couldn't go up."

"What was your thought, though?"

He sipped his coffee. "In theory, it'd be easier to go up two flights, get on the roof, and take the stairs down."

I took notes on my phone. "So would you go down?"

"Yep. I'd swing a leg over, squat, and swing down to the balcony below me. The glitch in that plan is the rails are not very stable." His eyes grew wide. "When I was a kid, my parents bought a roll-up ladder. We practiced fire drills. If the house caught on fire, I was supposed to open the window, anchor the rope ladder, and climb down. We lived in a two-story house, so it worked."

"Okay." I added this to my notes.

"If the circus was in town, I'd believe the killer was a trapeze artist."

"Yeah, I've wondered about rappelling down myself." Nope. I shivered at the thought. "There's no way I could do it."

"Did you notice if Carissa's patio furniture looked out of place?" Ian took another drink.

I thought back to the night of the murder. One patio chair had been cattywampus, and the red pillow had been on the floor, but did that really mean anything? "Maybe. Do you know if Carissa moved the rattan chair toward the rail to watch the sunrise?"

He finished his coffee and set the empty cup on a tall side table that matched his chair. "We weren't all that close, so I can't answer your question. I was trying to decide if the killer rappelled down by anchoring their rope to a chair, it'd still get pulled against the rail. But how did the killer get the rope back?"

I shook my head. "Maybe I need to watch more videos on the topic."

"I ordered pizza the other night and shared it with Carissa, but we ate at my place. Let me rephrase that. Carissa ate the salad I ordered and only one little slice of veggie pizza. I tried to discuss basketball with her."

"Ah, yes. March Madness. I lived in Lexington, Kentucky, for years. It's a big deal."

"Yeah, but she didn't care. She seemed down, and I asked what was wrong. Carissa said she'd done something mean for money. She was desperate to move to Atlanta for a fresh start, but she'd hurt someone. And she had regrets."

It had to be connected to her lies about Paul, unless she'd tried to ruin someone else too. "What else did Carissa say?"

"I don't remember her exact words, but if she tried to fix the situation, her life might be in danger. She was scared and maybe in over her head."

"That's not too far from Fox Island. It doesn't appear to be a secret. Did she really think she'd be safe there?"

Ian threw his hands up. "Apparently."

"If I needed to get away from bad people, I wouldn't go blabbing all over town where I was headed."

"Carissa was a dreamer. Not a realist." Ian stood. "I'm sorry I couldn't help more. I need to hit the road."

"Thanks so much for your time, Ian. If you think of anything else, will you give me a call?"

"Yes, ma'am." He reached for his cup and opened the sliding glass door.

I followed him through the apartment.

"If I see that guy around, I'll let you know."

"Or maybe call the cops first. Then me." I grinned at him.

"Okay. Stay safe."

"You too." I left him and headed to the beach access. When I made it to the beach, there weren't many people around. There was a bite in the breeze, and I shivered.

A man jogged by, but it wasn't the person I'd spotted in the parking lot.

I called Bess.

"Good morning. Will you be at work this morning?"

"Yes. I'm on the beach near Carissa's apartment. It's possible I saw

Brandon."

She sighed. "I wish you'd leave that child alone."

I looked both ways. "He's a grown man with an addiction problem. I've taken Tom off my list of suspects, and even though I've ruled Brandon out, it's possible he knows something."

"What are you talking about?"

I explained about the guy wanting to get Carissa's drugs. "Will you go with me to talk to Tom? Brandon could be in trouble and not realize it."

"He's gonna be heartbroken, but let me give him a call."

"Thanks." I disconnected. The cool breeze made me wish I'd worn a heavier sweater.

"Who you talking to?" A sweaty Brandon jumped out of the dune grass and loomed over me.

Chapter Forty-Nine

My heart leapt at the sight of Brandon. "Oh, you scared me."

He glowered at me. "You didn't answer my question."

"That was Bess King, my business partner."

"I know who she is. Are you following me?" He perspired despite the cool March morning.

"I discovered you asked Carissa for her extra drugs. You need to get help, Brandon."

"I'm not an addict anymore."

I scooted out of the dune area and toward the open space of the beach, hoping to be seen by somebody. Anybody. Where were the people? "I don't think it works that way. I think you're an addict, then you're a recovering addict, but it never goes away. You can live without taking drugs or drinking alcohol, but if you slip, it's possible you could spiral out of control again. I don't really know you, but I know there are people who care about you. You're not alone."

"It doesn't feel that way."

"Did you have a fight with Carissa? Maybe it got out of hand. You strangled her, then stuck her in the tub to make it look like she drowned? I'd be terrified if I accidentally killed someone. It makes sense you left the scene of the crime."

"I didn't kill her." He hung his head. "But I did want her stash. We were in the same support group, and she said she had oxys from after her surgery."

My ringtone sounded.

Brandon pointed to it. "Answer it and put it on speaker."

I swiped and switched to speaker mode. "Bess, we're on speaker mode. I found Brandon."

"Hi, Brandon. Your dad's going to meet Kate and me in a few minutes. Would you like to join us? I'll bring breakfast and coffee."

His shoulders drooped. "Fine."

"Bess, why don't you and Tom meet us at Sammy's Smoothies?" It was close enough we could walk. There was no way I'd give Brandon a ride in case he had a hidden weapon.

"Okay. I'll text Tom."

I carried the phone without disconnecting the call.

"Brandon, do you know who killed Carissa? Were you maybe around the night she was murdered?"

He looked toward the ocean. "I went by her place to ask one more time. I didn't want to buy off the street. It'll kill my dad if I get busted again. That's why I was so persistent with Carissa. It seemed like my safest option, and she needed money."

"What happened?"

"I was about to knock, but she was arguing with a woman. It seemed my best move was to leave and try again when she'd be in a better mood." He shuffled from one foot to the other.

I adjusted my stance to hear him better. "Where'd you go?"

"There's a picnic area and playground with a view of Carissa's building. It was dark, and there weren't any families around. So I sat at the table and waited."

"How long?"

He shook his head. "Not sure. Long enough to doze off. When I woke up, the light was still on in Carissa's apartment. While I considered going back, someone wearing black stepped onto the balcony."

"How do you know what the person wore?"

"The building has lights going up the outside. When it's not turtle season, the lights are on. I assumed it was Carissa wearing one of her dance outfits. Then the person reached out. I couldn't see a rope, but there must have been one because the person climbed to the roof."

"Hmph. It seems risky. Could you tell if it was a woman or man?"

He stuffed his hands into the pockets of his dirty khakis. "Like I said, I thought it was Carissa."

"What'd you think she was doing?"

An older couple walked by, holding hands. For a second, I wondered if that would be Reid and me one day.

"She had lined up a job in Atlanta, and I thought maybe she was practicing some acrobatic thingy. No job would be worth that to me, though."

"Could it have been a man?"

He lifted his hands. "Maybe."

"Let's go to the smoothie shop."

Brandon didn't move. "Dad's going to be furious. I failed again."

"He loves you. Just hold on to that."

He turned and trudged to the path.

I walked beside him to Sammy's Smoothies.

Bess and Tom stood on the sidewalk in front of the shop. The pastor's shoulders slumped. He looked more defeated than angry.

Brandon stopped in front of his father. "Hi, Dad. I'm sorry."

The man took his son in his arms and hugged him.

Tears sprang to my eyes. They didn't need an audience for this very private and raw moment. I walked into the shop and sat at a table for four.

Bess joined me. "Tom's a good man. He'll give every last penny he has to try and save his son."

"I'd do the same for Ethan. By the way, thanks for ratting me out to my son."

"Someone needs to get through to you. Did Brandon say anything?"

"Yes, and he'll need to tell the police." I reached for a paper napkin and wiped at a tear. "He's innocent, but he saw the killer."

"Who is it?"

"I still don't know, and he wasn't close enough to identify the person, but they escaped by climbing up to the roof."

The men joined us, and we ate breakfast in relative silence. Then Tom promised to drive Brandon to the police station.

I called Paul.

"Hey, what's up?"

"Tom and Brandon Cross are on their way to see you. Brandon has some crucial information related to Carissa's death."

"I'll clear my schedule and be ready the moment they arrive."

Chapter Fifty

At the store, I drew up plans to organize Izzy's art studio while Bess made contacts and scheduled three appointments. Despite my amateur murder investigation, our business was growing.

I gathered a variety of supplies and loaded the back of Bobby's Cherokee. It was amazing how easily the containers fit in the vehicle. They looked nice and tidy. In the past, when I loaded up my Beetle, the items were usually crammed into the space.

Bess joined me in the parking lot. "Would you like some company?"

Relief flooded through me. "Yes. I'm going to the art gallery to show Izzy the plans for her studio. I'm a little nervous to be around her after the accident."

"It wasn't an accident."

"You're right." My phone rang. "It's Paul. Do you mind if I answer?"

"Go ahead. I'll lock up." She sashayed away.

"Hey, Paul. What do you think about Brandon's story?"

"We haven't talked yet. You should know Officer Collins found the truck that ran you into the marsh. It'd been reported stolen. We've got a crew dusting it for prints now."

"Drat. It could've been anyone then."

"Don't get discouraged. We're getting closer."

"Thanks for the update."

"My job is to serve the public. Talk to you later."

Bess returned. "I'm ready."

It was a short drive to the art gallery, and Bess helped me carry in a variety of organizational supplies.

"Look, the coffee shop is closed. That smoothie was tasty, but it doesn't have the same kick."

"I know what you mean." I avoided discussing Marie.

Izzy appeared, and her eyebrows shot up. "Oh, hi, ladies. Did we have an appointment?"

"No, but I was hoping to show you a preliminary sketch. It won't take long."

"Good, because I don't have much time. Come back to my office." She led us to the room and stood by the credenza. "Show me what you have."

I opened the sketch pad and laid it down. "You have a great space, and I thought we could place your three easels here, here, and here." I pointed to the plan and explained my vision.

Bess displayed a variety of containers, and Izzy signed off on everything. She either really liked it, or she was in a hurry to get rid of us.

On our way out, I tapped on France's open office door.

She looked up. "Hi, Kate. Bess. What can I do for you?"

"I wanted to see how the organization plan is going now that you've lived with it for a few days." The desk was clear of junk, and I didn't see trash scattered around the room like before. However, there were packages wrapped in brown mailing paper. They were mostly rectangles with a depth of about two inches, making me think they were paintings. Had Izzy sold that many of her paintings? It seemed like a lot, but what did I know? Maybe tourists bought them and requested they be mailed.

"I remember you saying the system will work if I follow through, and I'm doing better. It'd be a shame to have your expertise go to waste." France's comment pulled me out of my musings.

Bess said, "Be sure to tell your friends if you like it. We'd appreciate any referrals you send our way."

This was my opportunity. "Speaking of friends, I heard your boyfriend has a concert tonight."

France broke into a smile. "Yes, Ryan, or should I say, Anchorman, is the main act."

"Have the local concerts led to bookings in bigger cities? Like Atlanta or Charlotte?"

"He has an agent now, so that's progress." France pointed to her phone. "I've got to make a call, but thanks for stopping by."

"Have a good weekend." I waved.

Bess followed me. "Bye, France."

Once we made it into the SUV, I looked at my friend. "What do you think?"

"My brain is spinning. Like how do they run an art gallery without more employees? The front greeter is only part-time, and often there's nobody at the welcome desk. Wouldn't you think Saturday is a busy day to visit the gallery? It makes me think we need a person to be on hand to greet people or answer the phone when we're out of the office. My biggest concern is about Marie. I sure hope those bad women didn't kill that poor girl."

I bit back a smile. Bess certainly was hyper this morning. "I can't say much, but she's safe."

"Un-huh. That tells me she might've been in danger."

I backed out of the parking lot. "Did you notice all the brown packages against the wall?"

"Yep. One was ripped, and I could see it was a painting."

"Could you see enough to tell if it's one of Izzy's? I'm wondering if the packages are going in or out."

"I didn't see any shipping stickers, but there wasn't time to really examine them."

"Oh, Bess. It just hit me. If Brandon didn't get drugs from Carissa, who is his dealer?" I pulled into a gas station and called Paul. "He's not answering."

"Do you want to swing by the police station?"

My heart beat faster. "Yes, I think it's important to see if there might be a link to the two from Jamaica."

Bess waved her fingers. "You best hurry because I feel like Tom and Brandon will go to the nearest rehab after their meeting with Paul."

Chapter Fifty-One

Officer Drake Collins met us in the front room of the police station. "I'm sorry, but I can't let you interrupt Chief Wright during an interview."

I met his gaze. "Okay, but he needs to ask Brandon who he bought the drugs from when Carissa wouldn't give him her supply. Specifically, was it Jason Nesbitt or Deshane Palmer?"

"I'll try to get your message to him." He lowered his voice and leaned close. "But it's only because you're the chief's sister."

"I appreciate it, and thanks for finding the truck that ran me off the road."

"It's my job. Are you staying here or going?"

Bess was standing at the sign-in window, speaking to the receptionist.

"We'll leave you alone." I walked over to Bess. "You ready?"

"Kate, this is Ruby Jeffers. We sing in the choir together. She's going to ask if there's money in the budget to help her get her office better organized."

"Hi, Ruby. It's nice to meet you." We chatted for a couple of minutes before leaving.

Back in the SUV, I looked at Bess. "I should be doing more."

"You've talked to Ian, Brandon, Izzy, France, and Tom this morning. I'd say you've made progress."

"You're probably right. Let's go to the office."

"I've got a better idea. Let's head to Island Perk. We can leave your Jeep at the apartment and walk to work."

"Sounds like a plan." I drove, and Bess hummed an unfamiliar tune. I had agreed to focus on work after my busy morning, but a sense of urgency stirred in my soul. I needed to do something, and fast. Too bad I didn't know what that something was.

The street was lined with vehicles, and I had to park my brother's SUV behind the apartment building. The lot was secluded for being in the middle of town, but it was impossible to ignore the noise of tourists.

"I guess college kids have hit town." Bess paused to allow a group of girls wearing bikinis walk past us.

"Spring break. That makes sense. Is it going to be like this all week?" We crossed the street and walked to the coffee shop.

"No, it'll get worse. These students are probably from Georgia colleges and universities. Soon, we'll have kids from other states descend on us."

I laughed. "It's a different way of life here. In Lexington, most of the students leave town during school breaks."

"Look at that line." Bess pointed to the coffee shop.

"Do you mind ordering me something? I need to run home and go to the bathroom."

"Take your time. I'll be here for a while."

I jaywalked because it seemed easier than fighting the crowded sidewalks, and my apartment was directly across the street. I walked up the steps and pulled my keys out.

The door was open, and I knew for a fact I hadn't left it that way. Should I enter or run?

Chapter Fifty-Two

I called Paul. Once again, he didn't answer. I called Reid.

"Hey, Katie. How are you this fine spring morning?"

"It's been a busy one, and I'll catch you up later, but right now, my apartment door is wide open. I've been gone for a few hours, and I know it was locked when I left."

"Take a breath. Did you call Paul?"

"He won't answer."

"I'm on my way, but call the police. It's not safe for you to enter by yourself. Go where there are plenty of people."

"Spring break has hit Fox Island. It won't be a problem to surround myself with people."

"Good. It'll take me five minutes to reach you."

We hung up, and I called the police. They promised to send someone straight away, and I hoped it'd be that nice Officer Collins.

Instead of returning to the coffee shop, I stood on the sidewalk and watched my place. Sand Piper Apartments. There were eight apartments in the old complex. Had one of the neighbors seen who entered my place? The building was over seventy years old, and I'd never seen a security camera in the public areas.

A police siren blipped, and a patrol car stopped in the middle of the street. Officer Diaz got out of the official vehicle. His long-legged pace covered the distance in seconds. "Ms. Sloan, the dispatcher said you've had an intruder."

"Yes. My door is open."

"Stay back." He entered the apartment, and his hand hovered over the gun on his belt.

Bess elbowed me. "I can't leave you alone for two minutes without the cops getting involved."

"My door was open." I raised my hands in a helpless gesture.

"I'm glad you didn't do something stupid like going inside alone."

"Thanks, I think. Where's the coffee?"

"You're more important than a cup of coffee. As soon as I heard the siren, I pushed my way out of Island Perk. I hope the fire marshal doesn't see how many are crowded in there."

I smiled at Bess. No doubt she was trying to lighten the mood so I wouldn't be so freaked out.

Reid ran up the street, swerving around students. He placed his hands on my shoulders. "You okay?"

I nodded. "Officer Diaz is inside now."

"Good." He glanced at Bess. "Hey. I'm glad you were here with Katie."

I placed an arm around each of their shoulders. "What would I do without you two?"

Officer Diaz came to the doorway. "Ms. Sloan, would you come inside?"

Bess gave me an encouraging pat on the back. "I'll get the coffee this time."

"Thanks." I turned to Reid. "Would you come inside with me? I want to make sure I hear everything Emerson says."

"You bet." He held my hand, and we walked to the door.

The officer blocked our entry. "Ms. Sloan—"

"Please, call me Kate."

He nodded. "Okay, Kate. Did you leave a mess behind this morning?"

I replayed my actions. Shower. Dress. Folded the quilt on the couch. "No. Why? Uh oh, did you see my murder board? Whoever broke in probably saw it too. This could be bad."

Reid said, "Take it easy. You're safe. Give Emerson time to explain."

"Bear, I'm glad you're here, but you two should brace yourselves." The police officer looked at Reid, then stepped back for us to enter.

I walked into my apartment, and my heart dropped. Pillows had been tossed, drawers were open, chairs were tipped over, pictures hung crooked on the wall, and books were scattered all over the floor. The notes and pictures I'd taken for my amateur investigation had been torn to pieces and scattered like confetti. I gulped. "Whoever did this must have had plenty of uninterrupted time to create so much chaos."

Emerson removed a little notepad from his pocket. "How do you think they got inside, Kate?"

I threw my hands up. "This isn't the most secure place in town. I chose to live here temporarily, and they allow me to rent for a month at a time."

"A crime scene team will be here soon."

"Okay. I'll be at work today." With a shaky hand, I pulled a business card from my slim crossbody bag. "Here's my contact information in case you don't have it. At this point, I'm almost numb."

The cop nodded. "I'll let you know when it's safe to return."

"Thanks." I headed outside and took in a deep breath of sea air.

Reid hung back for a couple of minutes, and I stood there. Laughter and cigarette smoke filled the air. People walked around me. The sound of waves calmed me a little. The beach had always been my refuge, but had I made a terrible mistake by moving back to Fox Island? My family and good friends lived here, but had it been a horrible decision to come home? Some said you could never go back. Were they right?

Bess exited the coffee shop, carrying a cardboard tray with three coffees. She motioned with her head to meet up the street.

Reid appeared and rubbed my back. "I'm grateful you didn't arrive when the intruder was destroying your place."

Reid, Bess, and my family were the reasons I'd returned to Fox Island. It wasn't a mistake. "Yeah, I'm thankful too. Thanks for coming when I called."

"Anytime, Katie. I always want to be there for you."

For the moment, I'd enjoy the comfort provided by these special people. Later would be soon enough to figure out if anything important was stolen.

Chapter Fifty-Three

After work, Reid picked me up, and we drove to the latest Fox Island music festival. Six food trucks lined up near the entrance offering barbecue, fish tacos, Greek food, burgers, waffles, and dessert.

Reid whistled. "I guess we have the spring breakers to thank for so many dinner options."

"Oh man, I could go for a beef gyro." My mouth watered just thinking about it.

"Greek food truck, here we come." We got in the back of the line.

"Hey, tonight we don't have to pretend we're a couple." Oops. Was that too forward? Why hadn't I kept my mouth shut?

"Oh, Katie. You sure don't know how to keep a straight face."

"What do you mean?"

"I read instant regret the moment you finished your sentence. We've waited too long to be together. You're my girl, even if you're fifty-three years old."

"Does this mean we're going together?" I used finger quotes for the expression.

"Katherine Wright Sloan, will you be my girlfriend?"

"I'd be honored, Reid Calhoun Barrett."

He drew me to him and kissed me so good my toes curled.

"Whoo-hoo!" A kid behind us called out.

People clapped and cheered.

We ended the kiss and laughed. Reid looked at the group of mostly college kids. "The moral of the story, guys, is to never give up on the love of your

231

life."

More cheers sounded from the young men, and the line moved forward.

In a few minutes, we found ourselves sitting at a picnic table set up near the trucks.

I smiled at Reid. "That was fun."

"Yeah, it was. Not every man gets his own cheering section when he asks a woman to be his girlfriend."

I squeezed his hand. "I would've said yes no matter what."

"Good to know."

Music started in the distance, and a female voice belted out an old Billy Joel song.

We ate and listened to the music. Reid finished first. "Would you like dessert?"

"No, this is filling me up. But you go ahead."

"It can't hurt to see what they're serving." Reid moseyed off.

I finished my food and watched the crowds walk back and forth. Some people strolled away from the merchandise booths, carrying packages.

Reid returned. "I got a chocolate chip cookie. Do you want half?"

"I'm truly stuffed. Do you want to walk around while you munch on it?"

"Sure. I suppose we're heading to the art area."

"You got it." I stood and threw away my trash. "Hey, why don't we walk behind the vendors?"

Reid studied the setup. There were three rows of people selling crafts, foods, and various items, and they were arranged to form two aisles. There was space to squeeze between the two inner rows of booths. "I don't see why we can't. It's not roped off."

"Great." I reached for my boyfriend's hand, and happiness filled me. Reid Barrett was my boyfriend. It was so silly to feel like a giddy schoolgirl, but I couldn't help myself.

His grip was warm and comforting. He led us down the grassy open space. "What do you hope to find?"

"Whenever I've seen Jason and France, they've been in the shadows or at the back of the crowd. Suppose there is a deal going down tonight?"

Reid drew to an abrupt stop. "I don't like the thought of you being in danger."

"I know. Will you feel better if I text Paul?"

"Not to be overly dramatic, but it's probably a good idea in case we disappear into the dark of night."

I pulled my phone out of my purse and texted my brother. *Reid and I are at the music festival behind the vendor aisle. I'll be in touch if we see something suspicious.* "Done."

I moved ahead of Reid and stepped over a large clear tote full of baby clothes. A glance at the booth proved they were selling clothing for small children. We continued forward without any luck, so we walked to the other side of the merchant area. This space was more crowded and darker, but I continued my mission. The first booth featured ceramics made by local artists.

A large figure came rushing toward me like a defensive football player intent on sacking the quarterback. I froze.

Reid placed his hands on my shoulders. "Move, Katie."

We both dodged away from the man, but he still managed to bump into me.

I latched onto Reid and remained on my feet. "Jason?" I don't know why it surprised me to see him. Although my plan had been to surprise him and not the other way around.

His gaze darted from me to Reid. "Ms. Sloan, are you okay?"

"Yes. What about you? Why are you in such a hurry?"

He bent down and picked up a large manilla envelope. "I'm fine."

Reid said, "You don't look fine. Are you in trouble?"

Clapping sounded in the distance, and the female singer broke into another song.

Jason shook his head. "It's nothing."

"Let us help you. What's in the envelope?"

He tightened his grip on it. "Please, forget you saw me, or you'll be in danger too."

Ah ha. He was in trouble. "Are you protecting your cousin? Give us a chance to help you two."

"Nobody can help me. I must go." His voice was devoid of emotion.

Reid held up a hand. "The only way for you to be safe is to trust someone. We're on your side."

"Wrong. Nobody can help. Please, let me move past you." His eyes were wide, and perspiration ran down his face.

I said, "Where's Deshane?"

"They have her. If I do what they say, she'll be safe."

"Jason, we won't hold you against your will, but we're on your side. If you change your mind, call me." I passed him my business card.

"Thanks." He jogged away.

I looked at Reid. "I guess now we need to keep our eyes open for Deshane."

"On it."

We continued our mission and passed Izzy's area. She was dressed to the hilt and speaking to Mayor Washington and his wife. Izzy had one hand on the mayor's arm and was waving the other arm in a dramatic fashion.

Reid whispered into my left ear. "Keep moving before she catches us."

I picked up my pace until we were out among the crowds. "You still scared of her?"

"James is a married man, and you saw how flirty she was. Louise Washington is a local real estate agent, and I've worked with her on a couple of projects. She's not going to put up with Izzy's shenanigans for long."

"Would you introduce me to her one day? When I was selling real estate, I often tried to help clients see how to make the best use of small spaces. Maybe we can work with her on hard-to-sell homes."

"I think you'll like Louise. She was the first Black real estate agent on the island, and she's faced some battles building her business. She's got a moral work ethic."

"Good to know."

The performance ended with an announcement that Anchorman would soon take the stage. The crowd cheered.

Reid said, "What now?"

"Please, let's walk by Izzy's booth and see how she reacts."

CHAPTER FIFTY-THREE

He dropped his head. "I was afraid you'd say that."

I laughed. "Talk about being overly dramatic."

"Lead the way."

I took a deep breath, reached for Reid's hand, and walked toward the Fox Island Art Gallery's booth, determined to find a clue to the mysteries of Fox Island.

Chapter Fifty-Four

Izzy was by herself when we arrived. She frowned when we made eye contact, but I could tell the moment she spotted Reid. A smile filled her face. "Good evening. Y'all must really enjoy festivals. I've seen you more than anybody else."

"There's not much to do in my little apartment, and I like getting out and meeting people." I hoped my expression looked innocent.

She touched Reid's arm. "Are you helping Kate find a place to live?"

Reid backed away and draped his arm around my shoulders. "I thought you knew. We've found a house for Katie, and we've got plans to remodel it as soon as the papers are signed."

Izzy lifted her nose and waved her fingers in a dismissive way. "I've been so busy lately. It must've slipped my mind."

"I know you aren't selling Jason's work at the gallery, but what about the festival?"

"No. His art doesn't seem to appeal to my clientele."

I nodded. "That's too bad because I'd really like to buy a couple of his pieces. Will you carry his cousin's sculptures?"

"They are too primitive for my taste."

"Maybe I can buy directly from Deshane. Do you know how I can reach out to her?"

Izzy's eyes darted around as if trying to find anybody else to talk to.

Reid cleared his throat. "Izzy, you didn't answer Katie's question. Are you okay?"

"I'm fine, but I'm here to sell my artwork. I don't have time to answer

236

your questions."

I said, "Is France working tonight?"

"No, I gave her the night off. Unless you want to purchase one of my paintings, I'd appreciate it if you moved along."

"Okay. I'll reach out to you next week about your studio."

"Fine."

Reid kept his arm around my shoulders as we walked away. In the clearing, I looked around. Most of the crowd were strangers to me.

"Well, that was rude. You really ticked her off." Reid chuckled.

"Yeah. I can't believe she hired me to work on her studio."

"She knows talent when she sees it."

"Thanks." I yawned. "Would you mind if we skirt the crowd, and if we don't see anything interesting, we'll head home?"

"I'm bushed, and you've had a long day too. Let's roll."

The concert began, and the people crowded in front of the stage. It was hard to distinguish faces, so we decided to amble down the last aisle of merchants before heading out.

There was no sign of France or Deshane, but Pastor Tom and Bess stood near a card table with pamphlets in their hands.

"Hi, y'all." Bess greeted us with a smile. "Let me guess. You two aren't here for the concert."

"What can I say? I'm determined." I shifted my gaze to Tom. "How's Brandon?"

"After this morning's conversation with the police, he asked me to take him to another treatment facility. I allowed him to research, and he picked one on the outskirts of Savannah. This time he seems to want to get better. I pray this is the miracle I've been hoping for."

Bess reached over and patted his shoulder. "It'll be different this time. Just you wait and see."

"I hope you're right." Tom turned his attention to us. "We're handing out information about the dangers of drug abuse. The pamphlets are geared to victims as well as their families and friends. With spring break beginning, it seemed like a good time to get active."

Reid said, "You're doing good work."

I opened my phone and scrolled to the fuzzy picture I'd taken of Jason and Deshane. "These two are in trouble. If you happen to see them, would you please try to convince them to get help?" I showed Tom the picture first because Bess had seen it at least once. It couldn't hurt for her to refresh her memory though, so I passed it to her next.

Tom pointed to my phone. "Would you send me a copy? People usually consider me to be a safe person. I'll watch for them."

"Thanks." We exchanged information, I sent him the picture, and we headed for Reid's truck. "Oh, no. I just realized my apartment hasn't been released yet. I better call Paul."

"He never replied to your text, did he?"

"No, and that's rather strange." I dialed his number and pushed speaker mode.

"Sis, I'm kinda busy here tracking down a suspect."

"Sorry. Call me when you can." I hung up and met Reid's gaze. "I hope he's not chasing Jason."

"At this point, it's out of your hands."

"You're right. Do you think I should contact Officer Diaz and ask him?"

"He might be working with Paul. I've got a better idea." He opened the passenger door for me, and I hopped in. I was too tired to ask about what he had in mind. I closed my eyes, trusting Reid and his plan.

Chapter Fifty-Five

"Wake up, sleepy head." Reid's voice, combined with a nudge, pulled me out of a dream about decorating my new home.

"Wow, I only meant to close my eyes. Where are we?"

"We're at my mom's place. You can spend the night here."

"I can't impose like that." I had no necessities with me. No toothbrush, clothes, or any of my toiletries. "Why don't you take me to Bobby's?"

"When Mom heard about your apartment, she told me to invite you to stay here. Tomorrow you can find out about your apartment."

"But—"

"Please, don't argue. You need to rest. If you're tired, you can't make good decisions."

"Okay. I appreciate Joy's offer. Does this mean you two are okay?"

He chuckled. "Are you trying to pry info out of me about my dad?"

"Not so subtle, hunh?"

"Nope. Not even a little. Come on." He led the way to the house.

Joy opened the door for us. "Welcome."

The great room was a colorful oasis. A blue couch anchored by a bright floral rug. Paintings filled the walls with bouquets of flowers. Throw pillows on the couch and comfy side chairs continued the theme of flowers. The neutral wood coffee table hosted various vases of flowers. The woman knew what she liked, and she hadn't been afraid to showcase her love of flowers.

Joy pulled me close and hugged me hard and long. "Baby girl, what are we going to do with you? I can't believe everything you've been through these past few days."

Her kindness brought tears to my eyes, and I missed my own mother something fierce.

Reid disappeared into the kitchen.

I pulled back from Joy. "I so much appreciate you letting me stay here."

"Of course. You're welcome anytime. Are you hungry? Thirsty?"

Reid appeared carrying two glasses of water. "I thought you might be thirsty."

"Thanks." I accepted his offering. "Joy, if it's all the same to you, I think I'd just like to go to bed."

"Right this way."

"Katie, hold on just a minute. Your vehicle's still at the apartment. What time would you like me to pick you up?"

"Seven-thirty? If they won't let me in the apartment, I can run over to Island Perk and grab coffee before heading to work."

"I'm going to gather a few things to make you more comfortable. Reid, bring her to the big guest room when you're finished talking." Joy winked at her son, then left us standing in her great room.

"Sorry if she embarrassed you. My mother's never been known for her subtlety." Reid shook his head.

"To know Joy is to love Joy. Don't ever apologize for your mom."

He put his glass on a turquoise side table and took my face in both of his hands. His lips touched mine, and my entire body came alive. "I hope you can get some sleep tonight."

I laughed. "After that kiss, if I'm able to sleep, it'll only be sweet dreams."

"I'll show you to your room." Reid led me to the guest room and told his mom goodnight before leaving us alone.

Joy held up an extra-large T-shirt with a picture of Fox Island Lighthouse on it. "You can sleep in this. I laid out towels and a few toiletries in the bathroom. Can you think of anything else you need?"

"No, ma'am. This is so nice of you."

"It's my pleasure. May I ask you a question?"

I had no idea what was on her mind. "Sure."

"Has my son declared his intentions to you yet?"

I sat on the bed and laughed. "Yes, he did. We're officially dating only each other."

She propped her hands on her hips. "Thank goodness. I always thought you two would be good together."

"I heard Mr. Barrett was back in town."

"I should've known you'd turn the conversation to me." She sat on the end of the bed. "Yes, Sam is back in town. Yes, he wants me back. He's apologized and explained why he left. Before you ask, it wasn't another woman. He'd fought in the Vietnam War, and it messed with his brain. Sam came home a hot angry mess. He often lashed out and apologized later. You know, many of our soldiers were fighting in the jungles one day, and the next day, there were plopped back into their normal lives. There wasn't a long trip home on a Navy ship to decompress. As time went by, Sam grew worried he might harm Reid or me. For a while, he lived on the streets. He found temporary jobs to survive, and he lived in a shelter occasionally. He was able to get counseling a few years ago, and he's ashamed of how he treated us. Sam worked through the frustration and anger, and he believes it might be time to reconcile."

I kicked off my shoes. "How do you feel?"

"Sam took possession of my heart years ago, and I'm not sure I ever recovered. No offense to my other three husbands. They were good men, but—"

"They weren't Sam." I patted her hand. "I understand better than you'd imagine."

"Yes. I expect you do. We've both suffered from the star-crossed-lovers syndrome." She stood and stroked the top of my head. "There's a phone charger on the bedside table. I'm glad you and Reid are together. Goodnight."

"Goodnight, Joy."

After plugging the cord into my phone, I placed my spoon ring and watch on the bedside table and changed into the T-Shirt. It was as soft as a shadow, and I burrowed into the bedding. All thoughts of murder disappeared.

Chapter Fifty-Six

The alarm woke me up Sunday morning, and I discovered there were four missed calls on my phone. I took a quick shower, dressed, and pulled my hair into a messy bun.

Paul, Tom, and Bess had all reached out to me while I slept. It wasn't seven yet, but they were all early risers. I returned my brother's call first.

"Sis, if it hadn't been for Reid, I would've put out an all-points bulletin on you. Why didn't you tell me where you were?"

"I did call, but you were in hot pursuit. Have you made an arrest?"

"No, but we questioned Jason Nesbitt. He's been told to stick around."

"What'd you learn?"

"Nothing new."

"That's disappointing. So, can I return to my apartment?"

"Yeah, but be prepared. It's probably a wreck after the fingerprint team finished."

"Believe me, it was trashed before they started. Thanks."

"Next time you call, I'll listen."

"Unless bullets are flying. Then I'll understand if you blow me off. Bye." I gathered my meager belongings and followed the aroma of coffee to the kitchen. If the coffee didn't wake me up, the bright kitchen would. Upper olive cabinets over salmon lower cabinets popped against the white walls. The stainless steel appliances gave a modern edge to the bohemian space. "Good morning, Joy. I hope you didn't get up early on my account."

"No, I've already been for a walk on the beach. How'd you sleep?" She wore a flowery long top over black leggings and moved in the most graceful way, as if floating through the kitchen.

"Good. In fact, I didn't hear any calls come through last night." I'd really conked out, or else I'd been sleeping on my good ear.

"It's a lovely morning. Why don't you take your coffee onto the back deck?"

I doctored my coffee with a little creamer and sugar, then headed to the deck. I sipped my coffee, then called Bess.

"Girl, you scared me to death when I couldn't reach you. I finally had to call Reid. Why didn't you answer your phone?"

"I'm sorry, but I slept right through your call. If it makes you feel any better, I missed Paul's calls too. What's up?"

"Tom and I met Jason and Deshane. I spotted them and made a point to have a discussion. I played it real cool, though. They listened politely to my spiel, but neither one appeared to be impaired. What do you think that means?"

"Neither used drugs recently? Maybe never? I saw Jason earlier in the evening. He was stressed. How did he appear with you?"

"Hmm." Bess paused. "I would say intense more than anything."

"It's good they were together." He must've completed the deal to get her back. "Did you see France?"

"Can't say that I did."

"Izzy said France had the night off, so maybe Jason got a break from her. Wait a minute. He was in a hurry when we saw him, and he was carrying an envelope." Had he exchanged the envelope for his cousin? When had Paul questioned Jason? Before or after the possible exchange?

My phone vibrated. "Bess, I've got another call. I'll see you at work."

"Bye."

I tapped my screen to answer the other call. "Hello."

"Ms. Sloan, this is Jason Nesbitt." His voice shook.

My heart leapt. "Jason, what's wrong?"

"I need to talk to you. Can you meet me at Burt's Gym?"

"Yes, but I don't have my car. I'll get Reid to bring me. He's the man you've seen me with. Is that okay?"

"Yes."

"I'll be there as soon as possible."

"Thank you." He hung up.

I called Reid.

"Good morning. I'm almost there."

"I'll wait for you in the driveway. Jason wants to meet us, and I don't want him to change his mind."

"I'll be there in two minutes. Tops."

I hurried inside and said a quick goodbye to Joy.

"Here are three coffees to go in safe travel mugs. All have cream and sugar, and if one of the people in your group doesn't like it, tough." She winked and handed me a bag with the drinks.

"How'd you know?"

"Sorry, I couldn't help but overhear your conversation. Be safe, hon." She gave me a quick hug, and I headed for the driveway.

Reid pulled up about the same time my feet hit the concrete.

I opened the door and handed him the bag. "Good morning. Your mom sent sustenance."

"Perfect. Now tell me what's happening."

Chapter Fifty-Seven

I t didn't take long to reach the gym, but I had time to tell Reid as much as I knew. He pulled behind the building and shut off the truck. "Are we supposed to go inside?"

"I don't know."

The thick back steel door opened, and Burt Fitzpatrick stuck his head out.

We exited the truck, and I carried the flat-bottom bag of coffees.

Burt eyed us. "Bear, what are you doing here?"

"We're planning to meet someone. You probably know him. Jason Nesbitt."

"Yep. Poor guy is in a world of hurt." Burt motioned us to enter. "Jason's in my office."

We followed the owner of the gym down a shadowy hall. "I've got people working out in the main rooms. I'll keep watch, and you three should be able to have a private conversation in there."

I glanced toward the workout area and spotted treadmills, medicine balls, power plates, kettle balls, free weights, battle ropes, hanging ropes, and equipment I was unfamiliar with. I continued to the office and knocked on the door before entering. "Jason? It's me, Kate. Reid's here too."

He appeared from behind a coat rack holding pairs of boxing gloves instead of jackets. "Thank you for coming."

Burt closed the door behind us.

"Here's some coffee." I opened the bag and passed a red insulated cup to each man. "Oh, there are muffins too."

Reid nodded, "Probably blueberry. They're Mom's favorite."

Jason drank his coffee but ignored the muffin. "They've got my cousin. I got her free once, and they took her again."

"Poor, Deshane. Have they made any demands?"

The Jamaican groaned. "Yes. They want me to deliver drugs to the Port of Savannah. I don't know how to do that, and I don't want to do it either. France thinks they need to use different ways for moving the drugs."

The situation had to be more involved than walking into a post office to mail a package. "Can you back up a second? How are they transporting drugs?"

"In the art just like always. They think the police only believe drugs from Jamaica go to Europe."

Reid leaned against the wall. "Most drugs come into the United States through Mexico."

I said, "Let's start at the beginning. Are you saying you and Deshane brought drugs into America hidden in your art? Why?"

He moved to the swivel chair behind the desk. "Here's the short answer. Deshane had a boyfriend back home. He's a drug dealer. And he was abusive. My cousin wanted to escape from him. She begged me to come to America with her for a fresh start. She thought she'd made contact with a good person, and they promised to sell our artwork."

I sat across from him. "How does this connect to the drug business?"

He splayed his hands on the uncluttered desk. "She didn't know her boyfriend intercepted the messages. He worked a deal with the gallery and placed drugs in her metal sculptures. They also hid bags of heroin in the frames of my pictures."

My heart dropped. "How?"

"We thought we were smart and gathered our art in my apartment. Her boyfriend broke into my place and hid the drugs in the pieces. I don't know how we didn't get stopped at the border." He dropped his head into his hands.

"What happened next?"

"Izzy had a sailor bring us here on his motorboat. It was very big. We

246

were on the boat for six days. Deshane was sick every single day. When we arrived, France met us. She paid the sailor, then brought us to the gallery. We opened the art in her office. She pulled a pouch of heroin out of a blue heron sculpture and accused us of using the gallery to deal drugs. We were shocked. Then she showed us another small bag of drugs. She blackmailed us to keep us under her control, but she was the bad person."

Reid said, "Why didn't you try to call the police?"

His eyes grew big. "They would not believe us. We're foreigners in your fine country. France is a well-respected citizen. It would not go well for us."

"I'm so sorry. You must've been terrified." Would the police have believed his story? I folded my hands together. "So, you didn't feel free to tell the police. Then France and her gang kept you under their control by blackmailing you."

"Yes. I am afraid it is so."

Reid sat in the other rickety chair beside me. "You could've only brought a limited supply of drugs into the country. What kept the supply going?"

"They sent me back for more but kept Deshane here. France threatened to harm my cousin if I didn't bring back more art and drugs. What choice did I have?"

"How'd you get the drugs when you returned home?" No condemnation came from Reid's even and smooth voice.

"I went home and painted like crazy. It was not my best work, but what choice did I have? Deshane had more sculptures at my place. Her old boyfriend arrived, hid the drugs, then drove me to the boat that would bring me here." Jason's jaw tightened. "He also sent money to be cleaned."

"Laundering money? I always imagined it was a more sophisticated process using banks or casinos. It makes sense to send money with you because it's a small operation." Reid rubbed his chin.

"Changing out the money is the reason for the festivals. Izzy gives a discount to customers who pay cash. Now you know, and we must find Deshane."

I said, "Do you have any idea where she could be?"

"No, but the art gallery has an attic. We hid there once when the police came to question France and Izzy. There is also the outbuilding at Izzy's home." He pointed at me. "You've been there. The other night I heard you."

"Oh, the art studio. I wondered what was going on, but Izzy rushed me away."

"Yes. Izzy was very mad at me that night for dropping my duffle bag. Later, I overheard something when she returned to the building. She told someone that you were a big problem. She also told the person on the phone to take care of you."

I gasped. "That was the night I was run off the road and into the marsh."

Reid stood up abruptly. His chair fell to the floor, and his fists were clenched. "Izzy was behind the attempt on your life. The police need to question her."

Jason held out his hands. "No. They might hurt my cousin."

"Stay calm. We don't want any harm to come to her. Jason, do you know who killed Carissa Ruffalo?" I expected to hear France's name.

"You mean the dancer?"

"Yes." Reid returned to his seat, but the clench of his jaw told me he hadn't calmed down much.

"She also wanted to leave. At first, it was to go back to dancing. Then she wanted to get away from France and Izzy. They offered her a lot of money to get the policeman out of the picture."

"Why?" My heart raced.

"The chief of police had been snooping around the gallery. Izzy was certain he knew they were dealing drugs. To put a stop to his investigation, they forced Carissa to say they were going to get married. She started the rumor, but her heart was tender. She wanted to take away her lies. I believe that is why she was murdered. It is why I am afraid for my cousin. She wants to break free from the evil women."

I said, "So, who killed Carissa?"

"I will tell you, but you must promise to save my cousin. And there can be no help from the police."

I exhaled. It was a big request and one my brother would heartily oppose. My next step could help prove Paul's innocence, but it could also put a rift in our relationship.

Chapter Fifty-Eight

Grim determination took a hold of me. "We'll find Deshane."

"Wait, Katie." Reid reached for my hand. "There are so many possibilities for this to go sideways. What if we put Deshane and Jason in more danger than they face now?"

I focused my gaze on Jason then Reid. "He's afraid of the police, and it could be with good reason. We can't promise that Paul won't arrest him."

"I hear ya, but we also can't promise one of us won't get shot."

Jason's head bobbed from one of us to the other like a person watching a tennis match.

"True, but we really don't have another option."

Reid rolled his head. "Oh, Katie. The things you can get me to do. All right. I'm in."

"Thank you." I squeezed his hand.

Jason said, "It is all settled. Yes?"

I took a deep breath and let it out slowly. Paul would be furious, but I didn't see another viable option. "Yes, but first, who killed Carissa?"

"The singer. Anchorman."

I sank back into my wobbly chair. "You're kidding. I had hoped he wasn't involved. I guess it makes sense, though. He used to date Carissa, and now he dates France. She must've conned him into doing her dirty work."

"France asked me to kill the woman, but I refused. It took some fast talking to make her agree that I was more valuable as a person to bring drugs to her. I even told her it was safer to use me than to get involved with a Mexican cartel. I didn't want to keep transporting drugs, but it's better than killing a woman." He stood. "Now we rescue my cousin."

"Okay, but after two cups of coffee, I need to visit the restroom. Do you know where it is?"

He gave me directions, and I hurried. I needed to alert someone, but a text might be risky. What if Jason asked to see my phone? I'd also given him my word to not call the police. My store had an answering machine, and it'd be easy to claim I was calling in sick. I dialed and pressed the number three to leave a message. I kept my voice soft. "Bess, I won't see you at church. If I don't show up for work tomorrow, call Paul. Ryan Ford murdered Carissa. France and Izzy are involved in the drug trade. Deshane Palmer is missing. Reid and I are going to try to find her, but please don't tell Paul yet. I'm counting on you. Love ya."

I took care of business and hustled back to the office. Burt was in the hall and moved to let me walk past. Instead, I stopped in front of him. "I noticed your ropes for climbing. Do many people use them?"

"Some do. Why?"

"Specifically, have you seen Ryan Ford, Izzy Reynolds, or France Granger train on them?"

He nodded. "France is a rockstar on the ropes. Izzy has never darkened my door, and Ryan hasn't been here in years."

"Thanks. I better scoot." I entered the office. "Where to first, gentlemen?"

Muffin crumbs had fallen onto the desk. I pulled a wipe out of my purse and cleaned the space.

Jason said, "I need to ride with you. May we go to Izzy's house first?"

Reid stood. "Sure."

On the drive, Jason rode in the backseat. The three of us discussed possible plans and excuses if we were caught on Izzy's property. After bouncing around different scenarios, I angled myself into the passenger seat so I could look at both men. "If Izzy is there, we'll say I needed Reid to help me measure the studio so I can build a supply shelf. Jason, you stay hidden in the truck. If no one is home, the three of us will find a way to enter the studio. If we're caught, we'll stick to the shelf story. We can adlib, but that's our main spiel."

"I have a key." Jason dug into the pocket of his khakis and retrieved a metal key.

"Wow, that's downright impressive." Reid chuckled, then he pulled onto Izzy's property.

"I will hide now." Jason unfastened his seatbelt and lay on the floor.

Reid pulled to a stop at the front door. "Showtime. Are you ready?"

Not really. "What's the expression about in for a pound—"

"In for a penny. We can do this."

A sense of dread slowed my footstep as we walked to the front door. I pressed the doorbell and waited.

Chapter Fifty-Nine

Nobody answered Izzy's door after three attempts, and there was no sign of her black Volvo. "What do you think, Reid?"

"Looks like it's time to inspect the studio. I'll get Jason."

I walked to the side of the house and followed the little path Izzy had led me on the night of my accident.

Reid and Jason caught up.

"Follow me." Jason led us to the back of the building and unlocked the door. "This is where we were hiding the night you were here."

The rooms were dark, unlike the studio area. There were twin beds, a desk, and a bathroom. "You stayed here?"

"Only sometimes. It's too far for us to walk."

Reid said, "We need to check every square inch of this place. If Deshane isn't here, we need to skedaddle."

I said, "I've got the front room. Reid, will you see if there's a hidden area or attic?"

"Yes, ma'am." He winked at me.

I entered the studio. Sunlight streamed inside. One canvas had been painted in black, gray, and dark purple. The image projected anger, and I shivered. In the kitchenette, I opened all the cabinets. Deshane was small, and there was a slim chance she was hiding in one of the spaces. No such luck, so I entered the bathroom. The shower curtain was drawn closed. My heart beat faster. If I found Deshane in there, she better be alive. With shaky fingers, I whipped open the curtain.

Empty.

What a relief. With shaky legs, I returned to the men. "Any luck?"

"No. Every minute she's away from me, I grow more worried." The big man wore a forlorn expression.

Reid said, "Let's go."

The three of us hustled out of the building, only pausing for Jason to lock the door. We ran to the truck, and Reid took off.

He glanced at me. "I saw a security camera on the back corner of the house. If it works, Izzy will know we were here."

"Stick to our story. We were measuring to build a cabinet."

He gripped the steering wheel and focused on driving. "Where to next?"

"Fox Island Art Gallery seems the most likely place, but it could be the most dangerous."

Reid pointed to the back. "Jason's phone is ringing."

I hadn't heard it, but I kept quiet while he talked.

"Yes, yes, yes. I want to see my cousin again." He was silent for long moments. "Yes. I will meet you there. Goodbye."

"What's wrong?" Butterflies fluttered in my belly.

"Izzy and France know we were at the studio."

Reid glanced back. "It sounds like you're supposed to meet them."

"Yes. At the marina. In one hour. With the dirty money. If I do not go, they will kill my cousin."

"That doesn't give us much time. Where is the money?"

"My locker at Burt's Gym."

Reid turned the truck around and headed back in the direction of the gym. "We've got to call the police. This thing is bigger than the three of us, and we don't have much time."

"No, no. We cannot involve your police."

My phone vibrated, and Paul's name appeared. "Too late. This is Paul."

Chapter Sixty

"Hi, Paul."

"Katie, what's happening? And don't get dodgy with your answers. Bess called me."

"Man, that stinker. Why isn't she at church?" Next time I'd have to confide in somebody else. Ha, there wouldn't be a next time.

"She's protecting you. How do you know Ryan Ford murdered Carissa?"

"First, are you looking for him?"

"Yes. I've got people searching as we speak. Your turn."

"Izzy and France are definitely involved. We're with Jason Nesbitt. They have his cousin, and she's in danger."

"I'll put out a BOLO for Deshane Palmer. Hold on."

Reid continued driving to the gym.

"Sis, I'm back. Why don't you bring Jason to the station so we can question him?"

"Two problems with that. He can give you enough information to stop the drugs flowing into Fox Island, but he and his cousin need to be granted immunity."

"No promises, but I'll see what can be done."

"You need to hear his whole story, but it will have to wait. France and Izzy demanded we meet Ryan at the marina if we want to see Deshane alive."

"What happens if Ryan is arrested before then?"

I perspired. "I don't know. You're the expert in these kinds of situations."

"Nobody is an expert in these circumstances. We've got to do the best we can."

"Our plan is to grab the money needing to be laundered, then bust it over to the marina."

Paul huffed. "We don't have much time. Call me when you have the money. Meanwhile, I'll be working on a plan to get some of my people over there in disguises."

The call ended, and I updated Reid and Jason on what Paul had said.

Jason wasn't happy, and Reid tried to calm him.

Something nagged me. A memory, or possibly a clue. But deep down, something told me I needed to figure it out before we reached the marina.

Reid pulled behind Burt's Gym, and the guys ran inside.

I remained in the truck with my eyes closed, trying my best to decide what bothered me. I replayed our earlier conversation with Jason while we were in Burt's office.

There hadn't been time to inspect the art gallery's attic. I texted Paul the information, but the anxious feeling didn't dissipate.

I closed my eyes and tried to remember if I'd seen anything in the art studio.

Jason jumped into the backseat with a black sports duffle bag.

Reid slid into the driver's spot. He touched my arm. "Katie, are you okay?"

I glanced at him. "Yeah, but there's something we're missing. I'm trying to remember what. Did you two find the cash?"

"Yep. I guess we're on the way to the marina."

Jason leaned forward. "Please, hurry."

Burt ran out of the building. "Stop."

Reid lowered his window. "We're kinda in a hurry."

"Bear, how can I help?" The dark-haired man wearing a green T-shirt with the name of his gym gripped the windowsill.

My heart warmed. The retired wrestler wanted to help the Jamaican artist.

I leaned toward him and spoke before Reid could answer. "Do you have a boat?"

"Of course."

I said, "We're meeting the bad guys at the marina. It could be dangerous, though."

"It takes a lot to scare me. I'll head there now." He turned and jogged to a red truck with big wheels.

Reid shifted into reverse, and Burt spun out, leaving us in his dust.

Reid chuckled. "Now there's a man you always want to be on your side."

Chapter Sixty-One

Reid slowed his truck as we headed down the dusty pot-hole-filled road.

Paul hadn't called back, so I texted him an update.

An old truck painted red, white, and blue bounced past us. A wrestling emblem on his back window made me suspicious that Burt had reached out to a friend.

"Interesting." Reid pointed to the truck. "There's another one about to pass us."

"Talk about calling in the calvary." A white pickup with fishing poles sticking out of the passenger window also breezed by us.

Reid moved his wrist and glanced at his speedometer. "At the rate, I'm getting passed, you'd think we were driving in a school zone."

Jason said, "Do you think Ryan will be suspicious when he sees so many people at the marina?"

Reid said, "It's a beautiful day. We'll hope nobody becomes suspicious."

I faced forward, still struggling to remember the potential clue. Had it been in the art studio?

I had opened cabinets in hopes of finding Deshane, but that'd been a flop. There had only been shampoo and soap in the shower. One easel held a dark painting. It'd been a boat in a storm at night on the water. The depressing scene caused me to wonder who'd buy the thing, but was there a clue in the painting?

Black. Gray. Deep purple.

"We're here." Reid's announcement pulled me out of my trance.

In the back, Jason clutched the bag. His head was bowed, and I didn't interrupt in case he was praying.

Jason lifted his head. "I'm ready to fight for my cousin. I am not helpless. I have you two. You're my new friends. I'm not alone. So yes, I am ready to take a stand."

Soon, we stood in the parking lot, looking toward the marina.

Jason's phone rang. This time he answered it on speaker mode. "Hello."

"Hi, Jason. Leave your friends behind. The two of us are going on a little trip."

"No. Where is Deshane?" Jason's voice sounded serious and confident.

"I'll tell you after I get the cash. Come on. We're going to take a morning boat ride."

"No. My cousin first, then I will go wherever you say."

I typed a note into my phone and flashed it for Jason to read. *Once he has you alone, he might throw you overboard.*

He read the note and whispered, "I can't swim."

"Hey man, are you paying attention?" Ryan's tone was angry. "The clock's ticking on your cousin's life, man. Get down here."

"I'm coming."

I hung back, but Reid stayed with Jason until they reached the first boat. Reid snagged a life jacket off it and fastened it onto our new friend. The men gave each other a man-hug, and Jason walked to a boat.

The scene made me feel like I was watching a pirate movie, and the good guy was walking the plank.

Reid returned to me. "This may be the worst thing I've ever had to do. Jason's a grown man, but he seems so innocent. He's a kind soul."

"I guess it's not surprising he got pulled into the drug smuggling operation."

Jason reached the boat, but he hesitated before stepping onto it. He looked back and waved at us.

"Oh, man. I pray this isn't the last time we see him." I waved back.

The man waiting on the cabin cruiser wore shorts and a hoodie. His face was concealed, but we knew it was Ryan. The guy held a hand out for Jason.

When they connected, Ryan pulled Jason onto the boat. My friend hit the dock and rolled into a ball, holding the duffle bag to his middle.

I looked around for a policeman. To spot one of Paul's people would've made me happy. To be fair, I didn't know all his employees. In the distance, I saw men fishing in a red rowboat. Down the way was a green ski boat where Burt and another hulking man appeared to be getting ready for a trip.

Jason jumped up and held the money over the water. He argued with Ryan. The two circled each other on the aft deck. Ryan would lunge, but Jason would lurch to the side as if ready to drop the bag. At last, Ryan formed the timeout signal with his hands. He picked up his phone and appeared to make a call. When he slipped his phone into his pocket, Jason called me.

"What's wrong?"

"He said Deshane is tied up in the lighthouse."

"We'll get her."

Jason said, "Thank you. Whatever happens, thank you for your kindness." He hung up and faced off with Ryan again.

I looked at Reid. "Deshane is at the lighthouse. He wants us to rescue her. I think we should trust Burt and his people will watch out for Jason."

"I agree. Let's hurry." He grabbed my hand and ran.

I huffed and did my best to ignore the stitch in my side. I hadn't done this much running in years, and it was teaching me how out of shape I was.

Once we were in the truck, Reid took off before I buckled my seatbelt. "Are you going to call Paul?"

"Yes." I punched his number into my phone.

"Katie, what's going on?"

I updated him on our progress. "Where are you?"

"I'm with Officer Collins at the art gallery. We know Izzy Reynolds is in her office, but we don't have a handle on France Granger."

"I'll let you know if we see her at the lighthouse. Are you sure Jason is safe?"

"The Coast Guard is ready to lend a hand."

"Great."

"I'm also going to send help your way. The sheriff's department is willing to assist as well as the GBI."

"Thanks. I'll talk to you soon."

Reid pulled onto Lighthouse Lane so fast white dust billowed behind us. He screeched to a stop by the ticket booth, and we leapt out of the truck.

The smell of sunscreen was heavy. A breeze forced my hair to slap my face, and I pulled it back.

College kids traversed the area around the lighthouse, the restaurants, and the beach paths. Young families stood in line to purchase tickets to tour the structure, and we got into line behind them.

Reid tapped my shoulder. "The woman said the lighthouse is closed for maintenance. Visitors can tour the grounds for free today."

"I guess that explains how Deshane could be hidden in there." We reached the older lady. I leaned close to make sure we could hear each other. "I'm Kate Sloan. My brother is Police Chief Paul Wright. We believe a woman is being held captive in the lighthouse. Who's in charge?"

"Oh, dear. I'll have to call Mr. Tucker and have him meet you over there."

I glanced at Reid. "I don't guess she's talking about our legendary quarterback, Cash Tucker."

"None other. He's never bashful about sharing his glory days, but he's a good guy."

We jogged to the tall structure, and Cash met us at the entrance.

He looked from me to Reid. "Bear, what's the problem? Do we need to clear the grounds?"

"I think it's the safest option. We believe a young lady is being held prisoner in the lighthouse. The kidnapper may be armed and dangerous."

"On it." He stepped away.

"Wait, can you let us in?"

"Don't know what I was thinking." He shook his head and returned to unlock the door. "There aren't many places to hide. Good luck."

I took a deep breath. "If I remember correctly, there are about two-hundred steps to the top."

"Not quite. One-hundred-fifty-four to be exact." He entered the structure and poked his head into a room to the side. "Empty."

"Yeah, that would've been too easy."

"I'll lead the way." We began climbing the wide steps and circled around and around. Each landing was empty.

I gulped in air at each stop, then continued. After our third break, discouragement hit me. "Where is she? Do you suppose it's a trick?"

"Maybe." Reid placed one foot in front of the other.

There was a clatter, like metal on metal.

Reid looked back at me.

"I didn't do that. It sounds like a key or flashlight or something may have hit one of the metal strips on the steps."

"Umph." The sound came from above us.

"That's gotta be Deshane." I pushed past Reid on the narrowing steps.

He grabbed my arm. "Yes, but France could be with her. They probably heard us, and France may be growing desperate. Let's play it smart."

I nodded. "Right. What's your plan?"

"Text Paul and tell him we're sure she's in here. Then we will continue going up."

Chapter Sixty-Two

I shot off a message to my brother, then shoved the phone into the pocket of my jeans. "Ready."

We hugged the wall as we continued our climb up the lighthouse. The spiral wound tighter with each step.

I heard a creak, felt a breeze, then a door slammed.

Reid leaned toward my good ear. "If that's France with Deshane, she either went out to the catwalk—"

"Or she wants us to think she did. Isn't there a service room or a lantern room?"

"Yes. So, she could be waiting to attack us or lock us out on the catwalk."

My hands grew damp. "What should we do?"

"One of us should go out the door while the other hangs back a second to see if she's hiding in the lantern room."

"I'll go outside." I wasn't as strong as Reid, and it seemed like the safest option.

He caressed my cheek before continuing up the steps.

We reached the top landing. No sign of France or Deshane.

I pushed the door open and stepped outside. It closed behind me, and I stood facing the two women we'd been tracking.

France's arm was wrapped around Deshane's neck, and a gun was pointed at her temple. "Stay back, Kate. I'd say I don't want to hurt you, but it'd be a lie. I don't need much reason to pull the trigger on either of you."

I gripped the safety rail with one hand and took a step closer. If we could scoot away from the doorway, she wouldn't see Reid come out. "I'm only here to rescue Deshane. I wasn't planning to see you here too."

"Stay back."

I raised my hand nearest the building in surrender while keeping a tight grip on the rail. "I don't have a weapon. You could let Deshane stay here with me while you escape."

"Nice try. You'll call your cop brother, and I'll be arrested the minute I walk out of here."

Deshane's eyes darted in every direction like a wild animal cornered.

"Don't you rappel? I bet we could find a rope for you to climb down and make your escape." I inched my way closer.

"No, I'm a rope climber."

I nodded, hoping to pull off a poker face. "What happened that night?"

"Ryan went pretending to have a romantic evening. Carissa wasn't interested." France's hand shook, and the gun wobbled. "Ryan decided to drug her, hoping she'd give in to his suggestion to continue the fake engagement."

"Even if he talked her into staying, she might have changed her mind the next day."

France waved the gun around. "Exactly. She passed out, and he called me." Her voice grew shriller with each word. "By the time I arrived, we thought she'd overdosed. Nobody was more surprised than me when the coroner said she'd drowned."

Her words made me sick. If Ryan had just left the scene, would Carissa still be alive? "What'd you do then?"

"My ropes are always in my car. Ryan got them for me while I staged the scene. I filled the tub. Even used bath salts."

"To make it seem realistic. Smart. Is that when you hatched the plan to make it look like she drowned?" I continued to move toward the woman holding the gun on Deshane.

"Yes, but he had to lift the body and put her in the tub. We decided using the chain lock would make convince the cops she hadn't been murdered. Ryan secured my ropes on the top of the apartment building then threw them to me. I chained the door then exited by the patio and climbed up to freedom."

"Is Ryan part of your drug business?"

"It was his idea. I just happened to mention the gallery might have to close if we didn't turn a profit soon. He needed money because his singing career hadn't taken off. He suggested trafficking drugs." Her gun hand shook. "At first, I said no. One day, he came to my office and suggested it again. He has a buddy in Jamaica, and he knew the guy would get us started for a small fee. Izzy overheard our conversation, and she jumped at the opportunity. The gallery is only a business to me, but it's Izzy's whole world."

"You know what? The police will understand. You just got caught in the middle of Ryan and Izzy's crimes."

Her spine straightened. "Do you think so?"

"Yeah. I'll vouch for you." We'd only made it a third of the way around the structure, but maybe it'd be enough. I didn't want to end up all the way around the observation deck and back at the door.

Deshane's eyes grew wide, and she whimpered.

"Shut up." France tightened her grip on the young lady.

Reid appeared in my peripheral vision.

I said, "France, let me help you. I can either stay up here with Deshane, or she and I can go down and stall the authorities while you climb down the other side of the lighthouse."

She glanced over the rail, and my stomach did a little flip.

France whined, "I don't have a rope."

Ugh. "Please, let Deshane go. You can hold me as a hostage. I'll be more valuable to you. Think about it."

"You're right. Walk back to the door, and we'll let her go. Deshane, when you reach the ground, I want you to insist on seeing Chief Wright. Here are my demands. I want to be driven to the marina. I want a speedboat gassed up and ready to go. If he agrees, I'll release Kate. Make sure they know I'm holding Kate Sloan hostage. She's the chief's sister. If you don't do this, I'll kill her, and it'll be your fault."

Tears streamed down the young lady's beautiful cheeks. "I understand."

France pushed Deshane toward me and the door, and I backpedaled.

I got past the opening, and so did Deshane. France opened the door. "Hurry."

I could've gone back into the lighthouse with Deshane, but France might have shot at both of us. So, I stayed in place, allowing the young woman to escape.

Chapter Sixty-Three

I faced France, who pointed the gun at me. Deshane was on her way to safety. "Are we going to wait up here for your demands to be met?"

"Yes. I can keep an eye on things from here." She pointed in the distance. "The marina is over there, but I won't be able to see if they bring in a boat for me."

"You know they might confiscate one of the boats that is already there." I needed to get France to focus on me, so Reid could take her by surprise. "Where will you go?"

She laughed, and I had her full attention now. "In case I decide to let you go, I won't share my destination. You'll blab to your brother, and we can't have that."

Reid crept up behind France.

She must've felt his presence, and she whipped around.

I swiped at her gun hand.

She lost her balance but didn't drop the gun.

I kicked behind her knees, and her legs crumpled. She landed on the catwalk.

Reid dropped to the metal-grated flooring and reached for the gun. France kicked him in the chest. He grunted but fought for control of the weapon. I was the only one still standing. I stomped on France's arm.

She howled.

Reid got control of the gun, then stood.

The door burst open behind me.

"Katie, we're here." Paul's voice never sounded so good.

Relief flooded through me, and I slid past him. "France is the one who kidnapped Deshane. Reid has her gun now."

Paul handcuffed France and read her the same Miranda Warning I'd only ever heard on TV shows. This was real life. I shivered.

"Here's the gun." Reid handed France's weapon to my brother.

Two more cops joined Paul.

Soon, they led France down the one-hundred-fifty-four steps to a patrol car.

Reid and I followed at a much slower pace. He wrapped his arm around me at the first landing. "You did a good job up there. If all those mean kids on the school playground could've seen you in action."

I laughed. "Yeah, they wouldn't be calling me an easy out today."

He hugged me. "Let's go home."

Home. I liked the sound of that. The moment I'd returned to Fox Island, it had felt like home. Standing in Reid's embrace felt even more like home. "Yes, let's go."

Chapter Sixty-Four

Supper was at Joy's house that evening. Paul, Susie, and Bess joined us as we gathered around her farmhouse table. Snowball snoozed in the corner on a colorful throw rug. The Westie was officially Paul's dog now.

"It's not fancy, but it should fill you up." Joy passed platters and bowls of food around. "We've got baked chicken, green beans, cornbread, dirty rice, okra, and candied yams."

My stomach growled at the sight and smell of the wonderful food. Bess said a blessing, and we dug in. It wasn't until after we ate that our discussion turned to the murder and drug ring.

Paul draped his arm around Susie's chair and leaned back. "Today, we arrested France Granger, Izzy Reynolds, and Ryan Ford. They devised a plan to trap the others into participating in the drug ring. We've contacted the Jamaican authorities to deal with their partner over there."

I said, "Jason told me drugs were hidden in the picture frames and metal art sculptures that he and Deshane created."

"It's true. I believe they were innocent at first. They were thrilled to have an art gallery in the States interested in their work. When they got here, it was a different story."

I leaned forward. "Izzy wouldn't sell any of Jason's pieces to me. I asked him about selling directly, but he got nervous."

"Yeah. Izzy and France threatened to hurt Deshane if Jason didn't go along with their demands. After Carissa was murdered, Jason knew he better agree to anything they wanted. I'm surprised he confided in you,

Kate."

"Hey, who can resist me?" I winked, and everyone laughed.

Paul sat straighter. "As your little brother, I know how you can wear a person down."

"Well, I'm proud of you. The killer has been caught, and the drug ring has been brought to a stop."

"Right. For a while, I'd been suspicious of Izzy and France, but Ryan's involvement surprised me."

Reid said, "He seemed like a nice guy. I guess his ability to put on a show transferred to acting like a good person around all of us."

"Is Ryan the one who ran me off the road?"

Paul nodded. "Yes, and he put the snakes in your car."

"Hunh. I have no sympathy for him anymore. What a creep."

Reid chuckled and rubbed my shoulder. "What about Marie? Can she come back to Fox Island?"

"I'll discuss it with the Feds. We have the primary players arrested, and we have gathered enough evidence against them. There was a lot of finger-pointing when we questioned the three. I believe she'd be safe, but someone else will make the call."

Bess said, "I'm going to miss her and her coffee if she has to leave for good."

We all laughed. When the laughter faded, I looked at Paul. "I promised Mike Best an interview. He was good to us. Do you want to join me?"

"We can't reveal every detail until after the trials, but maybe he'll agree to multiple interviews. I'll join you."

"Sounds good. Then you can nudge me if I'm about to share too much."

Joy stood. "Who's ready for banana pudding?"

Her question was met with groans and declarations of being stuffed, but when she served dessert, we all ate our portion. The others left, but I remained with Reid to clean the dishes. I kicked off my shoes and attacked the items that wouldn't fit into the dishwasher. I washed, and Reid dried.

Joy appeared wearing fresh lipstick and a sweater. "I'm bushed and going to bed. Thanks for handling cleanup."

Reid did a double take and stopped drying the bright yellow serving bowl. "Um, you're not going to bed looking like that. Let me guess, you're going to meet Dad."

She batted her eyes. "Yes, but I don't have a curfew. Soon, you need to hear his whole story. Lock up when you leave." She sauntered out the back door.

I looked at Reid. "She has some valid points. You and I have gotten a second chance at love. Why can't your parents?"

"She never really recovered from his disappearance. I just hope he doesn't pull the same stunt again."

"We'll be here to support her if that happens. For now, let's give your dad a chance."

We finished the dishes in silence.

I placed our damp dishtowels in the laundry room, then returned. "I'd like to find the young couple who saved me from the marsh. His name is Liam Deloach, and I learned he works at the ice cream shop."

Reid patted his belly. "I hope you don't plan on us eating anything else tonight."

"No, I'd just like to thank him properly. Don't feel like you need to go with me."

"What else would I do on a Sunday night? I'll drive."

It didn't take long to reach Foxy Ice Cream Shop. Not only was Liam working, but so was his girlfriend, Charlotte. We sat at a table, waiting for the crowd to thin out.

When the place was empty, I walked to the counter. "In case you don't recognize me, I'm Kate Sloan."

Liam nodded. "Yes, ma'am."

Charlotte said, "Hey, you're the lady from the marsh."

"Right. Liam, it occurred to me you probably ruined your golf club while saving my life. Are you on the high school team?"

He smiled. "Yes, ma'am. I'm not number one, but I'm on the team."

I pulled a check from my purse. "This is a little thank you, and I want you to use it to replace your club. If either one of you needs a part-time job, I work at Let's Get Organized. I'll be happy to hire either one or both of you."

Liam shook his hands. "I can't accept your money. Helping you was the right thing to do."

His response surprised me. "But you need a new club."

"I've got this job, and soon I'll have enough to buy another driver."

Reid tapped my shoulder. "Don't steal his good deed. He didn't do it for the money."

A large family entered the shop, and I knew we needed to leave. "If you ever need anything, look me up. I can never thank you enough."

"You just did. Thanks for your offer, though."

Reid led me to the sidewalk. "What a week."

We stood away from the door and faced each other. "We've seen the worst and the best in people. It may have even brought Ethan and me closer. He says he's coming to see me."

"Great."

"Yep. I'll expect him when I see him, though. In the meantime, I'm ready for a little bit of normal."

"Me, too."

"Something tells me with fixing up a house, it's still going to be a while before I reach normal." I wrapped my arms around his neck.

Reid's arms circled my waist. "At least we're not going to be chasing after a murderer."

"That's for sure." I leaned toward Reid, and our lips met. The delicious sensations swirling through my body assured me normal was going to be great.

About the Author

Jackie Layton is the author of cozy mysteries with Spunky Southern Sleuths. Her stories are set in Texas, Georgia, and South Carolina. She lives on the coast of South Carolina, where she enjoys walks on the beach and golf cart rides around the marsh. Reading, gardening, and traveling are some of her favorite hobbies. She always keeps a notebook handy to write down ideas for future stories. Be careful what you say around her, because it might end up in a book.

SOCIAL MEDIA HANDLES:
  https://www.facebook.com/JackieLaytonAuthor
  https://www.facebook.com/Joyfuljel
  https://www.pinterest.com/jackielaytonauthor/
  https://twitter.com/joyfuljel

AUTHOR WEBSITE:
  https://jackielaytoncozyauthor.com/

Also by Jackie Layton

A Low Country Dog Walker Mystery Series:
   Bite the Dust
   Dog-Gone Dead
   Bag of Bones
   Caught and Collared
   A Killer Unleashed

A Texas Flower Farmer Cozy Mystery Series:
   Weeding Out Lies